Praise for *Class Trip*

"Stephen King once said, 'I'm a salami writer. I try to write good salami, but salami is salami. You can't sell it as caviar.' The Stephen King of France, in terms of genre, is Emmanuel Carrère. And he writes caviar. He refines a short tale of childhood anxiety—a boy's trip to ski school—into one long extravagant shudder."

—*Mirabella*

"With architectural precision, Carrère constructs the delicate framework of Nicolas's world . . . Chilling."

—*Time Out New York*

"Suffused with an atmosphere of menace . . . The aftereffects of *Class Trip* are potent."

—*The New York Times Book Review*

Praise for *The Mustache*

"A Kafkaesque foray into modern urban paranoia . . . A thriller with a literary pedigree."

—*Voice Literary Supplement*

"A ghostless but uncanny tale . . . gratifyingly unnerving."

—Harry Matthews

ALSO BY EMMANUEL CARRÈRE

Gothic Romance
The Adversary

Class Trip & The Mustache

Class Trip & The Mustache

Emmanuel Carrère

Translated by
Linda Coverdale/Lanie Goodman

Picador
Henry Holt and Company
New York

www.picadorusa.com

Picador® is a U.S. registered trademark and is used by
Henry Holt and Company under license from Pan Books Limited.

For information on Picador Reading Group Guides, as well as ordering,
please contact the Trade Marketing department at St. Martin's Press.
Phone: 1-800-221-7945 extension 763
Fax: 212-677-7456
E-mail: trademarketing@stmartins.com

Library of Congress Cataloging-in-Publication Data

Carrère, Emmanuel, 1957-
[Classe de neige. English]
    Two by Carrère: Class trip, The mustache / Emmanuel Carrère; translated by Linda Coverdale, Lanie Goodman.
        p. cm.
    ISBN 978-0-312-42233-2
    1. Coverdale, Linda. II. Goodman, Lanie. III. Carrère, Emmanuel, 1957– Moustache. English. IV. Title. V. Title: Mustache.

PQ2663.A7678.C4313   1998   97-43483
843'.914—dc21   CIP

Class Trip first published in hardcover in 1997 by Metropolitan Books. *The Mustache* first published in 1988 in simultaneous hardcover/paperback by Scribner, an imprint of Simon and Schuster, Inc.

P1

Contents

Class Trip & The Mustache

Class Trip

Translated by
Linda Coverdale

1

FOR A LONG TIME AFTERWARD—EVEN NOW—NICOLAS TRIED TO remember the last words his father spoke to him. His father had said good-bye at the front door of the chalet, telling him once again to be careful, but Nicolas had been so embarrassed by his presence, so eager for him to leave, that he hadn't listened. Convinced that everyone was laughing at them, he had hung his head resentfully, avoiding his father's parting kiss. At home he would have been scolded for such behavior, but he knew that here, in public, his father wouldn't dare.

Surely they had talked earlier, in the car. Sitting in the back, Nicolas had found it hard to make himself heard above the noise of the defroster going full blast to keep the windows clear. He had been anxious to find out if there would be any Shell stations along the way. Nothing on earth would have made him let his father buy gas anywhere else that winter, because Shell was giving out coupons you could trade in for a Visible Man, a plastic model whose whole front lifted up like the cover of a box, revealing a skeleton and internal organs you could remove and put back again, thus learning about human anatomy. The previous summer, Fina stations had offered air mattresses and inflatable boats; elsewhere the premiums had been comic books, of which Nicolas had a complete collection. He felt lucky, at least in this respect, since his father drove a great deal on his job and had to fill the tank every few days. Whenever his father went on the road, Nicolas asked to be shown the route on a map so that he could calculate the number of miles and convert it into coupons, which he stashed in a safe the size of a cigar box, with a combination known only to him. It was a Christmas present from his parents ("For your little secrets," his father had said), and he had insisted on bringing it along in his bag. He would have really liked to count up his coupons during the trip and figure out how many he still needed, but his bag was in the trunk and his father had refused to pull over, saying that they'd get it when they stopped for gas somewhere. In the end, there had been no Shell stations or any other reason to stop before they reached the chalet. Seeing how disappointed Nicolas was, his father had promised to drive enough between then and the end of ski school to win the plastic model. If Nicolas would entrust him with all his coupons, it would be waiting for him when he came home.

The last stretch of the trip had taken them along minor roads that had too little snow to warrant putting chains on the tires—another letdown for Nicolas. Before that, they'd been driving on the highway. At one point, the traffic had slowed, then come to a standstill for a few minutes. Nicolas's father had drummed his fingers on the steering wheel in frustration, grumbling that this wasn't normal for a weekday in February. From the backseat, Nicolas could see only a hint of a profile above the thick neck tightly encircled by the overcoat collar. The profile and the neck betrayed anxiety, and a bitter, thwarted rage. At last the cars began to move again. Nicolas's father sighed, relaxing a little bit. Probably just an accident, he said. Nicolas was shocked by the relief in his voice: as if an accident—since it would create a traffic jam only until help arrived—could be considered something desirable. He was shocked but also intrigued. Glued to the side window, he hoped to see crumpled metal, bloodied bodies carried away on stretchers in the glare of flashing lights, but he saw nothing, and his father, surprised, remarked that no, it must have been something else after all. The bottleneck gone, its mystery remained.

2

THE CLASS HAD LEFT FOR SKI SCHOOL THE DAY BEFORE, BY BUS.
Ten days earlier, however, there had been a tragic accident, pictures of which had been shown on the news: a large truck had crashed into a school bus, and several children had died horribly in the flames. A meeting was held the next day at school to prepare for the class trip. Parents were to receive final instructions concerning their children's belongings: what clothes were to be marked; the stamped envelopes to be provided for letters home; the phone calls, on the other hand, that were best avoided (except in an emergency), to help the boys feel truly off on their own, not tied by a thread to their families. Several mothers were distressed by this last instruction: the children were so young . . . Patiently the teacher repeated that it was in their interest. The main purpose of such a trip was to teach them how to stand on their own two feet.

Nicolas's father remarked, rather brusquely, that the main purpose of school was not, in his opinion, to cut children off from their families and that he wouldn't hesitate to call if he felt like it. The teacher opened her mouth to reply, but he pressed on. He had come to raise a much more serious question: the safety of the bus. How could they be sure there wouldn't be a catastrophe like the one they'd all seen recently on the news? Yes, how could they be sure, chimed in other parents, who'd doubtless been wondering the same thing without daring to raise the issue. The teacher admitted that, unfortunately, there was no way to be sure. She could only say that they were taking every precaution with regard to safety, that the bus driver was extremely reliable, and that reasonable risks were a part of life. If parents wanted to be absolutely certain that their children wouldn't be hit by cars, they'd have to prevent them from ever leaving home—and that wouldn't keep them from having accidents with household appliances or from simply getting sick. Some parents conceded the soundness of this argument, but many were shocked by the teacher's fatalistic attitude. She was even smiling as she spoke.

"It's easy to see they're not your children!" exclaimed Nicolas's father. No longer smiling, the teacher replied that she had a child, too, and that he'd taken the bus to ski school the year before. Then Nicolas's father announced that he preferred to drive his son to the chalet himself: at least that way he'd know who was behind the wheel.

The teacher pointed out that the chalet was almost three hundred miles away.

So what? He was determined to make the trip.

But it wouldn't be good for Nicolas, she insisted. Wouldn't help him fit into the group.

"He'll fit in just fine," said his father, and he laughed sarcastically. "Don't try to make me believe arriving in a car with his dad will make him an outcast!"

The teacher asked him to think it over carefully, suggested that he speak with the school psychologist (who would confirm her opinion), but admitted that the final decision was up to him.

In school the next day, the teacher attempted to talk to Nicolas about this, to find out whose idea it was. Treading carefully, as she always did with him, she asked what he would prefer. The question made Nicolas uneasy. Deep down, he knew perfectly well he'd rather travel on the bus like everyone else. But his father had made up his mind, he wouldn't change it, and Nicolas didn't want the teacher and the other boys to think he was being forced to go along with his father's wishes. He shrugged, said he didn't care one way or the other—it was okay the way it was. The teacher left it at that. She had done what she could, and since she clearly couldn't change anything, it was better not to make a fuss.

3

NICOLAS AND HIS FATHER REACHED THE CHALET SHORTLY BEFORE nightfall. The other boys, who'd arrived the previous day, had taken their first skiing lesson that morning and were now in the main room, on the ground floor, watching a film on alpine flora and fauna. This was interrupted by the arrival of the newcomers. While the teacher greeted Nicolas's father out in the hall and introduced him to the two instructors, the children in the room began to make a commotion. Nicolas watched from the doorway without daring to join them. He heard his father ask how the skiing was going and an instructor reply laughingly that there wasn't much snow, the kids were learning mostly how to ski on grass, but it was a start. Then his father wanted to know if they'd receive a certificate at the end of the course. An intermediate's star? The instructor chuckled again and said, "A beginner's snowflake, perhaps." Nicolas stood shifting from one foot to the other, his face impassive. When his father finally was ready to leave, Nicolas grudgingly allowed himself to be kissed but did not go outside to see his father off. From the hall, he listened with relief to the motor rumbling out on the driveway, then moving off into the distance.

The teacher sent the instructors to restore order and start the film rolling again while she helped Nicolas settle in. She asked him where his bag was, intending to carry it upstairs. Nicolas looked around; there was no bag to be seen. He didn't understand.

"I thought it was here," he mumbled.

"You're sure you brought it with you?" asked the teacher.

Yes, Nicolas definitely remembered that they'd put it in the trunk, between the tire chains and his father's sample cases.

"And when you arrived, you took it out of the trunk?"

Biting his lips, Nicolas shook his head. He wasn't sure about that. Or rather, yes: now he was certain that they'd forgotten to remove it. They'd stepped out of the car, later his father had gotten back in, and they hadn't ever opened the trunk.

"How silly," said the teacher, not at all pleased. The car had left barely five minutes before, but it was already too late to catch up with it. Nicolas felt like crying. He stammered that it wasn't his fault. "You could have at least thought of it," sighed the teacher. Relenting when she saw how miserable he looked, she shrugged and said it was a silly mistake but not a serious one. They'd figure something out. Anyway, his father would quickly realize what had happened. Yes, agreed Nicolas: when he opened the trunk to get his sample cases. Hearing this, the teacher was confident he'd soon return with the bag. Yes, yes, said Nicolas, torn between his desire to have his things back and his fear of his father's return.

"Do you know where he's planning to stop for the night?" asked the teacher.

Nicolas didn't know.

Darkness had fallen, making it unlikely that Nicolas's father would show up with the bag before morning. It was therefore necessary to make some arrangement for that night. The teacher and Nicolas returned to the main room, where the film was over and everyone was getting ready to set the table for dinner. Following the teacher through the door, Nicolas felt painfully like the new kid who doesn't know what's going on, the kid everyone makes fun of. He sensed that the teacher was doing what she could to protect him from any teasing or hostility. After clapping for silence, she announced in a joking tone that Nicolas—off in the clouds, as usual—had forgotten his bag. Who would lend him some pajamas?

Since each student's list had specified three pairs, anyone could have lent him some, but nobody spoke up. Not daring to look at the children gathered around them, Nicolas stayed close to the teacher, who repeated her appeal with a touch of irritation. He heard giggles, and then a voice he couldn't identify said something that made the others burst out laughing: "He'll pee in them!"

It was pure meanness, a random shot, but it hit home. Nicolas did still occasionally wet his bed, not very often, but even so he dreaded sleeping anywhere except in his own room at home. From the very start, this had been one of his greatest anxieties about ski school. At first he'd said he didn't want to go. His mother had requested a meeting with the teacher, who had reassured her that he probably wouldn't be the only one, and besides, that kind of problem often disappeared in a group setting. Just in case, it would be a good idea for him to take along one more set of pajamas and a drawsheet to protect the mattress. Despite these comforting words, Nicolas had watched nervously as his bag was packed: since they were going to sleep in dormitories, how could he place the drawsheet over the mattress without anyone noticing? This worrisome thought and a few others like it had tortured him before he left, but even in his worst nightmare he'd never have imagined what was actually happening to him: finding himself without his bag, the drawsheet, pajamas, reduced to begging in vain for a pair, mocked and stripped naked as soon as he arrived, as though his shame were written all over his face.

Finally, someone said he'd lend him some pajamas. It was Hodkann. That sparked fresh merriment, because he was the tallest boy in the class, while Nicolas was one of the smallest, so the offer almost seemed intended to poke more fun at him. But Hodkann put a stop to the jeers by saying that whoever

bothered Nicolas would have to deal with him, and everyone
knew he meant it. Nicolas gave him a flustered, grateful look.
The teacher seemed relieved but perplexed, as though she suspected a trap. Hodkann had great authority over the other
boys, which he exercised in a capricious fashion. In all games,
for example, they took their cues from him, without knowing
whether he would behave like a referee or a gang leader, dis-
pensing justice or flouting it cynically. Within the space of a
few seconds, he could be extraordinarily kind and extraordinarily brutal. He protected and rewarded his vassals but ban-
ished them without cause as well, replacing them with others
whom he'd previously disdained or mistreated. With Hodkann,
you never knew where you stood. He was feared and admired;
even adults seemed afraid of him. He was about as tall as an
adult, moreover, with a nearly grown-up voice and none of the
clumsiness of boys who shoot up too quickly. He moved and
spoke with an ease that was almost disconcerting. Although
he could be vulgar, at times he expressed himself extremely
well, with a richness and precision of vocabulary surprising for
his age. He received very good grades or very bad ones, without
seeming to care either way. On the form everyone filled out at
the beginning of the school year, he'd written, "Father: de-
ceased," and everyone knew he lived alone with his mother.
On Saturdays she came to pick him up at noon in a little red
sports car. Although she stayed in the car, it was easy to see that
she didn't look like the other boys' mothers, with her aggressive, made-up beauty, her hollow cheeks, her mane of red hair

that seemed hopelessly tangled. The rest of the week, Hodkann went to and from school on his own, by streetcar. He lived far away, and everybody wondered why he didn't attend a school closer to his home, but this kind of question, which would have been easy to put to someone else, became impossible if you were face-to-face with Hodkann. Watching him head off toward the streetcar stop, his book bag on his shoulder (he was the only one who didn't carry a school satchel strapped to his back), the children tried—each of them secretly, because no one dared talk about him in his absence—to imagine his ride, the neighborhood where he and his mother lived, their apartment, his room. There was something both improbable and mysteriously attractive about the idea that somewhere in the city there existed a place that was Hodkann's room. No one had ever been there, and he himself didn't go to the other boys' homes. He shared this distinction with Nicolas, in whose case, however, it was less peculiar, and Nicolas hoped that no one had noticed it. Nobody ever thought of inviting him or expected to be invited to his home. He was as timid and unobtrusive as Hodkann was bold and self-assertive. Ever since the beginning of the year, he'd been scared to death that Hodkann would notice him, would ask him something, and he'd had several nightmares in which Hodkann had singled him out for bullying. So he was quite worried when Hodkann—in a sudden fit of benevolence, like a Roman emperor in the arena—brought the pajama torture to an end. If Hodkann was taking him under his protection, that meant he might just as easily abandon him or hand him over to others whom he'd already turned against him. Many sought Hodkann's favor, but all knew it was dangerous, and Nicolas had managed not to attract his attention until now. Well, that was over. Thanks to his father he'd attracted everyone's attention, and he felt he'd been right about ski school all along: it was going to be a dreadful ordeal.

4

MOST OF THE STUDENTS ATE IN THE CAFETERIA, BUT NOT
Nicolas. His mother came to get him and his younger brother,
who was still in nursery school, and the three of them ate lunch
at home. The boys' father said that they were very lucky and
that it was a shame their classmates had to use the cafeteria,
where the food was terrible and fights often broke out. Nicolas agreed with his father and, when asked, declared that he
was glad to escape the bad food and the roughhousing. He realized, though, that his classmates formed their strongest
bonds between noon and two o'clock, in the cafeteria and on
the playground, where they hung around after lunch. While he
was gone, they'd thrown yogurts at one another, been punished by the monitors, formed alliances, and each time his
mother brought him back it was as if he were a stranger who

had to start all over again on the relationships he'd begun forming that morning. He was the only one who remembered them: too many things had happened during that two-hour lunch period.

He knew that the chalet would be like the cafeteria, but lasting two weeks, without a break or the possibility of going home if it turned out to be too hard on him. He was afraid of that, and his parents were too—so much so that they'd asked the doctor if he'd write an excuse for Nicolas. But the doctor had refused, assuring them that the trip would do him a world of good.

In addition to the teacher and the bus driver, who was also in charge of the kitchen, there were two instructors at the chalet, Patrick and Marie-Ange, who assigned teams to set the table after Nicolas had rejoined the other children: some busied themselves with the silverware, others with the plates, and so on. Patrick was the one who had spoken so lightheartedly to Nicolas's father about skiing on the grass. Tall, with broad shoulders, he had a tanned, angular face, very blue eyes, and long hair worn in a ponytail. Marie-Ange, a trifle chubby, revealed a broken front tooth when she smiled. Both wore green-and-purple track suits and little bracelets woven of multicolored threads that you tied on your wrist while making a wish and left on until they fell off by themselves, when your wish—supposedly—had come true. Patrick had a whole supply of these bracelets, which he distributed like medals to children he was pleased with. Just after Nicolas joined the group, he gave him one, which upset several boys who'd been hoping to get them. Nicolas hadn't done anything to deserve his! Instead of saying that poor Nicolas needed to be consoled because he didn't have his things with him, Patrick laughed and told the story of how when he and his sister were little their father always punished one when the other had been naughty, and vice versa, so they would learn early on that life could be unfair. Nicolas thanked him silently for not making him look like a crybaby, and as he went around the tables setting out the soup spoons Patrick had entrusted him with, he thought about the wish he would make. First he considered asking not to wet his bed that night, then asking not to wet his bed the whole time he was in ski school, but he realized that he might as well ask for his entire stay in the chalet to go well. And why not ask for everything to go well for the rest of his life? Why not wish that all his wishes would always come true? The advantage of a wish that was as general as possible, encompassing all specific wishes, seemed so obvious at first glance that he knew there was a catch, something like the story of the three wishes, which he knew in its nice version for children (with a peasant whose nose changes into a sausage) but also in a much grimmer variation.

Above his parents' bed at home was a shelf full of books and dolls in folk costumes. Most of the books were about herbal healing or do-it-yourself repairs, but two of them fascinated Nicolas. The first, a big green volume, was a medical dictionary that he didn't dare carry off to his room for fear it would be missed, so he had to read it in quick snatches, his heart pounding, while he kept an eye out through the half-open door. The other book was called *Tales of Terror*. The cover showed a woman from the back as she looked into a mirror, and in the mirror you could see a grinning skeleton. This one was a paperback, easier to handle than the dictionary. Without saying anything, figuring that his parents would confiscate the book and tell him he was too young to read it, Nicolas had sneaked it into his room, hiding it behind his own few books. When he lay sprawled across his bed on his tummy, immersed in its pages, he kept ready as a cover in case of emergency his collection of *Tales and Legends of Ancient Egypt*, in which he'd read the story of Isis and Osiris a good ten times. One of the scary stories told how an elderly couple discover the powers of a kind of amulet: the severed paw of a monkey, a shriveled, blackish thing able to grant three wishes to its owner. Without thinking or even really believing in what he's doing, the man asks for a certain sum of money he needs to repair his roof. The woman immediately upbraids him for his foolishness, saying he should have asked for a lot more—he has wasted the wish! A few hours later, there is a knock on the door. It's an employee from the factory where their son works. The man is quite distressed, he has ghastly news for them. An accident. Their son was caught in the gears of a machine and killed, torn to shreds. The manager of the factory would like them to accept some money for the funeral: exactly the amount the father had asked for! The mother howls with grief and now makes her own wish: that their son be given back to them! And so, at nightfall, the scraps of his dismembered body drag themselves to their door, little gobbets of bloody flesh twitching on the front steps while one severed hand tries to get into the house in which the horror-stricken parents have barricaded themselves. They have only one wish left: that this thing without a name should vanish! That it should die once and for all!

5

SIX COULD SLEEP IN EACH BEDROOM, AND THERE WAS ONE PLACE available in Hodkann's. Without asking anyone's opinion, he announced that Nicolas would take it. The teacher approved: although she was still worried about his sudden mood swings, she liked the idea of the biggest boy in the class looking after the smallest one like this. She felt somewhat sorry for shy, overprotected Nicolas. The rooms were furnished with bunk beds. Since Hodkann had assigned him to an upper bed, above his own, Nicolas climbed the ladder and wriggled into the borrowed pajamas, rolling up the legs and sleeves. The top came down to his knees; the pants swam on him. Going to the toilet, he had to hold the pants up with both hands. And he had no slippers, towel, washcloth, or toothbrush—things no one could lend him because they didn't have extras. Luckily, nobody paid any attention to him, so he was able to slip unnoticed through the bustling bathroom and be among the first ones in bed. Patrick, who was in charge of his room, came over to muss his hair and tell him not to fret: everything would be fine. And if there was anything wrong, he would come to Patrick and tell him about it, promise? Nicolas promised, divided between the real comfort this assurance gave him and the painful impression that everyone was waiting for something to go wrong for him.

When they were all in bed, Patrick turned out the light, said good night, and closed the door. They were left in the dark. Nicolas thought that a ruckus would break out immediately, a pillow fight in which he'd have trouble holding his own, but no. He realized that everyone was waiting for Hodkann's permission to speak. Hodkann let the silence last for a long while. Gradually their eyes grew accustomed to the gloom. Their breathing became more even, but there was still a feeling of expectation in the air.

"Nicolas," said Hodkann at last, as though they were alone in the room, as though the others didn't exist.

"Yes?" murmured Nicolas, like an echo.

"What does your father do?"

Nicolas replied that he was a traveling salesman. Nicolas was rather proud of this profession, which seemed to him prestigious, even a little mysterious.

"So he travels a lot?" asked Hodkann.

"Yes," said Nicolas, repeating something he'd heard his mother say. "He's on the road all the time."

He was working up the courage to mention the advantages

this meant for premiums from gas stations, but he didn't get the chance: Hodkann wanted to know what his father sold, what kind of stuff. To Nicolas's great surprise, Hodkann seemed to be asking questions not to make fun of him but because he was truly curious about what his father did. Nicolas said that he sold surgical supplies.

"Forceps? Scalpels?"

"Yes, and artificial limbs too."

"Wooden legs?" inquired Hodkann in amusement, and Nicolas sensed, like an alarm deep inside him, the threat of mockery closing in.

"No," he said, "plastic ones."

"He drives around with plastic legs in his trunk?"

"Yes, and also arms, hands—"

"Heads?" burst out Lucas, a red-headed boy with glasses whom Nicolas had thought was asleep, like the others.

"No," said Nicolas, "not heads! He's a traveling salesman in surgical supplies, not gags!"

Hodkann greeted this sally with an indulgent chuckle, and Nicolas immediately felt relaxed and gratified. Protected by Hodkann, he, too, could say funny things, make people laugh.

"He's shown you these artificial limbs?" continued Hodkann.

"Of course," said Nicolas, drawing confidence from this initial success.

"You've gotten to try one on?"

"No, you can't do that. Because it goes where your arm or

your leg was, so if you've still got your arm or leg there, you've got nowhere to put it."

"Me," said Hodkann calmly, "if I were your father, I'd use you for demonstrations. I'd cut off your arms and legs, I'd fit on the artificial ones, and I'd show you to my clients like that. It'd make a great advertisement."

The occupants of the neighboring bed cracked up. Lucas said something about Captain Hook in *Peter Pan*, and abruptly Nicolas felt afraid, as though Hodkann had finally shown his true face, one even more dangerous than he'd feared. The henchmen, fawning, begin cackling already, while the potentate nonchalantly searches his imagination for the most refined of tortures. . . . But Hodkann, sensing the threat in what he'd just said, removed the sting by saying with that surprising gentleness he sometimes showed, "Don't worry, Nicolas. I'm just teasing." Then he wanted to know if, when Nicolas's father brought back his bag the next day, they might be able to see those amazing artificial limbs, those sets of surgical instruments. The idea made Nicolas nervous.

"They're not toys, you know. He only shows them to clients . . ."

"He wouldn't show them if we asked him?" persisted Hodkann. "And if you asked him yourself?"

"I don't think so," replied Nicolas in a small voice.

"If you told him that, in exchange, no one would beat you up during ski school?"

Once more apprehensive, Nicolas said nothing.

"Fine," concluded Hodkann. "In that case, I'll find some other way." After a moment, he announced to the room at large, "Time to go to sleep."

They heard him tossing heavily in bed until he found a comfortable position, and everyone knew they shouldn't say another word.

6

ALL WAS QUIET, BUT NICOLAS WASN'T SURE IF THE OTHERS WERE
sleeping. Perhaps—scared of making Hodkann mad—they
were pretending, and maybe Hodkann was as well, lying in wait
for anyone who dared disobey him. As for Nicolas, he didn't
want to sleep. He was afraid of peeing in the bed and wetting
Hodkann's pajamas. Or even worse, of peeing right through the
mattress, since there wasn't a drawsheet, and wetting Hodkann
himself below. The smelly liquid would start dripping down
onto his tiger's face, he'd wrinkle his nose, wake up, and then
it would be awful. The only way to avoid this catastrophe was
not to fall asleep. According to the glowing hands of Nicolas's
watch, it was twenty past nine; wake-up was at seven-thirty,
which meant a long night ahead. But it wasn't the first time:
he'd had practice.

The year before, Nicolas's father had taken him and his

younger brother to an amusement park. Because of the difference in their ages, the two of them hadn't been interested in the same rides. Nicolas had been most attracted to the Ferris wheel, the haunted house, and the tunnel of terror, while his brother liked the merry-go-rounds for little kids. Their father had suggested compromises and was irritated whenever the children rejected them. At one point, they'd passed a wheel designed to look like a caterpillar turning a circle in the air at top speed. The passengers, clutching the safety bars of their little cars, found themselves hurtling skyward, suspended upside down by centrifugal force. The wheel turned rapidly, faster and faster; you could hear shrieking, and the people got off pale, with wobbly legs, but thrilled by the experience. A boy Nicolas's age remarked excitedly to him that it was cool, and the boy's father, who had gone on the ride with him, gave Nicolas's father a knowing smile to indicate that perhaps it was not so much cool as exhausting. Nicolas wanted to go on the ride, but his father showed him a sign by the ticket window saying that children younger than twelve had to be accompanied. "So come on it with me!" entreated Nicolas. "Oh please, come on it with me!" His father, who did not seem eager to be whirled around head over heels, begged off by pointing out that they couldn't take along his little brother, who'd be petrified, or leave him all alone, unsupervised. Then the father of the boy who'd just gone on the caterpillar kindly offered to watch Nicolas's brother during the three-minute ride. He looked something like an older version of Patrick, the instructor: he was wearing a denim jacket, not a heavy overcoat like Nicolas's father's, and he had a cheer-

27

ful face. Nicolas gave him a grateful look, then gazed hopefully at his father. But his father told the other man that there was no need to bother. When Nicolas opened his mouth to plead with him, his father shot him a threatening glance and gripped the back of his neck firmly to make him walk on. They moved away from the caterpillar in silence, Nicolas not daring to object while they were still within sight of the other boy and his father. He could imagine their astonished expressions behind his back: why such an abrupt departure in response to a kind offer? When he thought they were far enough away, Nicolas's father stopped and said sternly that when he'd said no, that meant no, and there wasn't any use making a scene in public.

"But why?" protested Nicolas, on the verge of tears. "What difference would it have made?"

"You want me to tell you why?" replied his father, scowling. "You want me to tell you? All right, you're old enough to have it explained to you. Except that you mustn't talk about it, not to your playmates, not to anyone. It's something I learned from the director of a clinic. The doctors all know about it but they don't want it to get around, so as not to frighten people. Not too long ago, in an amusement park like this one, a small boy disappeared. His parents didn't pay attention for a few seconds, and that was that. It all happened very fast—it's quite easy to disappear, you know. They looked for him all day long and that evening they finally found him, unconscious behind a fence. They took him to the hospital—they'd seen there was a big bandage on his back, with blood coming out—and the doctors knew what had happened, they could already tell what they'd see on the X ray: the little boy had been operated on, and one of his kidneys had been taken out. There are people who do that, can you believe it? Bad people. That's called trafficking in organs. They've got vans with everything they need for operations. They prowl around amusement parks or near the entrances to schools, where they kidnap children. The head of the clinic told me they preferred not to spread the information around, but it's happening more and more often. Just in his clinic alone, they've had a kid who had his hand cut off and another who had both eyes ripped out. You understand, now, why I didn't want to hand your little brother over to a stranger?"

After that story, Nicolas had a recurring nightmare that took place in an amusement park. He didn't remember all the details in the morning but sensed that the main thrust of the dream was pushing him toward some nameless horror from which he might never awaken. The metal framework of the caterpillar loomed over the wooden shacks of the park, and the dream was driving him toward it. The horror was lurking over there. It was waiting to devour him. In the second dream, he realized that he'd drawn closer and that the third time would probably kill him. They'd find him dead in his bed: no one would understand what had happened to him. So he decided to stay awake. Of course, he couldn't really manage that; his fitful slumber was disturbed by other nightmares, behind which, he feared, was hiding the one about the park and the caterpillar. He discovered, that summer, that he was afraid to fall asleep.

7

WITHIN THE FAMILY, HOWEVER, IT WAS SAID THAT HE TOOK AFTER his father, who slept badly but a great deal, with a kind of greediness. When he was home for several days in a row after being out on the road, he spent almost all his time in bed. After school, Nicolas would do his homework or play with his little brother, taking care not to make any noise. In the hall, they would walk on tiptoe; their mother was constantly putting her finger to her lips. At dusk, their father would emerge from his room in pajamas, unshaven, his face grumpy and puffy with sleep, his pockets stuffed with crumpled handkerchiefs and empty medicine wrappers. He looked surprised, and disagreeably so, to awaken there, to find these walls pressing in on him, to discover—pushing open the first door he came upon—a child's bedroom where two small boys, on all fours on the carpet, interrupted their game or their reading to look up at him anxiously. He'd manage an uneasy smile, mumbling disjointedly about fatigue, lousy schedules, drugs that wiped you out. Sometimes he would sit for a moment on the edge of Nicolas's bed, staring vacantly, rubbing a hand over his raspy beard or through tousled hair still creased from the pillow. He would sigh, ask strange questions, like what grade Nicolas was in. Nicolas would answer obediently, and his father would nod, saying that Nicolas was getting into serious schoolwork and should study hard to avoid having to repeat a grade. He seemed to have forgotten that Nicolas had already repeated a grade, the year they moved. One day, he asked Nicolas to come closer, to sit next to him on the bed. He put his hand on the back of his son's neck, squeezing gently. It was to show his affection, but it hurt, and Nicolas twisted his neck cautiously to break free. In a low, hollow voice, his father said, "I love you, Nicolas," which upset the boy, not because he doubted it but because this seemed such a strange way to say it. As though it were the last time before a long—perhaps a final—separation, as though his father wanted him to remember it his whole life long. A few moments later, though, his father didn't seem to remember it anymore himself. There was a blank look in his eyes; his hands were shaking. Wheezing, he stood up, his burgundy pajamas hanging loosely, all rumpled, and he fumbled his way out, as though he had no idea which door to open to get back to the hall, back to his room, back to bed.

8

NOW NICOLAS WAS THINKING (AND AT LEAST IT WAS HELPING KEEP him awake) about Hodkann's declared intention of seeing with his own eyes the samples stored in the car trunk. How would he go about it? Perhaps he'd find a way to stay in the chalet while the others went down to the village for their skiing lesson. Hidden behind a tree, he'd keep his eyes peeled for the car. Nicolas's father would get out, open the trunk to remove the bag, and carry it to the chalet. As soon as his back was turned, Hodkann would rush up, raise the lid of the trunk, then open the black plastic cases containing the artificial limbs and surgical instruments. That was undoubtedly his plan, but he wasn't aware that Nicolas's father always locked the trunk after taking something out of it, even if he knew he was going to be reopening it a few minutes later. Hodkann was so bold, though, that you could imagine him following Nicolas's father into the chalet and picking his pockets, stealing his key ring while he was speaking to the teacher. Nicolas saw Hodkann bent over the open trunk, forcing the latches of the sample cases, testing the blade of a lancet on the ball of his thumb, bending the joints of a plastic leg, so enthralled that he'd forgotten all danger. Nicolas's father was already leaving the chalet, walking toward the car. Another moment, and he would catch Hodkann. His hand would fall heavily on Hodkann's shoulder, and then—what would happen? Nicolas hadn't any idea. Actually, his father had never threatened dire punishment for touching his samples. Nicolas was certain, however, that even for Hodkann it would be a very tricky situation. The expression "to have a rough time of it" kept running through his head. Yes, if he got caught rummaging through the car trunk, Hodkann would have a rough time of it.

Hodkann's interest in his father bothered Nicolas. He even wondered if the other boy hadn't taken him under his wing to get close to his father, to win his confidence. He remembered that Hodkann didn't have his own father anymore. And when he was alive, this father, what did he do? Nicolas hadn't thought to ask, and anyway, he would never have dared. He couldn't help thinking that Hodkann's father had died violently, in suspicious, tragic circumstances, and that his life had led inexorably to such an end. He imagined him as an outlaw, dangerous, like his son, and maybe Hodkann had become so dangerous only because he had to deal with that, with the risks he ran for being the son of this father. Nicolas would have liked to ask Hodkann about him now. At night, with just the two of them, it would be possible.

It was a voluptuous thought, this nocturnal conversation with Hodkann, and Nicolas spent some time imagining how it would go. They would both leave the room, without awakening anyone. They would talk quietly in the hall or the bathroom. He pictured their whispering, the nearness of Hodkann's big, warm body, and he relished the idea that the tyrannical power wielded by Hodkann concealed a sorrow, a vulnerability that the other boy would confess to him. He would hear him confide, as though to his only friend, the only person he could trust, that he was unhappy, that his father had died gruesomely, dismembered or tossed into a well, that his mother lived in fear of seeing her husband's accomplices reappear some day, determined to avenge themselves on her and her son. Hodkann, so imperious, so mocking, would admit to Nicolas that he was afraid, that he, too, was a lost little boy. Tears coursing down his cheeks, he would lay that proud head on Nicolas's lap, and Nicolas would stroke his hair, speaking gentle words of consolation, consolation for this vast and hitherto unspoken grief that had suddenly burst out before him, for him alone, because only he, Nicolas, was worthy of this revelation. Between sobs, Hodkann would say that the enemies who had killed his father and whom his mother so dreaded might come to the chalet to take him away. To take him hostage or simply kill him, abandoning his corpse in a snowy patch of undergrowth. And Nicolas would realize that it was up to him to protect Hodkann, to find a hiding place where he would be safe when these bad men, who wore shiny dark coats, surrounded the chalet and silently entered, one at each door so that no one could escape. They would draw their knives and strike coldly, methodically, determined to leave no witnesses. The half-naked bodies of children surprised in their sleep would pile up at the foot of the bunk beds. The floor would be streaming with blood. But Nicolas and Hodkann would be hiding in a hollow in the wall, behind a bed. It would be a dark, narrow space, a real rat hole. They would huddle together, their eyes wide with terror and glistening in the shadows. Together they would hear, over the sound of their own breathing, the appalling din of the carnage: shrieks of horror, death agonies, the dull thud of falling bodies, windows shattering into glass shards that would embed themselves in already mutilated flesh, the curt laughter of the killers. The severed head of Lucas, the red-headed boy with glasses, would roll under the bed toward their hiding place, coming to a stop at their feet to stare at them in disbelief. Later, all would be silent. Hours would pass. The murderers would have left empty-handed, exhilarated by the massacre yet seething with vexation at having missed their prey. In the chalet, there would be only corpses, huge heaps of dead children. But the two of them would not leave. They'd spend the whole night crouched in their nook, entrenched in the heart of the slaughterhouse, each one feeling on his cheeks a warm trickling that might be blood from a wound or the other boy's tears. They would stay there, trembling. The night would have no end. Perhaps they would never come out.

9

NICOLAS'S FATHER STILL HAD NOT RETURNED BY THE TIME BREAK-
fast was over the next morning. The teacher glanced at her
watch. There was no point in waiting around for him and missing the skiing lesson. Nicolas could feel her eyes on him, and for
once the look in them was less than indulgent. Perhaps, he said
in a small voice, it would be best if he stayed at the chalet. He
hoped that Hodkann would volunteer to stay behind as well.
"We're not going to leave you all alone," announced the teacher
firmly. Patrick observed that nothing much could happen to
him, but the teacher said no, it was a matter of principle. In the
meantime, she asked Nicolas to go upstairs with her, as she
wanted to call his mother to inform her of the situation and
find out if she had heard from her husband. The telephone was
on the second floor, in a small wood-paneled office with a lovely
view of the valley from the window. The teacher dialed the

number, waited for a moment, and asked Nicolas in an annoyed tone if his mother usually left home very early in the morning. Nicolas replied contritely that no, she didn't, not usually. Actually, he was glad his mother wasn't answering. This phone call made him uneasy. Few people called them at home; on those rare occasions when the phone did ring, his mother approached it with obvious trepidation, particularly when his father wasn't there. If Nicolas was around, she shut the door so that he wouldn't hear, as though she feared receiving bad news and wished to spare him for as long as possible. The teacher sighed, then redialed the number, just in case she had made a mistake before. This call was answered immediately, and Nicolas wondered what had happened the first time. He imagined his mother in the position in which he had caught her several times: standing in front of the ringing telephone, wincing in dismay, not daring to answer it. When the ringing stopped, she'd seem relieved for a moment, but if the ringing began again, she answered right away, grabbing the receiver the way you'd jump into the water to escape a fire.

Nicolas studied the teacher's face nervously as she introduced herself and explained why she was calling. The phone was the old-fashioned kind, with an extra earpiece for someone to listen in. Noticing Nicolas watching her, she motioned for him to pick it up. He obeyed.

"No, " she explained patiently, "it's not serious. But it's inconvenient. I mean, without his bag he's got no change of clothes, no ski things, only what he's wearing, so we're not quite sure what to do with him."

She smiled at Nicolas to take the edge off that last remark, which had been made largely to provoke a reaction from his mother.

"But my husband will certainly bring back the bag."

"That's what I'm hoping, but since he hasn't shown up yet, what I want to know is, where can we reach him?"

"When he's out on the road, he cannot be reached."

"Really? He doesn't know in advance what hotels he'll be staying in? What happens if you need to talk to him urgently?"

"I'm very sorry. That's just how it is," said Nicolas's mother sharply.

"But he calls you occasionally?"

"Yes, occasionally."

"If he calls, then, would you let him know? The problem is, if he doesn't come today, he might get too far away . . . You have no idea what his itinerary is?"

"No. I'm so sorry."

"Well, all right," said the teacher. "Would you like to talk to Nicolas?"

"Thank you."

The teacher handed the receiver to Nicolas and went out into the hallway to give him privacy. Nicolas and his mother didn't know what to say to each other. As far as his bag was concerned, there was nothing more to be said; all they could do was wait for his father to bring it back to the chalet. Nicolas didn't want to complain or cause his mother any further worry, while she didn't want to ask questions that would increase a distress she had no means of alleviating. So she simply urged him to behave himself and do as he was told, the same advice she would have given him if nothing had been wrong. Nicolas had the bitter impression that if she saw him halfway down the throat of a crocodile she'd still keep saying, Have a nice time, be good, don't forget to dress warmly . . . As for dressing warmly, she could hardly say that now and was probably being careful not to remind him to wear the big sweater with the reindeer on it that she'd knitted for him.

Accompanying the teacher back downstairs to the main room, where the breakfast tables were being cleared, Nicolas pondered the mystery: he knew his bag was in the trunk of the car—he'd seen it wedged between the tire chains and the sample cases—and his father could not have failed to notice it when opening the trunk, which he'd certainly had to do last night or this morning, at the latest, when he called on his clients. So why hadn't he phoned? Why hadn't he shown up? He must have had some idea of the trouble he was causing Nicolas. Had he lost the phone number of the chalet? Or the keys to the trunk? Had they been stolen? Had the car been stolen? Or . . . had there been an accident? All of a sudden, this hypothesis, which Nicolas hadn't yet considered, seemed all too likely to him. To let him down like this, his father would have to be unable to come, unable to telephone. Perhaps the car had skidded on a patch of black ice, crashed into a tree, and his father was dying, his chest crushed by the steering wheel. His last conscious thought, the words he'd stammered to the uncomprehending rescuers, must have been, "Nicolas's bag! Take Nicolas's bag back to him!"

Imagining this, Nicolas felt his eyes fill with tears, and a great tenderness came over him. He didn't want it to be true, of course, but at the same time he would have liked to appear before the others in the role of an orphan, the hero of a tragedy. They would try to console him, Hodkann would want to comfort him, and he would be inconsolable. He wondered if the teacher had reached the same conclusion and was trying to conceal her alarm from him as long as some hope still remained. Probably not. Not yet. Nicolas envisioned the moment when the phone would ring. The teacher would calmly go upstairs to answer it; the children would be carrying on in the main room, making a racket. He alone would be on the alert, awaiting her return. And there she was, her face pale and drawn. The children kept up the commotion but she didn't order them to be quiet. She seemed to hear nothing, to notice nothing, to see only Nicolas as she came toward him, reached for his hand, led him away to the office. She closed the door behind her, shutting out the noise from downstairs. She took his face between her hands, gently, the palms cradling his cheeks; you could see her lips trembling, and she said falteringly, "Nicolas . . . Listen, Nicolas, you're going to have to be very brave . . ." Then they would both begin to cry, she would be hugging him, and it was sweet, incredibly sweet—he would have liked that moment to last all his life, to fill his whole life, leaving room for nothing else, no other face, no other perfume, no other words, only his name repeated softly, Nicolas, Nicolas, nothing more.

10

BEFORE THEY LEFT, THE TEACHER AND THE INSTRUCTORS MADE more coffee while they discussed what to do about Nicolas. He had remained with them, apart from the other children, having apparently settled into his role as a problem to be solved.

"Listen," said Patrick, "there's no need to agonize over this. If it turns out that his father has completely forgotten about the bag, that he's a hundred miles away, then if we wait for him to come back, it'll spoil the kid's stay here and everyone else's too. I suggest we take some petty cash and get him the basics, so that he can participate in everything like the others. Okay with you, little guy?" he added, turning toward Nicolas.

It was okay with him, and the teacher approved as well.

After lunch, during the rest hour when everyone was supposed to nap or read, Nicolas went outside with Patrick. The air was mild; sunlight glittered through bare tree branches. Since he hadn't seen any other vehicle parked on the muddy driveway in front of the chalet, Nicolas thought that they would get to the village in the bus and that the driver would feel strange about having only two passengers. But Patrick walked past the bus, which sat there like a sleepy dragon, and continued down the chalet's little service road for about a hundred yards. Slightly off to one side was a yellow Renault 4L, which Nicolas hadn't noticed when he'd arrived. "The carriage is here!" exclaimed Patrick, opening the door on the driver's side. He got in and slipped off his neck a long leather lanyard with the ignition key on it. Nicolas made as if to get in the back, but Patrick leaned across the front seat to open the door on the passenger's side.

"Whoa, there!" he said merrily. "I'm not your chauffeur!" Nicolas hesitated: he had always been strictly forbidden to ride up front in a car—his father wasn't one to break the law. "Get a move on, buddy!" Nicolas climbed in. "Anyway," remarked Patrick, "it's a pigsty back there." Nicolas peered at the backseat timidly, as if scared that a big dog hiding under the ragged plaid blanket was going to leap at his throat. There were some old cardboard boxes, a backpack, a small carrying case full of cassettes, a coil of rope, and some metal objects that must have been climbing gear.

"Better fasten your seat belt," said Patrick, turning the key in the ignition. The engine coughed. Patrick tried again, kept trying . . . Nothing. Nicolas was afraid Patrick would become cross, but he simply made a silly face and explained to Nicolas, "Patience. She's like that. You have to ask her nicely." Turning the key again, he pressed very lightly on the accelerator, and raising the other foot, he murmured, "Here we go, here we go . . . Good girl!" Nicolas couldn't hold back a little burble of excitement when the car started up and began rolling down the narrow switchback road.

"You like music?" asked Patrick.

Nicolas didn't know what to say. He'd never asked himself that question. They never listened to music at home, they didn't even have a record player, and everyone at school considered the music class a drag. The teacher, Monsieur Ribotton, made them do musical dictation exercises: he played notes on the piano for them to mark down on printed staves in special notebooks. Nicolas never got the notes right. He preferred the short biographies of great musicians Monsieur Ribotton dictated to the class, because at least they were in words, with letters he knew how to write. Monsieur Ribotton was a short man with a very large head, and although his pupils cringed before his violent temper, which had even led him—according to school legend—to throw a stool in a child's face, they thought he was ridiculous. They could tell that the other teachers didn't think much of him, that no one did. His son, Maxime, a sneaky, sweaty little dunce who wanted to be a police detective when he grew up, was in the same class as Nicolas, who didn't much like him but felt sorry for him anyway. One day, a boy sitting in the first row had stretched out his legs and accidentally dirtied the cuffs of Monsieur Ribotton's pants with the soles of his shoes. The teacher had flown into an enormous rage that had inspired neither fear nor respect, only contemptuous pity. With bitter, plaintive fury, he had announced that he was fed up with coming to school just so that someone could get his pants filthy, that he could scarcely afford them as it was, that everything was expensive, that his salary was pitiful, and that if the parents of the student who'd just dirtied his cuffs had enough money to pay for dry cleaning every day, good for them, but as for him, he didn't. His quavering voice made it seem as though he was about to burst into tears, and Nicolas had felt like crying, too, because of Maxime Ribotton, who had to endure the spectacle of his father humiliating himself in front of his classmates, shamelessly spewing out his appalling resentment at having been treated so cruelly by life. Nicolas hadn't dared look at Maxime, but afterward, during recess, he had been amazed to hear Maxime refer to the incident in a casual, joking way, assuring his listeners that they shouldn't be upset when his father threw a fit, that he calmed down pretty quickly. Nicolas had expected Maxime to leave the classroom without a word after that scene and never come back to school again. Then they would have heard that he'd fallen ill. A few kind children would have gone to visit him. Nicolas saw himself going along with them, choosing from among his own toys a present he could give to Maxime without hurting his feelings. He imagined the grateful look in the invalid's eyes, his wasted face and limbs racked with fever, but the gifts and friendly words would be to no avail. One day they would learn that Maxime Ribotton was dead. The band of good-hearted children would go to the funeral, and from then on it was to the grief-stricken father, old man Ribotton, that they resolved to be kind and to show their good hearts. They didn't behave rowdily in his classroom any-more or greet the names of the great musicians he pronounced so respectfully with idiotic rhymes: Stuck-in-the-dirt Schubert, for example, or Schumann the Moron.

Outside of those names, Nicolas didn't know anything about music, but rather than admit this to Patrick he answered eva-sively that yes, he liked it. He already dreaded the next ques-tion, which wasn't long in coming: "And what kind of music do you like?"

"Uh, Schumann . . ." he replied off the top of his head.

Both impressed and amused, Patrick grinned wryly and said that he didn't have that kind of music, just pop songs. He asked Nicolas to pick out a tape: all he had to do was get the little cas-sette case on the backseat and read the titles out loud. Nicolas did. He struggled to decipher the English words, but Patrick filled in the rest after the first stammered syllables and, at the third tape, said fine, that one would do. He slipped it into the tape deck and the music exploded, right in the middle of a song. The voice was hoarse, mocking; the guitars slashed like whips. There was a sense of brutality but of suppleness, too, like the lithe movements of a wild animal. On television, this type of music made his parents turn the sound down in distaste. Ordinarily, if anyone had asked his opinion, Nicolas would have said he didn't care for it—but that day he was thrilled. Next to him, Patrick was tapping out the rhythm on the steering wheel, moving in time to the beat, now and then humming along with the singer, joining in on an exuberant squeal precisely on cue. The car rolled along in perfect harmony with the music, speeding up when it did, sweeping through turns when the tempo slowed, and everything throbbed in unison: the tires gripping the winding road, the shifting gears, and most of all, Patrick himself, swaying gracefully as he drove, a smile on his lips, squinting against the sunshine glinting on the windshield. Nicolas had never heard anything as beautiful as that song. His whole body was caught up in it. If only his entire life could be like that, always traveling up in the front seat, listening to that kind of music. If only he could grow up to be like Patrick: as good a driver, just as relaxed, with the same free and easy way about him.

11

"OKAY," SAID PATRICK AS THEY ENTERED THE STORE, "TIME TO GET serious. What do you need?"

Only then, after the exhilaration of the car ride, did Nicolas remember what they'd come for, remember that his bag had been forgotten in the trunk of his father's car and that his father was probably dead.

"Can you tell me what was in your bag?" asked Patrick.

"Um, extra clothes," replied Nicolas, taken aback by the question. Patrick must have known what was in the bag because everyone had been asked to bring the same things. Each student had been allowed to bring along one or two items of his own choosing, though, like a book or a board game, and in Nicolas's case there had been the drawsheet recommended by the teacher in case he wet his bed. He didn't have the courage to mention this to Patrick.

"And also," he said thoughtfully, "I had my safe."

"Your safe?" exclaimed Patrick, astonished.

"Yes, a little safe, a present so I could keep secrets in it. There's a combination to open it and I'm the only one who knows it."

"And if you forget it, what happens?"

"Then I couldn't open it anymore. No one could ever open it again. But I know it by heart."

"But suppose you get bonked hard on the head and lose your memory? You've written it down somewhere, at least?"

"No. You're not supposed to. Besides, if I lose my memory, I wouldn't remember where I'd written it, either."

"True enough," admitted Patrick. "You're kinda clever, pal."

Nicolas hesitated, not daring to tell Patrick that actually there was a problem with the safe. His father had given it to him along with a closed envelope containing the printed combination, which his father had advised him to destroy after learning the numbers by heart. Nicolas had done that. But it had soon occurred to him that before giving him the envelope his father might have opened it, then skillfully resealed it, thus acquiring access to the safe. Perhaps he took a peek into it from time to time to find out what Nicolas was hiding from him. Perhaps that was the only reason he'd given it to him. Although Nicolas wasn't absolutely sure of this, he was wary and didn't keep anything more private than the gas station coupons in the safe. If Nicolas's father had opened it, he must have been disappointed. But it was more likely that he was dead. Nicolas wasn't certain, though, so he resisted the temptation to tell Patrick this and said instead, trying to sound casual, "I could give it to you, if you want—the combination, I mean."

Patrick shook his head. "No. You don't know me. I might just knock you out after you've told me and then go swipe your secrets."

"Anyway, they're in my father's car."

"I don't want to know. None of my business—the combination or what's in your safe." He grinned and, pretending to point a gun at Nicolas, demanded, "Whatcha got in the safe?"

"Nothing interesting," replied Nicolas glumly.

In the children's clothing section, Patrick picked out a thick woolen shirt and waterproof ski pants that Nicolas tried on in a dressing room while Patrick got together the rest of what was needed: two pairs of underpants, two T-shirts, two pairs of thick socks, one knit cap, and a toothbrush. The ski pants were his size but a bit too long. Patrick briskly rolled up the cuffs, saying they'd be fine, his mother could hem them later if she liked. Nicolas enjoyed this way of shopping, without spending hours hesitating between two styles, two colors, two sizes, frowning with that anxiety entailed in every decision his parents made. He would also have liked a green-and-purple jacket like Patrick's, but of course he didn't dare ask for one.

Patrick chatted briefly with the clerk at the cash register as he paid. She was a cheerful girl and it was immediately obvious that she thought he was cute, that she liked his ponytail, his long face and bright blue eyes, his effortless way of moving and joking around. "This young man belong to you?" she asked, pointing to Nicolas. Patrick answered no, but if no one claimed him within a year and a day, he'd be glad to keep him.

"We get along pretty well, the two of us," he added, and Nicolas said the words over again to himself, proudly. He wanted to tell the other kids, nonchalantly, that he got along pretty well with Patrick. He looked down at his bracelet, the one Patrick had given him, and promised himself that later, when he was out from under his parents' thumb, he'd let his hair grow into a ponytail.

Patrick put the music back on in the car, and while he was driving, swaying to the beat, he made another memorable pronouncement.

"So, doncha think we're kings of the road?"

It took Nicolas a few moments to understand what that meant: everything was going well for them, they were having a good time, there truly wasn't anything for them to worry about—and when he figured this out he felt a joyous exaltation, as though this were their own personal password, just between the two of them. He was afraid that his high-pitched voice would sound shrill when he spoke and betray his littleness, but he overcame this fear and managed to reply, as though it were of no particular importance to him, "That's right. We sure are kings of the road."

12

THE AFTERNOON SNACK WAS FOLLOWED BY PLAYTIME: CHARADES, steal-the-bacon, make-believe. But that day Patrick announced that they were going to do something different.

"What?" they chorused.

"You'll see."

He told a group of them to push the tables, benches, and everything else cluttering the room back against the walls. He turned out all the lights except the ones in the front hall, so that everyone could still see. The children were excited by these mysterious preparations, stifling giggles as they pushed the furniture aside, guessing at what was to come—they were going to play ghosts or hold a table-turning séance . . .

Patrick clapped his hands for silence. "Now," he said, "you're going to lie down on the floor. On your backs." There was a bit more laughing and confusion as they all complied. Only Patrick remained standing, waiting patiently for everyone to find a place. In a calm, unhurried voice, he told them how to make themselves comfortable: first, stretch out, trying not to arch your back but keeping the whole spine flat against the floor; turn your palms up toward the ceiling; close your eyes. "Close your eyes," he repeated almost dreamily, as though he himself were closing his, settling himself to fall asleep.

There was a moment's silence, broken by an impatient voice: "What do we do now?"

"You don't get it?" someone called out. "He's hypnotizing us!"

Scattered snickers greeted this remark, which Patrick ignored. After a little while, he spoke again, as though he'd heard only the first question. "We do nothing . . . We're always busy doing something, thinking about something. Now we're doing nothing. We're trying not to think of anything. We're here, that's all. We're relaxing. Hanging out together . . ." His voice grew even more serene and soothing. He walked slowly around the room, through the maze of supine bodies. Nicolas could feel rather than hear that Patrick was passing close to him. He half opened his eyes but shut them immediately, afraid of getting caught.

"Breathe slowly," said Patrick. "Use your stomach. Make your stomach go up and down like a balloon, but slowly, completely . . ." Several times in a row he repeated, "Breathe in . . . breathe out," and Nicolas sensed that all around, others were following along, joining in the rhythm. He thought he'd never be able to do it. When they had to blow into the balloon during the health checkup, he was always the one with the poorest lung capacity, and his chest felt as though it were in a vise that kept the air from circulating. He breathed in and out more rapidly than the others, in a raggedy way, gasping like a drowning person. Patrick went on speaking, however, in a voice that was strangely both more and more distant and more and more present. "Breathe in . . . breathe out," he was saying, and without understanding how, Nicolas suddenly found himself caught up in that communal respiration, a part of the wave that ebbed and flowed around him, enveloping him. He heard the other children's breathing and his own melting into it. His stomach gently rose and fell, obeying Patrick's voice. Inside him blossomed little hollows into which his breath was pouring the way the incoming tide fills the crevices of a rock.

"That's good," said Patrick after a moment. "Now you're going to think about your tongue." Somewhere in the room, a single child tittered. Nicolas reflected briefly that if everyone had laughed, he would have, too, and found it silly to think about one's tongue, but he went along with the others: he thought about his tongue touching his palate, the way Patrick said it should; he felt its weight, consistency, texture—moist and smooth in some places, rough in others. This sensation grew quite peculiar. The tongue became enormous in his mouth, a huge sponge he was afraid might choke him, but just as the thought occurred to him, Patrick dispelled this fear by saying, "If your tongue becomes too big and bothers you, just swallow some saliva." Nicolas swallowed, and his tongue shrank back to its normal size. He still felt it, though; it was bizarrely

present, as if he'd just become acquainted with it. Then Patrick
told them to think about their noses, to follow the flow of air
through their nostrils. Then to direct their attention behind
their eyelids, between their eyebrows, to the backs of their
necks. From there he went on to the arms, beginning with the
fingers (which he made the boys uncurl one by one), moving up
toward the elbows, then the shoulders. "Your arms are heavy,"
he said, "very heavy. So heavy they're sinking into the ground.
Even if you wanted to, you wouldn't be able to lift them . . ."
And Nicolas felt that it was true, he couldn't do it. He lay spread
out on the flagstone floor like a puddle, while his mind floated
over his inert body and yet inhabited it as if it were a house with
deep foundations, exploring the passages running through his
limbs, pushing open the doors of rooms that were dark, warm—
above all, warm. Heat was now his strongest sensation, and he
was not surprised to hear Patrick describe it, urging them to
welcome it, enjoy it, let themselves be invaded by this intense
but pleasurable warmth that flowed through their veins, swirled
at the surface of their skin, provoking faint tinglings and long-
ings to scratch that were best resisted. "But if you really want
to," added Patrick, "go ahead, it doesn't matter." How did he
know that? How was he able to describe these extraordinary
things Nicolas was feeling—at the exact moment when he was
feeling them? Was it the same for the other children? There was
no more laughter, only placid breathing, attentive to Patrick's
voice. All were visiting, like Nicolas, this mysterious territory
within them, all listening with the same confidence to their
guide. As long as Patrick was speaking, telling them where to go

(now it was the legs, the individual toes, the calves, knees, and thighs), nothing could happen. They were safe, deep inside their bodies. It went on and on. How long had it been going on?

Suddenly, Nicolas sensed that Patrick was leaning over him. He heard a knee crack faintly. Patrick had crouched down, and he now placed his hands—palms quite flat—high up on Nicolas's chest, just below the shoulders, where they remained perfectly still. Nicolas's heart began to pound and his momentarily tranquil breathing grew panicky. He didn't dare open his eyes and gaze into Patrick's, looming above him. Very softly, Patrick whispered, "Shh," the way one quiets a nervous animal, and his palms weighed a touch more heavily on Nicolas's chest, the fingertips spreading out toward the shoulders so as to press them farther down, to thrust Nicolas even deeper into the ground. Nicolas felt as though he were panting, dashing around helter-skelter inside himself, bumping into walls, and at the same time he knew that none of this showed on the outside. His body remained motionless, tense in spite of Patrick's efforts, which Nicolas guessed were meant to help him relax. He could hear Patrick breathing quite calmly above him. He thought of the Shell stations' plastic model, of its thorax cover you could remove to look inside. Patrick was leaning on this cover, he was trying to identify, to tame what was underneath, but everything was in turmoil: it was as though all Nicolas's organs had fled in terror as far as they could from the wall against which pressed these firm, warm hands, and yet Nicolas would have liked these hands to stay there. He could hardly restrain a groan when they relaxed their pressure, then slowly withdrew.

Patrick's knee cracked again when he stood up; the sound of his breathing grew fainter. Peeking through half-open eyelids, Nicolas turned his head slightly to see Patrick bending over another child, starting all over again. Nicolas closed his eyes. A sudden shiver ran through his body. Had his father taken the coupons out of the safe? Had he already gotten the plastic model when the accident occurred? Trying to calm down, Nicolas imagined once more how things would go: the telephone that would perhaps begin ringing now, while Patrick was silently pressing on someone else's chest; the rest of the evening, disrupted by the devastating news; then that night, the next day, his life as an orphan. All the same, he felt it wasn't right to let himself get caught up in such daydreams, which could bring bad luck. What if the telephone really did ring, if the things he'd imagined to make himself sad and console himself actually happened? It would be dreadful. Not only would he be an orphan, he'd be guilty, awfully guilty. It would be as though he'd killed his own father. One day, to illustrate his usual warnings about being careful, his father had told the story of a classmate who'd pointed a gun at a younger brother—all in fun, of course— without realizing that it was loaded. He'd pulled the trigger, and the bullet had struck his little brother in the heart. What happened next? wondered Nicolas. What did they do to him, this child murderer? They couldn't punish him; it wasn't his fault, and he'd already been punished enough. Comfort him, then? But how do you comfort a child who has done that? What can you say to him? Can you, can his parents hug him and tell him gently that it's all over, forgotten, that now everything will be fine? No. What, then? Try to lie to him so that his life won't be ruined, invent a less horrible version of the accident, and gradually convince him of its truth? The gun went off all by itself, he wasn't the one holding it, he had nothing to do with it . . .

"Very slowly," said Patrick, "you're going to start moving again . . . First your feet. Swing them in circles around your ankles . . . Like that . . . Nice and easy . . . You can open your eyes now."

13

THAT NIGHT, NICOLAS WENT FOR A RIDE ON THE CATERPILLAR. The grown-up who accompanied him wasn't his father but Patrick. They'd left his little brother with the father of the boy from the amusement park. Nicolas's brother was wearing his green slicker (with the hood up, even though it wasn't raining) and his red rubber boots. He waved good-bye to them while he held the hand of the other boy's father, who was still smiling. You couldn't see his face very clearly. Patrick had taken a seat way in the back of a car, with his knees resting against the metal sides, and Nicolas went to sit snugly between his long legs. The man in charge of the ride dropped the safety bar down across their laps and locked it in place. The caterpillar started moving, gliding in front of the little brother still waving his hand, and then, rising abruptly, it left the ground. Up in the sky, the caterpillar hung motionless, then hurtled into its descent. Nicolas felt himself sucked into a void that was somehow inside him as well. His stomach turned over; he was scared, trying to laugh. Now the caterpillar was going fast. It came around to ground level again, whooshing like a speeding train, and shot immediately back up into the air. This time he barely had a chance to see the ticket window, his little brother, the people around him; he and Patrick were once more flung into the sky (but harder, faster), once more stopped at that frightening place and moment marking the sudden plunge down the other side. Nicolas pushed with his feet against the ground rushing up at them and held tight to the safety bar, while Patrick gripped it, too, his big, tanned hands clenched at either side of the small wrists. The sleeves of his sweatshirt were rolled up, revealing ropy veins that stood out prominently on his forearms. Against his back, Nicolas could feel Patrick's hard belly contract in apprehension on the edge of the abyss just as his own stomach did, and then tighten even more, trying to resist in that instant when their free fall actually began. There was a moment's respite at the bottom, but then they'd already begun the climb back, already reached the crest, and the marvelous panic of the descent was upon them again. With Patrick's taut thighs squeezing his legs, Nicolas kept his eyes tightly shut. Just before reaching the top, however, he suddenly opened them and saw the entire amusement park, far below: tiny figures, human ants milling about on the ground, light years away. During that brief instant, his eye was drawn to one—no, two—of these figures, a man walking away and a small child holding his hand. The caterpillar was already streaking earthward, it was impossible to see anything, but Nicolas realized what was happening. The next time around, he stared down, wide-eyed with icy horror; the man leading off his little brother was already farther away. They would be lost to sight when the caterpillar dove again, and at its next ascent Nicolas was certain that he wouldn't be able to spot them anymore. They would have vanished. He was seeing— had seen—his little brother for the last time, at least as he was now, with his eyes, all his limbs, all the organs in his body still intact. What had just slipped away before Nicolas's helpless gaze was the last image he would have of the child: a chubby little figure in a slicker and red rubber boots, holding the hand of a man in a denim jacket . . . and it was useless to cry out. Even Patrick (against whose body his own was pressed) would not hear him, and even if he did, even if he had seen the same thing, it wouldn't make any difference. The ride lasted three minutes. There was no alarm button, and you couldn't get off once the ride had begun. For another minute and a half, two minutes, they were going to keep whirling around and around while his little brother disappeared behind a fence, led off by the man in the denim jacket to his accomplices in their white coats, and when the ride was over, when they'd climbed down unsteadily, it would be too late. Was Nicolas the only one who'd seen it? Or had Patrick, too? No, he hadn't seen a thing—it was better that way. When the ride stopped, he would lift Nicolas up from between his legs and clamber out of the car with a big grin, telling him again that they were kings of the road. For a few seconds longer he would remain unaware of what had happened, still able to smile. Nicolas envied him and would have given his life not to have opened his eyes, looked down, seen what he had seen, so that he might share Patrick's blissful ignorance and live one more minute with him in a world from which his little brother had not yet disappeared. He would have given his life to have that minute last forever, so that the caterpillar ride would never end. What had just happened, what was happening below would not exist. They would never learn about it. There would be nothing else on earth except the caterpillar turning faster and faster, the centrifugal force tossing them way up into the sky, pressing them tightly against each other, this hole gaping in his belly, sucking him up from the inside, filling itself for an instant only to open up again, going deeper and deeper, and Patrick's stomach against Nicolas's back, Patrick's thighs next to his legs, Patrick's breath against his neck, and the noise, and the void, and the sky.

14

THE DAMPNESS AWAKENED HIM, OVERWHELMING HIM WITH A
feeling of disaster. The sheet was wet, as were the pants and top
of his pajamas. Thinking he was back at home, he almost called
out in tears but stifled his cry in time. Everyone was asleep.
The wind whistled through the fir trees outside. Lying on his
stomach, Nicolas was afraid to move. At first he hoped that the
warmth of his body would dry the sheet and his pajamas before
morning came. No one would notice anything the next day unless they climbed up to look, to sniff at the covers. But he didn't
smell the characteristic odor of peepee. This smell was not as
sharp, barely noticeable. The consistency of the puddle was different, too, like tacky glue between his body and the sheet.
Worried, he stealthily slipped one hand beneath himself and
felt something viscous. He wondered if his tummy had come
open, letting this sticky liquid leak out. Blood? It was too dark

to tell, but he imagined an enormous red stain spreading across the bed, across Hodkann's blue pajamas. At the slightest movement, his insides would spill out. A wound would have hurt him, though, and he didn't feel pain anywhere. He was scared. He didn't dare raise his hand to his face, bringing that gummy stuff, that jellyfish secretion from inside him, close to his mouth, his eyes, his nostrils. He could feel himself staring, his face grimacing with fright at the idea that something ghastly was happening to him that had never, ever happened to anyone else, something supernatural.

In the book of horror stories where he'd found "The Monkey's Paw," he'd read about a young man who drinks a strange elixir, then watches his body gradually decompose, liquefy into a blackish slime. He isn't really the one who sees this, in the story—it's his mother, who is astonished that he won't leave his room anymore, won't let anyone in, and speaks in a voice that becomes clotted, curdled, dropping lower and lower until soon it's a kind of incomprehensible gurgling. Then he gives up talking, communicates through notes slipped under the door, messages on which the writing deteriorates as well, the last ones little more than desperate scribbles on paper covered with oily black stains. And when—beside herself with worry—the mother has the door broken down, all that remains is a revolting puddle on the floor, at the surface of which float two lumps that once were eyes.

Nicolas had read this story eagerly but without any real feeling of terror, as though it couldn't happen to him, and now something like it was happening to him, now this gluey pus was oozing from his body. It was worse than a cut, it was a leak, something seeping out of him. Soon it would *be* him. What would the others find in his bed in the morning?

He was afraid, afraid of them, afraid of himself. He had to run away, he thought, and hide, and dissolve off by himself, alone. It was all over for him. No one would ever see him again.

Cautiously, expecting every moment to hear a horrid slurping noise, he managed to lift his stomach off the sheet. Throwing back the covers, he crawled to the ladder and climbed down. Hodkann's eyes were closed. Nicolas tiptoed from the dormitory without waking anyone. Out in the hallway, the light switch gave off a tiny orange gleam but he didn't turn it on. At the very end of the hall, unobscured by shutters or curtains, the milky glow from the window overlooking the woods allowed him to orient himself. He went downstairs, his bare feet chilled by the tiles. On the second floor, all the doors were closed except the one to the small office where the teacher had called his mother that morning. He went in, spotted the telephone, and reflected that he could use it if he wanted. Talking quietly, in the dead of night, without anyone knowing—but to whom? It was also in this office that the teacher and the instructors kept all the notebooks of class records. He could have looked through them, hoping to find something about himself. On those rare occasions when he was left home alone, he used the opportunity to go through his parents' belongings, his mother's dressing table, the drawers of his father's desk, without knowing precisely what secret he was looking for but with the vague certainty that discovering it was a matter of life and death for him and that, if he did discover it, his parents mustn't ever find out. He was careful to put everything back exactly where it had been so they would not be suspicious. He dreaded not hearing the door creak when they came home, being caught, startled by his father's hand falling heavily on his shoulder. He felt shaky, and his heart raced with excitement.

bad relationship

He didn't linger in the office but went on down to the first floor. The pajamas were sticking to his thighs, his stomach. A phantom class was assembled in the dim light of the hall, après-ski boots lined up along the wall, jackets hanging on a row of hooks. The front door was closed, of course, but only with a bolt, which he simply slipped open. He pulled the heavy door silently inward and saw that outside everything was white.

15

THERE WAS SNOW ALL OVER. IT WAS STILL FALLING, THE FLAKES
spinning delicately in the wind. Nicolas had never seen so much
snow, and in the depths of despair he was filled with wonder.
The frosty night air stung his half-naked chest, a striking change
from the heat of the house sleeping behind him like a huge
sated animal, its breath warm and even. Nicolas stood still for
a moment on the threshold, caught a snowflake lightly in his
hand, and went outside.

Thrusting his bare feet into the as yet unblemished snow, he
crossed the top of the driveway. The bus looked like a drowsing
animal, too, the chalet's cub, nestled against its flank, dozing
with its big blank headlight eyes wide open. Walking past the
bus, Nicolas followed a path to the snow-covered road, turning
around several times to look at his footprints, which were deep
and, above all, solitary, spectacularly solitary: he was alone out

there that night, alone as he trudged through the snow with nothing on his feet, in damp pajamas, and no one knew it, and no one would ever see him again. In a few minutes, his tracks would have vanished.

Just after the first hairpin bend in the road, near where Patrick's car was parked, he stopped. He caught sight of a yellow light moving through the branches of the fir trees, down in the valley; then it disappeared. Probably the headlights of a car on the main road. Who was traveling at that late hour? Who, without knowing it, was sharing the silence and solitude of that night with him?

Upon leaving the house, Nicolas had intended to walk straight ahead until his strength gave out and he collapsed, but he was so cold that, almost unconsciously, he headed for Patrick's car as though it were a climber's hut. To reach it he had to wade through snow that was up to his knees. The door was unlocked. He climbed into the driver's seat and tucked his legs beneath him, trying to curl up in a ball in front of the steering wheel. When he touched the seat, it was already wet and freezing cold. He slid a hand between his skin and the waistband of his pajamas, but the viscous liquid had dried into a crust; the trickling he felt was only melting snow. Shivering, he cradled his hand down by his lower abdomen, between his navel and the thing he didn't like to mention because none of the names for it seemed like the real one to him: not *weewee*, which his parents used sometimes; nor *penis*, which he'd read in the medical dictionary; nor *dick*, which he'd heard at school. One day, in a corner of the playground, a classmate had gotten his thing out and shown Nicolas, for laughs, how it obeyed him. It stood up when he called to it, "Come on, Toto! Jump up, Toto!" Holding it between two fingers, he pulled it down like a lever, making it spring back against his belly. It had to have a name, though, a real name that Nicolas would learn later on.

He remembered the story of the Little Mermaid, which had been, with *Pinocchio*, one of his two favorite books when he was very young. There was a moment that had always had a strange effect on him, when the Little Mermaid, in love with the prince she has glimpsed during a storm at sea, dreams of becoming human so that he might fall in love with her. This is why she seeks a magic spell from the witch, who gives her a potion to make legs grow in the place of her fishtail—and takes the mermaid's voice in exchange. Now she must make the prince fall in love with a mute, and if she fails, if the prince has not declared his love to her at the end of three days, she will die. The part Nicolas liked best was when she had to spend the night alone on the beach after drinking the potion. She lay down on the sand with her fishtail covered with leaves and waited on the seashore beneath the distant, glittering stars for the metamorphosis to occur. There was a drawing in Nicolas's book that showed her like that, with long blond tresses hiding her breasts, and scales that began just below her navel. The drawing wasn't pretty, but you could imagine the incredible softness of her belly, beneath the fishtail. During the night, in pain, the Little Mermaid didn't dare look under the leaves, where what was still her was struggling with what she soon would be. It hurt, it hurt a great deal. She moaned softly, fearing to attract the attention of the fishermen who were chatting around their fire farther along the beach, mending their nets. Quite low, for herself alone, she tried to sing, so that she might hear her own voice one last time. When dawn came, she could tell that the battle was over, that the charm had done its work. She felt that there was something different under the leaves, that what she had been had become something else. She was afraid. Her soul was unbearably sad, and her voice had already died away in her throat. Slowly, feeling their way along, her hands moved down her body and there, below the navel, where ever since her birth the scales had begun, the silky skin continued. Nothing so affected Nicolas as this moment—quite brief in the book—which he could spend whole hours imagining, when the hands of the Little Mermaid first touched her legs. Curled up in his bed, the covers drawn snugly about him, he would play at being the Little Mermaid before he dropped off to sleep. He'd run his own hands along his thighs, along the soft skin on the inside of his thighs, skin so soft that the illusion was possible, that he could believe he was touching the Little Mermaid's thighs, calves, ankles, the graceful and so-slender ankles of the Little Mermaid, and together they would be drawn as if magnetized, the Little Mermaid and he, back up to the inside of the thighs, where hands were kept warm, and it was so sweet, so sad, this feeling, that he would have liked it to last forever and he always began to cry.

He was too cold now, he couldn't make the tears come, but it was even more like it was in the story. He wasn't home in bed but alone outdoors, beneath the cold and glistening stars, sur-

he's embarrassed about the pajamas and runs away

DENIAL

losing power and freedom

rounded by cold and glistening snow, and far from everyone, far from any help, like the Little Mermaid who understood at dawn that she no longer belonged to the world of sea creatures and would never, ever belong to the world of men. She was alone, completely alone, with no other comfort but her own warmth and the softness of her belly, and she coiled herself around this core, seeking refuge. Her teeth were chattering and she was sobbing with grief and dismay, for she already knew that she had lost everything and would have nothing in return. It would have cheered her to hear her own voice, but she no longer had a voice—that was gone, too, and Nicolas understood that the same fate awaited him as well. No one would ever hear his voice again. He would die of cold during the night. They'd find his body in the morning: blue, stiffened by a thin crust of frost, almost brittle. Patrick would probably be the one who discovered him. He would gather him up in his arms, lift him out of the car, and try to revive him with mouth-to-mouth resuscitation, but in vain. It would also be Patrick who would close his staring eyes, eyes filled with suffering and horror. It wouldn't be easy getting the frozen eyelids to go down, and everyone would be afraid to meet the terror-stricken gaze of the dead little boy, but Patrick would find a way. With the tips of his deft, tanned fingers he would know how to soften and gently close the eyelids, and his hands would linger on the now sightless face, a face forever at peace.

His parents would have to be told. The entire school would come to his funeral.

While he was imagining how the service would be (a comforting thought), a branch scraped the car's windshield, and fear gripped him once more. Fear not so much of an animal as of a murderer prowling around the chalet at night, ready to tear apart any child careless enough to wander away from its protection, its friendly slumbering warmth. Nicolas remembered the car, the headlights he'd seen on the road below, the traveler who alone was awake with him that night, and he remained on the alert for a noise, for the muffled crunch of a step in the snow. His hands were tucked away between his thighs, which trembled uncontrollably; one hand clutched that tiny thing without a name, and he wasn't crying, but his face was twisted in alarm. He opened his mouth to shout without making a sound, opened his eyes wide to make a mask of frightful anguish, so that those who found him would understand just from looking at him what he had suffered before dying a few yards away from them, in the snow and the darkness, while they were all fast asleep.

16

HE WASN'T EVEN AWARE THAT HIS WHOLE BODY WAS SHIVERING gently. He hadn't fainted, but the thoughts couldn't circulate anymore through the slowly freezing channels of his brain. Sometimes his mind felt sluggish, like a lethargic fish rising from placid, inky depths, approaching the thin skin of ice that covered the surface and leaving behind, just before vanishing back into the darkness, a tiny trace, a blink, an instantaneously erased ripple of astonishment: so that's what dying was . . . Diving lazily like that, into torpor, icy coldness, deep down to the calm black place where soon there would be no more Nicolas, no more body to tremble, no more consolation to seek, no more anything. He no longer knew if his eyes were open or closed. He felt the steering wheel against his forehead but saw nothing, neither the car door nor the stretch of snowy road and the fir trees framed in the window. At some point, however, a beam of light struck his eyelids: it moved around, going in different directions. Nicolas thought fleetingly of the nocturnal traveler, then of a gigantic deep-sea fish swimming around him, enveloping him in its phosphorescent aura. He would have liked to sink down, farther and farther down with the fish into the great depths, to escape from the traveler, to avoid seeing his face. He almost screamed when the flashlight beam blinded him as the car door was opened. A dark form leaned in, bending over him, and he seemed to choke on his own cry. A hand touched him as a voice said, "Nicolas, Nicolas, what's the matter?" When he recognized that voice, his entire body relaxed: muscles, nerves, bones, thoughts—everything began to melt, to flow endlessly, like tears, while Patrick was gathering him up in his arms.

He must have opened his eyes again, because he remembered the car door hanging open behind them while Patrick carried him back up the drive. In his hurry to get him inside, Patrick had neglected to slam the door shut, and the image of that door sticking out from the side of the car like a broken fin had fixed itself in Nicolas's mind. Later on, to make him laugh, Patrick and Marie-Ange told him that while they were rubbing him, he talked constantly about that door, saying that they had to go back and shut it. They were wondering if he'd survive, and he—he was concerned only that the door shouldn't stay open all night out on the road.

Then there had been light, Patrick's face, and Marie-Ange's, and their voices saying his name over and over. Nicolas, Nicolas. He was with them: their warm hands were moving over his

"fish out of water" The door symbolizes him being out of his comfort zone / open

body, rubbing him, wrapping him up, and yet they were calling him as though he were lost in a forest and they were part of a search party to find him. He lay in the undergrowth, wounded, losing blood, and heard their anxious voices in the distance calling, "Nicolas, Nicolas, where are you, Nicolas?" But he couldn't answer them. Once, steps rustled in the leaves: they were passing close by him without realizing it, and he couldn't make himself heard—they were already moving away, going off to search in another part of the woods. Later, Patrick picked him up again and carried him upstairs. They laid him down, put heavy blankets over him, held his head up so that he could drink something quite hot, which made him make a face, but Marie-Ange's voice insisted, said that it was good, he had to drink up. The glass was tipped and the burning liquid poured down his throat. Feeling began to return to his body, which was shot through by great, long shivers of such amplitude that they became voluptuous. He undulated under the covers like a big fish flapping its tail in slow motion. He kept his eyes shut, had no idea where he'd been taken, knew only that it was a safe place, that he was warm, that they were looking after him, that Patrick had come to save him from death and had carried him in his arms to this warmth and this safety. The voices around him had dwindled to murmurs; some slightly scratchy material was rubbing against his mouth. His body kept trembling with long, slow, convulsive movements that went down to the soles of his feet, where they lingered as though desirous of going farther, of stretching him out even more. He was so small, tucked into one end of the bed, cud-

REPETITION CYCLE

dled under the blanket as though he were in a cave, and the foot of the bed seemed infinitely far away, and higher too. It towered over him like a gigantic dune, rising way up into the sky and slanting down to vanish beneath his cheek. Down the vast slope of this dune rolled a black ball. It was only a small spot at first, when it left the summit, but as it descended it grew bigger and bigger, enormous, and Nicolas could tell that it would take up all the space, that there would be nothing left but it and that it would crush him. The humming sound it made grew louder as it came closer. Nicolas was scared but soon realized that he could make the black ball retreat whenever he liked, could suddenly send it all the way back to the top, condemned to a fresh descent that he would again be able to interrupt before he was smashed. *Just* before: all the pleasure lay in letting the black ball get as close as possible, in escaping from it at the very last moment.

Reference to Sisyphus' boulder myth where he would push a boulder up the hill and the watch it roll down. This is used for people who feel trapped.

75

17

HE FELT HOT, QUITE HOT, HUDDLED UNDER THE COVERS. HE WAS awake, but he put off the moment of opening his eyes, wishing to prolong the heat, the comfort. The insides of his eyelids were orange. From somewhere in the chalet—a washing machine, perhaps, or maybe it was his own ears—came a faint, soothing hum. The wash was going around and around behind its little porthole, tumbling slowly in the scalding water. Nicolas's knees touched his chin; the hand clutching the covers was pressed against his lips—he could feel the dry warmth of the knuckles. Somewhere in the bed was his other hand, somewhere in the lazy, toasty depths where his body lay all curled up. When he finally opened his eyes, the light was warm too. The curtains had been drawn, but behind them the sun was shining so brightly that the room was bathed in an orange glow sprinkled with tiny dots of light. Recognizing the table, the lamp shade, Nicolas understood that they'd installed him in the office where the telephone was. He let out a feeble moan, to hear the sound of his voice, then groaned again, louder, to find out if there was anyone around. Out in the hall, footsteps approached. The teacher sat down on the edge of his bed. Putting a hand on his forehead, she asked him softly if he felt better, if he hurt anywhere. She offered to open the windows, and the sunshine streamed gaily into the room. Then she went to get a thermometer. Did Nicolas know how to take his own temperature? He nodded. She handed him the thermometer, which vanished into the bed. Fumbling under the covers, still curled up in a ball, he pulled down his pajama pants and guided the thermometer between his buttocks. It felt cold and he had trouble finding the hole, but he managed, nodding again when the teacher asked him if everything was okay. She continued to stroke his forehead while they waited; after a moment, there was a faint ringing under the blanket. The teacher said that was enough time, and the thermometer made its way back to her. "Almost a hundred and three degrees," she read. "You should rest." When she asked him if he wanted anything to eat, he said no; something to drink, then—he ought to have fluids for a temperature. Nicolas drank, then withdrew into the warmth, the sweet and fuzzy sluggishness of fever. He played some more with the black ball. Later, the telephone awakened him. The teacher arrived as quickly as if she had been standing right outside in the hallway. She spoke for a few minutes in a low voice, smiling at Nicolas all the while, then hung up, sat on the edge of his bed to have him take his temperature again, and gave him more to drink. She asked him gently if he'd ever walked around at night before without realizing what he was doing. He said he didn't know, and she squeezed his hand as though satisfied with his answer, which both surprised and relieved him. Still later, he heard the bus rumbling out in the driveway, and in the front hall, his classmates returning with cheerful commotion from their skiing lesson. There were shouts, trampling footsteps on the stairs, laughter. The teacher asked everyone to quiet down because Nicolas was ill. He smiled, closed his eyes again. He loved being sick, having a fever, pushing back the big black ball just when it was about to flatten him. He loved these strange sounds—cracklings, buzzings—coming from outside or inside his body, he didn't know which. He loved being taken care of, without any responsibilities besides swallowing a little medicine. He spent a wonderful day, sometimes letting himself drift off into a teeming, feverish drowsiness, sometimes enjoying lying awake, absolutely still, listening to the bustling life of the chalet without having to take part in it. He heard a tangle of shrill voices downstairs at mealtime, plates being stacked, merriment, the tongue-in-cheek scoldings of the teacher and instructors. The teacher came up to see him every hour, and Patrick came once too. He felt Nicolas's forehead, like the teacher did, and told him he was really something else. Nicolas would have liked to thank him for saving his life, but he was afraid that kings of the road didn't do such things, that it would sound fake, soppy, so he kept quiet. At nightfall, the teacher told Nicolas that she had to call his mother again. She'd already called her that morning, while he was asleep, and now she had to bring her up to date on how he was doing. He could speak to his mother if he wished. Nicolas gave a long, drawn-out sigh, indicating that he didn't feel up to it, and heard only what the teacher reported. That he had a high fever, that it was too bad, of course, poor thing, but that no, he didn't need to be sent home. And there wasn't anyone who could take him home, either. Then she talked about sleep-walking. She said cases like this were not uncommon, but it was surprising no one had noticed it until now. Nicolas could tell, from what the teacher said, that his mother was protesting: he had never walked in his sleep before. Nicolas was annoyed by her insistence on defending him from this accusation, as though it were some shameful disease for which she might have been held accountable. He was quite content to have the teacher put the previous evening's events down to sleepwalking. That way, he didn't have to explain himself. It wasn't his fault, it wasn't a question of willpower. They would leave him alone. "I'd like to put Nicolas on the phone," said the teacher, hastening to add, after Nicolas looked at her imploringly, "but he's asleep right now." Nicolas flashed her a grateful smile before snuggling down into his bed again, wriggling his entire body, burying his face in the pillow and smiling, this time, all to himself.

18

NICOLAS SLEPT WELL, AND THE NEXT DAY WAS A PERFECTLY HAPPY one. In the morning, Patrick came into the office and, with the complicitous grin of a fellow king of the road, told him that he'd been monopolizing the teacher long enough: with all the snow that had fallen, there was no question of her missing any more skiing, and since they weren't going to leave him alone in the chalet, he'd be coming along too. Nicolas was afraid he would have to go skiing and tried to protest that he didn't feel well, but Patrick had already begun getting him dressed by adding several layers of warm clothing on top of his pajamas, an outfit that made him look, exclaimed Patrick gleefully, like the Michelin tire man. Announcing, "Last layer!" he plopped the pudgy figure down on the bed and swaddled it in the blanket. When he finally picked up the bundle, only Nicolas's eyes could be seen. Thus burdened, Patrick went downstairs and made a grand entrance into the main room, where breakfast had been cleared away and the children were getting ready to leave. "Here's a bag of dirty laundry!" joked Patrick, and Marie-Ange burst out laughing. The others crowded around them. In Patrick's arms, Nicolas felt as though he had climbed a tree to escape a pack of wolves. They could growl, slaver, claw the trunk all they liked—he was safe on the highest branch. He noticed that Hodkann was not among the encircling wolves but off on one side, reading, without seeming at all interested in what was happening. They had not spoken to each other for two days.

In the bus, Patrick arranged a kind of bed for him from two seats and a big pillow. Marie-Ange said that he was a real pasha and that Patrick was going to spoil him rotten if this kept up. Behind Nicolas, the others snickered a bit, but he pretended not to hear.

"And now, off to the bistro!" said Patrick when they'd arrived in the village. He picked Nicolas up again, still wrapped in his blanket, and carried him to the village café, which was at the foot of the ski slopes. Chatting with the café owner, a big man with a mustache, Patrick installed Nicolas comfortably on a banquette near the window, which overlooked—through a balcony with wooden balusters carved in the shape of fir trees—the modest hill where beginners had their lessons. The children were already putting on their skis and waving their poles around, and Marie-Ange and the teacher seemed overwhelmed. Nicolas was glad to have escaped all that. Patrick gave him a bunch of old comic books (not very interesting, but something to do) and asked what the gentleman would like to drink.

"Give him a mug of mulled wine," chuckled the owner. "That'll get him back on his feet in a hurry!"

Patrick ordered Nicolas a hot chocolate, ruffled his hair, and went outside, passing in front of the window to rejoin the group. They all turned toward him confidently, as though he alone could solve every problem—defective bindings, lost gloves, incorrectly buckled boots—and always with a joke and a smile.

Nicolas stayed in the café for the three hours the skiing lesson lasted. He was the only one there, aside from the owner, who readied the tables for lunch without paying him the slightest attention. Nicolas felt fine propped against his pillow, swathed in his blanket like a mummy. He had never felt so fine in his life. He hoped that his fever would last long enough so that everything would stay the same the next day, and the day after that, and all the other days of ski school. How many more were there? He'd already spent three days in the chalet, so there must be ten left. Ten days of being sick, excused from everything, carried around in blankets by Patrick—it would be marvelous. He wondered how he could prolong his fever, which he could feel letting up already. His ears weren't buzzing anymore, and he had to make a real effort to shiver. Now and then he groaned weakly, as though he'd half fainted and were once again beyond the control of his conscious mind. Perhaps, now that he was supposed to be a sleepwalker, he might be able to go outside at night again, to stretch out his illness and keep everyone worried about him.

The business about sleepwalking had been a lucky thing for him. He'd been afraid of reproaches, but thanks to this explanation, no one had blamed him for anything or even expected anything of him. He was more to be pitied, actually. He was suffering from a mysterious illness: they didn't know when it might strike again or how to prevent it. Yes, it was really a lucky thing. The teacher would convince his parents in spite of their misgivings. Nicolas walks in his sleep, they'd whisper at home. Of course, they wouldn't say it in front of him; when a child is seriously ill, no one talks about it in front of him. How serious was it, being a sleepwalker? The benefits were clear, but were there any real drawbacks? He'd heard people say that it was extremely dangerous to awaken someone who was sleepwalking. But how was it dangerous? For whom? What could happen? Was there a risk the sleepwalker might die or else go crazy, try to strangle whoever had awakened him? If he did something bad—really awful—during a fit, would it be his fault? Certainly not. Another advantage of sleepwalking was how hard it was to expose a faker. To claim you have the flu, you have to have a fever, which can be checked, whereas if Nicolas were to start walking around every night with a vacant stare and his hands held out in front of him, people might suspect that he was pretending in order to make himself interesting or to have an excuse for doing forbidden things, but they could not accuse him of faking if there was the slightest doubt about it. Unless, of course, there were some special ways of finding out. Somewhat uneasily, Nicolas imagined his father opening the trunk of his car to produce a device with dials and needles, a helmet he would strap onto Nicolas's head, something that would prove irrefutably, if Nicolas got out of bed at night, that he was completely conscious, that he was responsible for his actions and was trying to fool everyone around him.

Ever since Nicolas had fallen ill, there had been no more mention of his father. The first day, they had expected him to return or at least to telephone. That seemed to go without saying, for they assumed he would open his trunk and find the bag there. But as he'd given no sign of life, they'd simply stopped counting on him and wondering when he would arrive. If this silence had meant he'd had an accident, as Nicolas had thought, they would have discovered him by the roadside during the last three days. His mother would have been informed, and therefore he'd have found out too. Even if it had been decided to put off telling him, he would definitely have sensed from the way people were acting that something serious had happened. But no. It was curious, this mystery—plus the fact that everyone had so quickly lost interest in it, no longer seemed to notice it. Even Nicolas, at a loss for explanations, had stopped puzzling over it. He hoped only that his father would not return, that ski school would continue the way it was, with every day like this one, and that his fever would last and last. He looked outside, through the fogged-up window and the carved fir trees. On the beginners' slope, Patrick had lined up poles for the children to zigzag around. Some could ski already, and they teased those who couldn't. Maxime Ribotton came down the hill on his backside. Nicolas was warm. He closed his eyes. He felt comfy.

19

THE POLICEMEN WORE NAVY-BLUE SWEATERS WITH LEATHER shoulder patches but no coats or jackets, and Nicolas's first thought, as he sat bundled in his blanket, was that they must be terribly cold. When they'd pushed open the door, a chilly draft had swept into the café—you expected to see a flurry of snow following close on their heels. The owner had gone down into the cellar through a trap door behind the bar, and almost a minute went by before Nicolas decided it was up to him to greet the new arrivals. Under different circumstances, this role would have intimidated him, but his fever and especially the fact that he'd been declared a sleepwalker inspired him with the boldness of someone who feels forgiven in advance, unfettered by the consequences of his actions. From his corner, rather loudly, he called out, "Hello!" Busy brushing snow from their boots, the policemen hadn't noticed him and now looked around to see where the voice had come from, as though expecting to find a parrot's cage hanging somewhere. For a moment Nicolas thought he'd become invisible. To help them, he wriggled a bit. The blanket fell down about his shoulders. Then both men spotted him at the same time, cozily ensconced near the misty window. They exchanged a quick, almost alarmed glance, and hurried over to him. In spite of the fever and the sleepwalking, Nicolas was afraid that he'd made a stupid mistake, that he'd just jumped into the lion's mouth, that perhaps these weren't real policemen. Standing there looming over him, they studied him wordlessly, then glanced at each other again. The taller of the two shook his head, and the other one finally spoke to Nicolas, asking him what he was doing there. Nicolas explained, but now that the brief alert he had provoked was over, his answer didn't really seem to interest them anymore.

"Okay, so you're not by yourself," concluded the taller man, relieved. At that moment, the café owner popped out of the trap door. The policemen joined him at the bar, abandoning Nicolas. Their manner was grave: a child had disappeared from the hamlet of Panossière, a couple of miles away. They'd been looking for him for the past two days, without success. Nicolas realized what the policemen had hoped for when they'd first seen him, and he thought that in a way they'd come pretty close: two days—that meant the child had disappeared right when he himself had almost vanished.

When he was younger, Nicolas had read the *Secret Seven* adventure series, and he remembered that some stories had begun like this: one of the child detectives, overhearing a grown-up conversation, would nose out a mystery, which the band would then solve. He imagined himself outpacing the official investigation, finding the lost little boy and taking him to the police station, explaining modestly that it hadn't been so difficult: simply thinking about it had done the trick, and then he'd been lucky, of course. Raising his voice to make himself heard and trying not to sound screechy, he asked how old the boy was. The policemen and the café owner turned toward him in surprise.

"Nine years old," replied one of the officers, "and his name is René. You haven't seen him, by any chance?"

"I don't know," said Nicolas. "Do you have a picture him?"

The policeman seemed more and more astonished at Nicolas's interest in the inquiry, but he replied evenly that he happened to have some fliers that had just been printed up for distribution throughout the surrounding area. He pulled a bundle from a bag and showed one to Nicolas.

"Look familiar?"

The photo was in black and white, poorly reproduced. Still, you could tell that René had blond hair, a Dutch-boy cut, and glasses; his smile revealed a wide gap between his front teeth, unless it was simply that one of them was missing. The text stated that he had last been seen wearing a red jacket, beige velour pants, and new après-ski boots. Nicolas studied the flier for some time; he could feel the policeman watching him, intrigued, probably torn between irritation at this kid playing the big shot and awareness that they shouldn't overlook even a single lead. Nicolas made the pleasure last awhile, finally shaking his head and saying no, he hadn't seen him. The officer was going to take the flier back, but Nicolas offered to hang it up at the chalet where his class was staying. The man shrugged. "The way things are going for us, why not?" remarked his colleague, who was leaning back against the bar, and Nicolas got to keep his prize.

The café owner, clearly bored by all this concern, said that the boy must have run away from home for a few days, nothing really serious.

"Let's hope so," replied one of the officers. The other one, the man leaning on the bar, sighed.

"Fliers like this make me feel sick. Because here you're seeing just one of them, and there's still a good chance we'll find the kid. But back at the station we've got a bulletin board full of them, and some are from a few years back. Three years. Five years. Ten years. We looked, and then in the end, naturally, we had to stop looking. We haven't a clue where the kid is. The parents haven't a clue. Maybe they keep hoping—anyway, they think about it all the time. Can you imagine? How can you think about anything else after something like that?"

The policeman had been speaking in a subdued, toneless voice, staring at the photo and shaking his head as though he might start banging it against the counter at any moment. His colleague and the café owner seemed embarrassed by this show of feeling.

"You're right, it's hard," agreed the owner, attempting to change the subject, but the policeman kept shaking his head and talking.

"What can they tell themselves, the parents, huh? That their kid's dead? That he'd be better off dead? Or else that he's out there somewhere, alive, that he's older, bigger? You know, you see the description—the jackets, the boots, height three feet eight inches, weight sixty-eight pounds—and then you look at the date, it's seven years ago. The kid's been three feet eight inches tall and sixty-eight pounds for seven years. What's that supposed to mean?" The policeman almost burst into tears but regained his composure. He sighed deeply, as if emptying himself out, apologizing to the others, and then, in the tone of voice one might use to say, "It's finished, it's all over, don't get upset about it," he repeated softly, "Hell, what's that supposed to mean?"

20

NICOLAS'S TEMPERATURE HAD GONE DOWN, IN FACT HE WASN'T
sick anymore, but everything continued according to his wish,
as though he was going to be feverish until the end of ski
school, as though once this niche had been selected, it was
more convenient to have him stay in it. The teacher and the instructors didn't even try to justify his quarantine by taking his
temperature or giving him medicine. They seemed simply to
have forgotten that he might have taken skiing lessons like the
others, eaten at the table with them, slept in a dormitory. Anyone entering the small office that had been his room for two
days now found him lying on the couch, nestled in his blanket,
engrossed in a book (or daydreaming, more often than not),
and whoever was using the phone or looking for some papers
would smile and say a few pleasant words to him, as though he
were a household pet or a much younger child. The door was

left ajar. Sometimes a classmate would stick his head in, asking if he was all right, if he needed anything. These visits were brief, not unfriendly, but pointless. Hodkann did not come to see him.

The afternoon of the day the policemen had shown up at the café, Lucas poked his head around the door to say hi to Nicolas, who called him into the office and asked him for a favor: Nicolas wanted Hodkann to come up, he needed to talk to him. Lucas promised to tell him and left. From downstairs came the muffled thud of falling bodies: Patrick was giving the class an introductory lesson in karate.

Nicolas waited until that evening, in vain. Was it that Hodkann didn't want to come or that Lucas hadn't given him the message? Suppertime arrived, then bedtime. There was the usual din, which lasted awhile, then all was quiet. The teacher and the instructors had gotten into the habit of chatting while they sipped herbal tea and smoked a cigarette before going to bed; their voices floated up now from the main room, but the words were unintelligible. It was then that Hodkann came into the office.

He hadn't made a sound, and Nicolas was startled: before he'd had time to plan anything, Hodkann was standing in front of him in pajamas, with a grim look in his eye. His expression indicated that he wasn't used to being summoned like this by a mere pup and that he hoped he hadn't gone to all this bother for nothing. Hodkann waited without a word. It was up to Nicolas to speak first, but preferring to keep silent as well, he drew from under his pillow the flier about the missing boy, which he unfolded to show to Hodkann. The small bedside lamp shed a soft orange light around the room; there was an almost imperceptible hum, too, that must have been coming from the light bulb. They could still hear the placid murmur of grown-up voices downstairs, occasionally enlivened by Patrick's hearty laughter. Hodkann nonchalantly examined the flier Nicolas had handed him. They were engaged in a kind of duel that would be lost by whoever spoke first, and Nicolas realized that he should be the one.

"There were some policemen in the café this morning," he said. "They've been looking for him for two days."

"I know," replied Hodkann coldly. "We saw the flier in the village."

Nicolas was floored. He'd thought he was letting Hodkann in on a secret, and everyone knew it already. They must be talking about nothing else in the kids' rooms. He would have liked Hodkann to give him back the flier—it was his only advantage, the only valuable card he had to play, and he'd stupidly begun by giving it away. Now Hodkann was going to ask why he'd sent for him, what he had to say, and Nicolas had already told him everything. Hodkann's anger, his crushing contempt, would fall on Nicolas. Holding the flier, Hodkann stared at Nicolas with the same chilly wariness as before. He seemed capable of going on like that for hours, never tiring of the distress he caused his victim, and Nicolas realized that he'd never be able to stand the tension.

Then, in his unpredictable way, Hodkann changed his tactics. His expression softened, and he sat down familiarly on the edge of the bed, next to Nicolas, saying, "You've got a lead?" The wall of hostility had crumbled in an instant: Nicolas wasn't afraid anymore; on the contrary, he felt united with Hodkann in that trusting, whispering complicity he'd often dreamed about, the kind that bound together the members of the Secret Seven. At night, by the gleam of a flashlight, while everyone else was asleep, they were trying to solve a terrible mystery . . .

"The police think he just ran away from home for a few days," he began. "At least, they hope so . . ."

Hodkann smiled with affectionate irony, as if he knew his Nicolas well and could tell exactly where he was heading. "And you," he said pointedly, "you don't buy that." He glanced down at the flier still lying unfolded on his lap. "You don't think he looks like that kind of kid."

This idea hadn't occurred to Nicolas; he found it a flimsy one, but having nothing else to fall back on, he nodded in agreement. Hodkann had accepted his invitation to join in the search for René, to follow the trail of the mystery. Nicolas already envisioned the two of them discovering secret passages, exploring damp tunnels strewn with bones, and since they didn't have a single lead, there was no point in being picky. Then a thought struck Nicolas out of the blue, dazzling him. His father had told him never to breathe a word about it, never to betray the trust the clinic directors had placed in him, but Nicolas couldn't have cared less: Hodkann and René were worth it.

"There is one small possibility," he said hesitantly, "but . . ."

"Let's have it," demanded Hodkann, and Nicolas blurted

out the story of the traffickers in human organs who kidnapped children to mutilate them. In his opinion, that's what had happened to René.

"And what makes you think so?" asked Hodkann. There wasn't a trace of skepticism in his voice, only the liveliest interest.

"You mustn't tell anyone," explained Nicolas, "but the night I went outside, I wasn't sleepwalking. I couldn't fall asleep at all, and then from the hall window, I saw a light out in the driveway. A man was walking around with a flashlight. That seemed weird to me, and I went down. I hid so he wouldn't see me and I followed him to a van parked on the road. It was a white van, exactly like the ones where they have their secret operating rooms. The man got in and drove off. The headlights weren't on—he didn't even start the engine, just let the van begin rolling down the hill on its own, so there wouldn't be any noise. That seemed fishy to me, you know? I remembered that story about the organ traffickers and I figured they must be prowling around the chalet in case someone came out all by himself . . ."

"If that's true, you had a close shave," muttered Hodkann. He was hooked, Nicolas could tell. This new role was enjoyable: it had all come to Nicolas in a flash, he was improvising, but a whole story was already taking shape before him and everything that had happened during the last few days could be explained, beginning with his own illness. He recalled a book in which the detective also pretended to be sick, even delirious, in order to allay the suspicions of the criminals and keep a close eye on them. That's just what he'd been doing, too, for

several days now. In the book, the detective's assistant—very
resourceful but not quite as smart—continued the investigation on his own as best he could, thinking the detective was
out of the game. In the end, admitting he'd been faking, the
detective abandoned the masquerade, and it turned out that
by staying in bed he'd come closer to solving the mystery than
his assistant had by shadowing and interrogating everyone.
Caught up in his story, Nicolas actually thought it plausible
that he and Hodkann might play out similar roles, and even
more astonishingly, Hodkann seemed to go along with this as
well. They both imagined the organ traffickers spying on the
chalet (that huge store of fresh bodies, of livers, kidneys, eyes),
waiting for a chance that never came and making up for it with
a child from the neighboring village, little René, who'd had
the misfortune to be discovered alone nearby. It all fit. Horribly, it all fit.

"But why shouldn't we tell anyone about this?" asked Hodkann, suddenly worried. "If it's true, it's very serious. We'd have
to tell the police."

Nicolas looked him up and down. That night, it was Hodkann who was asking timid practical questions and he, Nicolas,
who was silencing him with cryptic replies.

"They won't believe us," he said, lowering his voice still further to add, "and if they did, it would be worse. Because the
organ traffickers have accomplices in the police force."

"How do you know that?" asked Hodkann.

"From my father," answered Nicolas firmly. "Because of his

job, he knows lots of doctors." And as he spoke, forgetting that
everything was based on a lie he had told, he had another idea:
perhaps his father's absence was somehow involved. What if
he'd spotted the traffickers? What if he'd really and truly tried
to follow them? What if they'd taken him prisoner—or killed
him? Although it was fairly shaky, he confided this hypothesis
to Hodkann anyway and, to strengthen it, invented more details: absolutely nothing must be said about this, either, but his
father was investigating on his own, without the knowledge of
the police. Using his job as a cover and taking advantage of his
connections in the hospital business, he was on the trail of the
traffickers. That was why he'd come to this area, under the
pretext of driving Nicolas to the chalet: his informants had
tipped him off about the presence of the van where the secret
operations were performed. The hunt was desperately dangerous. The quarry was a powerful, unscrupulous organization,
and he was going up against them alone.

"Wait a minute," said Hodkann. "Your father's a detective?"

"No, no, but . . ."

Nicolas broke off, and this time he was the one to wear a
look of grim determination, studying Hodkann as if gauging
his ability to handle the whole story. Hodkann waited. Nicolas
realized that Hodkann didn't doubt any of what Nicolas had already told him, and he pressed on, somewhat unnerved by his
own words.

"He has a score to settle with them. Last year they kidnapped my little brother. He disappeared in an amusement park and was later found behind a fence. They'd taken out a kidney. Now do you understand?"

Hodkann understood. His expression was solemn.

"No one knows this," continued Nicolas. "You promise me you won't talk about it?"

Hodkann promised. Nicolas enjoyed the effect his tale was having on Hodkann. He'd envied the prestige the other boy had derived from his dead father—a man who'd died a violent death—and now he, too, had a daredevil father, an avenger running a thousand risks, embroiled in an intrigue from which he had little chance of escaping alive. At the same time, Nicolas wondered anxiously what would come of that night's crazy extravagance, the torrent of fantasies he couldn't take back now. If Hodkann talked, it would be a complete catastrophe.

"I was wrong to tell you that," he whispered. "Because now you're in danger too. They'll be targeting you."

Hodkann smiled, with that mixture of jauntiness and irony that made him irresistible, and said, "We're in the same boat." At that moment, they slipped back into their former roles: Hodkann was once again the big kid to whom the little one had wisely entrusted his perilous secrets, the protector who would look out for him, taking things in hand. They heard chairs scraping over the flagstones of the main room, then the teacher and the instructors coming upstairs. Hodkann placed a finger to his lips and dove under the bed. An instant later, the teacher looked in at the half-open door.

"Time to sleep, Nicolas, it's late."

Drowsily, Nicolas said okay and reached over to turn off the lamp.

"Everything's all right?" asked the teacher.

"Just fine," he replied.

"Good night, then." Back out in the hall, she turned off the light there as well. Her footsteps faded away; he heard a door creak, a faucet running.

"Perfect," whispered Hodkann, plopping down on the bed again near Nicolas. "Now we need to make our plan of action."

21

AS SOON AS THE BUS PULLED UP ON THE VILLAGE SQUARE, AT THE bottom of the slope where the skiing lessons were given, Nicolas could tell that something serious had happened. About ten people, men and women, were gathered in front of the café, and even from a distance, sorrow and rage were clearly visible in their faces. Unfriendly looks were directed at the bus as the driver parked it. Frowning, Patrick said he'd go see what was going on. The teacher told the children to stay in their seats. Those who had spent the entire ride from the chalet singing a funny song about summer camp fell silent of their own accord. Patrick went over to the group in front of the café. He had his back turned, with his ponytail streaming over the hood of his jacket, so the children couldn't see his face, only that of the man to whom he was talking, who answered angrily. Two women next to him joined in, one sobbing and shaking her fist. For a few minutes, Patrick just stood there, and no one said a word inside the bus. Since the defroster had stopped working when the engine was turned off, the windows were steaming up; the children wiped the glass clear with their hands or jacket sleeves to see what was happening. They usually fooled around like that, drawing pictures, writing words, but Nicolas realized he was trying not to, trying instead to make a clear circle representing nothing, as though everything risked being insulting to the people gathered outside, who seemed capable, if provoked by the slightest gesture, of tipping the bus over, burning it and all its passengers. Finally Patrick came back. He seemed troubled now, not as outraged as the villagers, but clearly upset. The teacher immediately went to meet him, to hear what he had to say without the children listening in. Then Hodkann broke the silence, voicing not a suspicion but a certainty they all more or less shared.

"René's dead."

He'd said "René," not "the missing boy," as if everyone knew him, as if he'd been one of them, and now Nicolas felt overwhelmed by the anguish that waiting had kept at bay. Patrick and the teacher got back on the bus. The teacher opened her mouth, but instead of speaking, she closed her eyes, bit her lips, and turned to Patrick, who gently laid a hand on her arm.

"There's no point in trying to hide it from you—something very serious has happened. Something awful. They found René, the boy who disappeared in Panossière, and he's dead. That's it." He sighed, to show how hard it had been for him to tell them.

the kids are
traumatised

101

"Someone killed him," said Hodkann from the back of the bus, and once again it was less a question than an affirmation.

"Yes," Patrick replied curtly. "Someone killed him."

"They don't know who?" asked Hodkann.

"No, they don't know who."

The teacher moved the handkerchief she held clenched in her fingers away from her lips and with great effort managed to speak. Her voice shook.

"I would assume," she quavered, "that some of you believe in God. So I think those of you who do should say a prayer. That would be good."

There was a long silence. No one dared move. The windows were so fogged up nobody could see outside anymore. Nicolas clasped his hands and tried to recite the Lord's Prayer silently to himself but he couldn't remember the words, not even the beginning. He seemed to hear, far away, his mother's voice pronouncing snatches of it that he was unable to repeat. Once she'd taught catechism class. When they moved, that was the end of that, and she no longer made him and his little brother say their prayers at night. He pictured himself (but it was absolutely impossible: simply imagining the gestures frightened him) putting his hand in his jacket pocket, pulling out the flier he'd gotten from the policeman, unfolding it—oh, the rustling of the paper!—and looking at the photo of René. He wondered what he'd do with it in the hours, the days to come, wondered whether he'd risk getting it out, keeping it, putting it somewhere. If he'd had his little safe, he could have stashed it there, buried the whole thing, and then forgotten the combination. If someone found it in his pocket or caught him studying the photo, wouldn't that give away what Hodkann and he had played at the previous evening?

Their nighttime conversation and his own fibs now seemed to him like a crime, a shameful, monstrous participation in the crime that had actually taken place. He could see René's chubby cheeks, his pudding-bowl haircut, the gap between his front teeth or else the space where he'd lost one of them. He must have put it under his pillow and waited to see what the tooth fairy would bring. Behind his glasses, his eyes were filled with terror, the terror of a small boy over whom a stranger is bending—to kill him—and Nicolas could feel René's expression clinging to his own face, his mouth opening in an endless, soundless cry. He would almost have been relieved if a policeman had searched his pockets and found the flier that would give him away. A policeman—or René's father, crazed with grief, ready to kill in his turn and doubtless ready to kill him if he learned what Hodkann and he had been up to. Were René's parents there, in the crowd gathered in front of the café and now hidden behind the wall of misty windows? Were they all still there? What was Hodkann doing? Was he praying? Were the others all around them praying in that chapel of mist? Would there be an end to this silence, this horror that gripped them all and in which, unbeknownst to everyone, he was so deeply involved?

22

THERE WAS NO SKIING LESSON. THEY DROVE BACK TO THE CHALET
and tried to get through the rest of the day. Probably a time
would come when they could return to normal life, think
about something else, but each of them sensed that that moment was still far in the future and would not arrive during ski
school. There was nothing they could do, however, except wait
for it. As playing was out of the question, the teacher decided
to assemble the class for a dictation exercise, followed by
arithmetic problems. Since some time still remained before
lunch and they were all expected to write at least one letter to
their parents during their stay, she suggested that they set to
it. But after passing out a few sheets of blank paper, she
changed her mind. "No," she murmured, shaking her head.
"It's not the right time." Standing in the middle of the room

clutching the packet of paper so fiercely that her knuckles turned white, she looked exhausted.

Hodkann chuckled nastily and called out, "Let's write a composition, then. About our happiest memory of ski school . . ."

"Enough, Hodkann!" exclaimed the teacher, and then she almost shouted it, "Enough!"

Hodkann was the only one of the children bold enough to speak, reflected Nicolas. It was as if the fact that he had lost his father had given him that right. Later, during lunch, when even the clatter of cutlery seemed muffled in cotton, Nicolas asked Patrick if they'd found René near the chalet. Patrick hesitated, then said no, he'd been found over a hundred miles away.

"That means one thing, at least," he added, "which is"— he hesitated again—"that the murderer isn't in this area anymore."

"It also means," continued the teacher, "that there's no reason to be afraid. It's terrible, it's awful, but it's over. You're not in any danger here."

Her voice broke on the last word; the tendons of her neck stuck out like taut strings. She looked around at the children sitting at their lunch, as though defying them to challenge this reassurance.

"But he must have been killed here," insisted Hodkann. "He didn't travel a hundred miles on his own."

"Listen, Hodkann," said the teacher, in a pleading tone edged with a kind of hatred, "I'd like us to stop talking about this. It happened, there's nothing we can do about it, we can't change a thing. I'm truly sorry that at your age you all should have had to cope with something like this, but we must stop talking about it. Simply stop. All right?"

Hodkann merely nodded, and the meal continued in silence. Afterward, some of the boys began to read or draw, while others gathered for a game of Authors. Those who wished to play hide-and-seek were told to stay indoors and under no circumstances to go outside.

"I thought we weren't in danger anymore," remarked Hodkann flippantly.

"That's enough, Hodkann!" yelled the teacher. "I asked you to be quiet, so if you can't manage that, go upstairs to your room, by yourself, and I don't want to see you again before supper!"

Hodkann went upstairs without arguing. Nicolas would have liked to go with him, so they could talk, but the teacher would never have allowed that, and besides, Nicolas wanted to avoid drawing attention to a compromising complicity between the two of them. At the moment, each was better off looking out for himself. Nicolas stayed in a corner, pretending to read a magazine. Whenever he turned a page, he thought he heard the flier crinkle in the pocket of his jacket, which he was still wearing on the pretext of feeling cold. Bundled up like that, he seemed to be waiting to be called away, never to return again. The little boy's body, lying broken on the snow, floated before his eyes. But perhaps there hadn't been any snow where he'd been found. Had the murderer killed him there or here? Even if the killer had won his trust with presents or promises, which was how they operated, these bad men Nicolas's parents had always warned him about, it was hardly likely that René would have let himself be driven so far away without protest. Living or dead, he must have made the journey in the trunk, and it was even worse to think that he'd still been alive. Shut up in the dark, not knowing where he was being taken.

Nicolas's father had once told him one of those hospital stories he brought back from his trips. A small boy was to have had a minor operation, but the anesthetist had made a mistake, and the child had been left permanently blind, deaf, mute, and paralyzed. He must have come to in utter blackness. Hearing nothing, seeing nothing, feeling nothing with his fingertips. Buried in a slab of endless night. With no idea that people were hovering desperately around him. In a world that was close by but cut off forever from his own, the doctors and his parents peered in distress at his pasty face, not knowing if there was anyone behind those half-closed eyes who could feel and understand things. At first he must have thought that he'd been blindfolded, perhaps put in a body cast, that he was in a dark, quiet room, but that eventually someone would come to turn on the light, set him free. He must have trusted his parents to get him out of there. Time passed, though, impossible to measure, minutes or hours or days in silence and darkness. The child shrieked and couldn't even hear his own cry. At the core of this slow, unspeakable panic, his brain struggled to find the explanation. Buried alive? But he didn't even have an arm anymore to stretch out toward the coffin lid above him. Did he ever suspect the truth? And René, tied up in the trunk, did he guess what was happening? He felt the bumps in the road, he pitched around, bruising himself on the corner of a suitcase, touching an old blanket with his fingers. In his mind's eye, did he see the silhouette of the driver behind the wheel? Did he imagine that moment when, having parked in some isolated spot in the woods, the driver would get out, slam the car door, walk around to the trunk, open it? First a thin streak of light, which grows wider; a man's face bends over him, and then René knows with absolute certainty that the worst is about to begin and that nothing can save him. He remembers his happy childhood, the parents who loved him, his pals, the present the tooth fairy brought him when his front tooth fell out, and he understands that this life ends right there, with this atrocious reality that is more real than all that has come before. Everything that has already happened is only a dream, and here is the awakening, that cramped space in which he lies bound, the click of the key in the lock of the trunk, the glimmer of light revealing the face of the man who will kill him. That instant is his life, the sole reality of his life, and there is nothing left but screaming, screaming with all his might, a scream that no one will ever hear.

23

THE CHILDREN HAD THEIR AFTERNOON SNACK, AND THEN PATRICK decided to have another session of relaxation. "To try to make your minds go blank," he said. But Nicolas couldn't make his go blank, and even with his eyes closed, he sensed that the others around him weren't managing it either. Lying on the floor, their limbs outstretched, they were all afraid of looking like the dead child. As before, Patrick spoke to them soothingly, telling them to empty themselves out, to feel heavy, heavy, to sink into the ground, to let themselves melt into it. One after the other, he named the parts of the body that were to grow heavy, but this time, simply hearing these words was upsetting, inspiring thoughts of being tortured. When Patrick mentioned their arms, calves, spines, the soles of their feet, a sensation of warmth in their fingertips, he spoke kindly and patiently, his voice enveloping them in tenderness, trying to reassure them,

to tell them that all these pieces of themselves were friends,
working together for their common good, but still the muscles
would contract so that everything felt stiff, tight, tense, the
way one is when besieged on all sides and even inside oneself.
Patrick said to breathe calmly, deeply, evenly, to let the wave fill
and empty the abdomen, ebbing and flowing, but their air was
cut off, as it had been in the throat of the strangled child. Temples throbbed; fingers clutched at the floor. Ears buzzed with
strange noises, difficult to identify: dull thumps, a clanking that
probably came from the radiator near where Nicolas was lying
but that also sounded like a car careening over a pothole or a
"sleeping policeman," a speed bump in the road. Nicolas's father liked that expression, which made him laugh; it was one of
the few things that did, the idea of driving over a policeman.
The car jolted about inside Nicolas, in that dim, rough landscape, that treacherous terrain full of chasms in the depths of
which sloshed liquids secreted by squishy glands with unknown
names. The car made its way through his body, twisting as
though on a winding road through those tepid, viscous things
in his belly, crossing the pass of the diaphragm (where an almost
unbearable weight pinned him down), climbing through the
cavernous gorge of the lungs toward his throat, heading for his
mouth: he was going to spit it out, with its horrid battered cargo
in the trunk. Lying right next to the window, near the burning-
hot radiator, Nicolas heard the engine rumble louder and
louder, closer and closer. As it approached him, he could see
the underside of the car the way you see it in a garage, when it
goes up on the lift. All that rusty metal, blistered by overheat-

ing, was going to run him down, dribbling oil and blood over him just as a spider wraps its living prey in gluey secretions. Outside the window, tires squeaked on the snow. The engine stopped; one car door slammed, then another. Patrick said to keep going, to pay no attention, but they couldn't keep going: rubbing their eyes as though awakening from a nightmare, several children had already gotten up and gone to look out the window at the van parked in front. Now the police were knocking on the chalet door.

That's it, thought Nicolas: they're coming for me. He looked around for Hodkann, with the wild idea that they might flee together before they were captured, but then he remembered Hodkann had been sent to his room. By this time the teacher was greeting the policemen, ushering them upstairs to the little office that had been Nicolas's domain before his life had fallen apart. Then the teacher called to Patrick and Marie-Ange to come up as well, and Patrick made the children promise to keep quiet while they were on their own. No one would have dreamed of acting up. Each boy remained silently frozen in the pose he'd held since being surprised by the arrival of the van. They listened intently, hoping in vain to hear what was being discussed in the office, the door of which was closed to them for the first time since they'd arrived at the chalet.

"What do you expect they're saying?" someone finally asked, in a shaky voice.

"What do you think they're saying?" someone else replied disdainfully. "They're conducting their investigation!"

This exchange loosened their tongues. Maxime Ribotton

announced self-importantly that his father supported the death penalty for sadists. A voice asked what that was, a sadist, and Maxime explained that it was what people were called who committed these kinds of crimes: raping and killing children. They were monsters. Nicolas didn't know what raping meant, and probably wasn't the only one, but he didn't dare ask and in any case guessed that it had something to do with the thing without a name, between his legs, that it was a kind of torture having to do with that—the worst of all, maybe having it cut or torn off. He was impressed by the confidence with which Maxime, usually so apathetic, handled these questions. "Monsters!" the boy repeated, cackling, as though he and his father had one of these creatures in their power and were preparing, before lopping off his head, to give him a taste of his own medicine. In Hodkann's absence, he had come into his own as a kind of star, talking in a loud voice, telling other stories about children who'd been abducted, raped, murdered, stories he'd read in his father's newspaper, a special one devoted entirely— if Maxime was to be believed—to that. The "bad men" spoken of in Nicolas's home (with an agonized but evasive insistence that never spelled out in what way, exactly, they were bad) seemed to be, more than Schubert, Schumann, and dirtied trousers, the main topic of conversation in the Ribotton household, and now that the topic had finally come up, Maxime the sullen dunce was in his element.

During this discussion, Nicolas was off by himself near the door to the hall, where he was suddenly startled to see Hodkann rush down the stairs and over to the front door. Their eyes met:

there was something imperious in Hodkann's look, as though his life—and even more—depended on Nicolas's discretion. Without a sound, he slipped out of the chalet. Only Nicolas had seen him go. At the instant Hodkann closed the front door behind him, the office door opened. The policemen, the teacher, and the instructors could be heard as they now descended the stairs. Ribotton and the others stopped talking.

"This kind of investigation," sighed one of the policemen, "is complicated and time-consuming. You look and you look, you've no idea in what direction to move, and when you find something, most of the time it's because the guy panicked and slipped up." The five adults all seemed worn out. They glanced into the room where the boys, now hushed, were waiting, and the other policeman, the one who had spoken about missing children with such helpless anger in the café, shook his head again and muttered, "A kid that age . . . Holy Virgin, pray for us." Moved by the same thought, the teacher closed her eyes tightly; it was a tic she had developed since that morning. Then the policemen left. Nicolas and the others watched through the window as the police van negotiated the snowy parking area and headed down the tree-lined driveway to the road. No one used the drive except the occupants of the chalet, but the policemen put on their blinker anyway before they turned.

24

NICOLAS WAS THE ONLY ONE WHO HAD ANY IDEA HODKANN WAS gone. He didn't know what he was scared of, but he was terribly scared of whatever it was. Just the night before, when they'd talked over what they called their plan of action, Hodkann had thought (or pretended to think) that he might be able to come up with some clue by carefully searching the area around the chalet—even though three feet of snow had fallen since René's disappearance—or by casually asking the villagers if they'd happened to notice any strange vans around lately. A worried Nicolas had urged him over and over to be careful. He would have preferred that Hodkann not question anyone—even casually— and that, on the pretext of pursuing their investigation, they simply continue each night their secret whispered conversation, made thrilling by an impending danger that would have lost nothing in Nicolas's eyes by remaining make-believe. Now that the tragedy had occurred, what was Hodkann up to? What would happen if he hadn't returned in an hour? Or by tonight? If he disappeared too? If they found his dismembered body in the snow tomorrow? Nicolas would be guilty of having kept quiet. By speaking up in time, which meant immediately, he might be able to prevent the worst from happening.

It was growing dark out; the lights had been turned on. Nicolas hovered around Patrick, looking for an opportunity to talk to him privately, but every time he had a chance he hung back and let it slip away. It occurred to him that they might all of them be lured outside the chalet, one by one, each child going off alone in search of the one before, and in the end it would be he, Nicolas, who would find himself alone, truly alone, waiting until the man who had killed them all decided to come in and finish the job. Nicolas would watch the front-door latch slowly open—and it would be time to confront that nameless evil he'd always felt skulking around him and which was now closing in.

When they began setting the table for supper, the teacher remembered Hodkann off in his room and craned her head up the stairwell to shout that he could come down now. Nicolas shivered, but what happened was what he least expected: Hodkann strolled down and joined them as though he hadn't been out of his room all afternoon. When, how he'd gotten back inside—this Nicolas never found out.

Supper was eaten in an atmosphere of gloom that no one tried to dispel, after which they went to bed, earlier than usual. "Try to sleep well, guys," said Patrick. "Tomorrow is another day." Nicolas headed for what had become his room, but the teacher told him he wasn't sick anymore and could rejoin the others.

When he went to get his pajamas, left rolled up in a ball beneath the sofa cushion, he lingered for a moment in the office, which had ceased to be his special place ever since the policemen's visit. The soft light of the small lamp beneath its orange shade made him feel like crying. To hold back the tears, he bit down on his wrist, the one around which Patrick had tied the bracelet, now somewhat frayed. He thought once more about the day his family had moved, a year and a half earlier. The decision to leave the town where he'd spent his earliest childhood had been made very quickly, with a haste that had completely baffled him. His mother had kept telling him insistently, vehemently, that he would be much happier where they were going, that he'd make plenty of new friends there, but her agitation, her fits of anger and tears, her way of brushing aside, as though it were an enemy, the lusterless hair that would immediately fall back over her face like a curtain—these things made it almost impossible for Nicolas to believe her words of reassurance. He and his little brother had stopped going to school, and she kept them home all the time. Even during the day, the shutters remained closed. It was summertime: they stifled in a climate of calamity, siege, and secrecy. Nicolas and his little brother had asked for their father, but he'd gone on a long sales trip, she said; he would be joining them in the other town, in the new apartment. On the last day, when the boxes the movers would be coming for after their departure had all been packed, he'd sat

in the middle of his empty room and cried the way you do when
you're nine and something dreadful is happening that you just
don't understand. His mother had wanted to take him in her
arms to console him, repeating over and over, Nicolas, Nicolas,
and he knew that she was hiding something from him, that he
couldn't trust her. She had begun to cry, too, but since she
wasn't telling him the truth, they couldn't even really cry
together.

25

BEING BACK WITH THE OTHERS ALSO MADE THE SECRET MEETING
Nicolas had to have with Hodkann more difficult. Where had
Hodkann gone, and to do what? With the teacher keeping her
eye on him, Hodkann hadn't broken the dismal silence at the
supper table and had gone to bed without even brushing his
teeth, without speaking to anyone, turning toward the wall like
a wild animal best left undisturbed. Stretched out on the upper
bunk, as still as a statue lying on a tomb, Nicolas wondered if
Hodkann was asleep or not. An hour passed like this. Finally
Hodkann whispered, "Nicolas," and slipping quietly from the
bed, signaled him to follow. Nicolas climbed down the ladder and
tiptoed out to join him in the hall.

As Nicolas went by him, Lucas sat up suddenly, grunting,
"What are you up to?" But Hodkann stuck his head in the door
and simply hissed, "Shut up!" Lucas didn't need to be told

twice. Just to be safe, they moved away from the bedroom, going over to the window at the end of the hallway. Hodkann hoisted himself easily onto the sill, sitting with his back to the casement. His silhouette stood out clearly against the black and white masses of fir trees drooping beneath their burden of snow, while his face remained in darkness. Nicolas was afraid of this darkness.

"So?" he murmured.

"Your father has a gray R25, right?" asked Hodkann tonelessly.

Nicolas realized that what felt so chilly on his forehead was what the horror stories he liked to read in secret called a cold sweat. He didn't reply.

"Yes," continued Hodkann, "it's a gray R25, I remember very well. When the policemen came this afternoon, I sneaked down from the bedroom and listened at the office door to what they were saying. They were talking about the things that were done to René, and I'd rather not tell you about it. It still makes me sick. And then they asked if anyone had seen a gray R25 in the area. The teachers said no—they must've not remembered, or maybe they didn't pay attention when your father was here. So I thought things over, and when I could tell they were about to leave, I came downstairs fast, ahead of them, and went to wait for them out on the road." After a brief pause, Hodkann added, "I told them everything."

He fell silent again. Nicolas didn't move. He stared at this face of darkness.

Then Hodkann's tone changed. Now he was trying to justify

what he'd done without giving up any of his authority. "Listen, Nicolas," he whispered, "I had to. I know I promised you I wouldn't talk about it, but your father's in danger. That's obviously why they're looking for him, can't you see? The traffickers might be holding him prisoner right this minute. Maybe they've already killed him," he said with sudden brutality, as if to shake some sense into Nicolas. "But if they haven't, there's still time to find him, and we can't do that, not by running around looking for footprints in the snow. This isn't the Secret Seven, Nicolas—these guys are monsters. Nicolas, listen to me," he insisted, almost begging. "If there's any chance of saving your father and we let it go by, don't you think you'll feel bad about it for the rest of your life? If it's your fault he dies? Imagine your life after that."

Hodkann broke off, seeing that his argument was having no effect on Nicolas, who remained motionless. Hodkann gave up with a shrug. "Anyway, it's done." Then, slipping down from the window sill, he reached out to take Nicolas's hand. Sadly, softly, he murmured, "Nicolas . . ." Nicolas stepped back to avoid his touch. "Nicolas, I understand," Hodkann assured him, stroking his hair, trying to get Nicolas to lay his head on his shoulder, and this time Nicolas gave in. Standing pressed to Hodkann's chest while the other boy kept stroking his hair and quietly repeating his name, Nicolas felt the warmth of Hodkann's immense body, white and soft, as soft as an enormous pillow from which protruded only that hard, nameless thing jutting out against his belly. But Nicolas was tense, stiff, as though frozen in ice, while all was flaccid and empty between his legs. There was nothing there, a void, an absence. He stared over Hodkann's shoulder, out the window, at the dark mass of fir trees bending beneath the snow, and beyond, into the blackness.

26

THE NEXT MORNING, THEY FOUND NICOLAS HUDDLED BENEATH
the open window, through which snowflakes swirled into the
hall. He was awake, and his teeth were chattering, but he didn't
say a word. Once again, as though he no longer had any other
choice, Patrick carried him to the couch in the office. This time
the teacher seemed more irritated than concerned. All right,
Nicolas was a sleepwalker and you couldn't blame him for being
upset after such a trying day, but she was upset, too, and worn
out. She had no intention of going along on the big excursion
Patrick had planned for the boys; she had hoped to get some
rest, alone in the chalet, and could have done without having
to take care of a sick and moody child. Since Nicolas clearly
didn't seem able to be up and about, however, he was allowed
to reclaim his place on the office couch for the time being, and

the teacher retired to her room. The class left with Patrick and Marie-Ange. Only Nicolas and the teacher stayed behind.

Hours went by. Nicolas had pulled the covers over his face, and without moving, almost without feeling anything, he waited. He would have liked to experience once more the delicious warmth of a fever, his cocoon of obliviousness, but he wasn't feverish, just cold and scared. The teacher didn't bring him anything to drink or come to talk to him. There was no lunch. She was probably asleep. He didn't even know where her room was.

He must have been drowsing, too, because he was awakened by the telephone. It was already dark, but the others hadn't come back yet. The receiver jiggled slightly in its cradle. It rang for a long time. It stopped, then began again. The teacher came in, and telling Nicolas that he might perfectly well have answered it himself, she picked up the receiver. Her face looked sleepy, puffy, and her hair was mussed.

"Hello?" she said. "Yes, it's me . . . Yes, he's right here."

She glanced at Nicolas without smiling. Then she frowned. "Why? Has something happened? . . . I see . . ."

She set the receiver down on the desk. "Would you mind leaving me alone for just a minute, please?" Nicolas got up and slowly left the room, keeping his eyes on her. "You should go downstairs, you'll be more comfortable," she added when he'd reached the hall, and she shut the door. Nicolas went as far as the stairs and sat down on the top step, hugging his knees to his chest. He heard nothing of what was being said in the office, but perhaps the teacher was simply listening silently to her caller. At one point he thought about standing up, tiptoeing over . . . but he didn't dare. When he leaned against the railing, the wood creaked sharply. A few yards away, a band of orange light gleamed beneath the office door. Nicolas thought he heard a muffled sound, as if someone was trying to stifle a sob. Although the conversation lasted a long time, he couldn't manage to hear anything else. Everything was drowned in a well of silence. Deep down, water glimmered darkly.

Finally he heard the receiver clatter softly into its cradle. The teacher did not come out of the office. She was probably standing in the same position, her hand still resting on the receiver; she was squeezing her eyes closed, trying not to scream. Or else she had lain down on the couch and was biting the pillow that still bore the imprint of Nicolas's head. A few days earlier, when he had imagined her learning over the phone about his father's accidental death, she had first sent him away, as she had just done, but afterward she had left the office, come toward him, taken him in her arms. She had wept over him, saying his name again and again. It was a wrenching scene, but a touching one, infinitely sweet, and now it could never take place. Now she was afraid to come out, afraid to see him, afraid to speak to him. She would have to come out, though—she couldn't stay in that office for the rest of her life. Cruelly, Nicolas imagined her distress, the unbearable anguish that had overwhelmed her after she'd hung up the phone. She was perfectly still; so was he. She must suspect that he was there, quite near, that he was waiting for her. If he were to knock on the door, she would call to him not to come in, not now, not yet . . . Perhaps she'd turn the key—yes, she'd lock herself in rather than show him her face and see his own. If he wanted, it would be easy to scare her. Simply speaking would be enough, out in the silent hall. Or humming. Humming something light, innocent, relentless, like a counting rhyme. She wouldn't be able to stand it, would start shrieking behind the door. But he didn't hum, didn't budge, didn't say a thing. It was up to her, not him, to take charge of the course of events, since events would have to follow their course. Gestures would have to be made, words spoken. Harmless words, at least, useful only for keeping up pretenses, for acting as if nothing had changed, as if the phone call had never taken place. Perhaps she was going to get out of it that way, by pretending it hadn't happened. By waiting for another phone call, waiting for someone else—someone braver— to answer it. It would be Patrick. The policeman who had phoned earlier wouldn't understand—he'd say that he'd already spoken to the teacher, told her all about it, but she would shake her head, close her eyes, swear in the face of all the evidence that someone else must have answered instead, someone pretending to be her.

It grew dark. Snow fell on the fir trees outside the window where Hodkann had spoken to Nicolas. There was noise downstairs. The class was back. Lights, shouts, hubbub. The long walk must have brought a glow to their cheeks, and for a few moments, perhaps, the class had forgotten the horror of the previous day. For them it was yesterday's horror, which would recede with each passing hour, soon fading into a memory their parents would take care not to revive. The mothers would speak of it among themselves in hushed voices, with knowing, pained expressions. But for Nicolas it would always, always be like it was now, at the top of the stairs, waiting until the teacher found the courage to come out.

On his way upstairs, Patrick found him sitting on the steps in the gloom of the hallway.

"What are you doing here, buddy?" he asked kindly. "You'd be better off in your office."

"The teacher's in there," mumbled Nicolas.

"Ah, really? And she doesn't want you around?" Patrick laughed and whispered, "She must be phoning her boyfriend!"

He knocked on the door, for form's sake, and as Nicolas had foreseen, the teacher asked, "Who is it?" in a strange voice. Since it was Patrick, she opened the door, but closed it immediately behind him. Now the two of them were holed up inside, thought Nicolas. Soon they'd all be in there, everyone but him, each one trying to shift onto someone else the burden of having to go see him and talk to him. To tell him the truth? No, they wouldn't be able to. No one could tell that truth to a little boy. Someone would have to, though. Nicolas waited, feeling almost curious.

Patrick stayed in the office for a long time, but he, at least, was brave enough to come out and sit on the steps next to Nicolas. When he took the boy's wrist to see what kind of shape the bracelet was in, his hands shook.

"It's holding up fairly well!" he said, and then, unnerved by the silence, he launched into some story about Mexican gener-

· als and Pancho Villa that Nicolas didn't understand at all, that he didn't try to understand, but that must have been meant to be funny because Patrick kept making these fake-sounding chuckles. He was talking for the sake of talking, doing his best, and Nicolas thought it was nice of him. If he could have, Nicolas would have interrupted him and said, looking him straight in the eye, that all this stuff about Pancho Villa was fine but not really necessary and that he wanted to learn the truth. Patrick could sense this and suddenly stopped telling his story, even though he wasn't anywhere near the end. Without trying to cover up his failure, he gulped like someone drowning and said very quickly, "Listen, Nicolas, there's a problem at home . . . It's too bad about ski school, but the teacher thinks—and so do I— that it would be best if you went home . . . Yes, that would be best," he added, just to say something, anything.

"When?" murmured Nicolas, as though that were the only thing he needed to know.

"Tomorrow morning," replied Patrick.

"Someone's going to come get me?"

Nicolas wondered whether or not he'd rather the police came for him.

"No," said Patrick. "I'm the one who's taking you. Is that okay? The two of us get along pretty well."

Grinning weakly, he ruffled Nicolas's hair; the boy bit his lips to keep from crying as he thought about the kings of the road. It must have been a relief to Patrick that Nicolas had questioned him only about practical details, not about the reasons behind their trip. Perhaps he found it peculiar that Nicolas didn't seem all that astonished. Still, the child did ask, in a barely audible voice, "Is it serious, what happened at home?"

Patrick thought a moment before replying, "Yes, I think it's serious. Your mother will tell you about it."

Nicolas began to descend the stairs with downcast eyes but Patrick held him back, squeezed his shoulder hard, and, trying to smile, said, "It'll be okay, Nicolas."

27

AT SUPPER, DURING WHICH THE TEACHER DID NOT APPEAR, Maxime Ribotton (who didn't want to lose his new topic of conversation) started talking again about sadistic child killers and the things he and his father would like to see done to them. Patrick told him sharply to be quiet. Hunched over his plate, Nicolas ate the scalloped potatoes the cook had fixed to help the hikers get back their strength. To show their appreciation at the end of the meal, Patrick suggested that they all shout, "Hip, hip, hurrah!" three times, and Nicolas shouted along with the others.

Then he asked Patrick if he could sleep in the office on his last night. Patrick hesitated before giving his permission, and Nicolas understood that it was because of the telephone. He went upstairs to bed before the others did, without saying good-bye to them and without anyone noticing except Hodkann, who hadn't taken his eyes off him all evening. But Nicolas had never returned his gaze.

No one, apparently, was aware that he was leaving.

Fifteen minutes later, Patrick came up to see him and said they'd be hitting the road early the next morning. He should get a good night's rest. Did he want a pill to help him out? Nicolas said yes, swallowing it down with a sip of water. It was the first time he'd ever taken a sleeping pill. He knew you could die if you took too many at once. During the time when they moved and his father was gone for so long, Nicolas had looked all over for the bottle his father used, but he must have taken it with him, or else Nicolas's mother had locked it away in a drawer.

Patrick sat down on the edge of the bed, as if to talk to Nicolas, but couldn't find the words. No one would ever again be able to find any words to say to him. Patrick was reduced to the same meager gestures as before, the hand squeezing Nicolas's shoulder, the sad, affectionate little half-smile. Patrick didn't dare say "It'll be okay" again, probably sensing how hypocritical it would be. He sat quietly for a minute, then stood up. He had gathered together Nicolas's new things, the ones he'd bought for him at the store, and had put them in a plastic bag he placed at the foot of the bed, ready for the morning. He turned out the lights and left. Nicolas remembered his own bag, carefully packed a week earlier for his trip to ski school. The police must have found it in the car trunk, must certainly have searched through it. He wondered if they'd managed to open his little safe, and he wondered what they'd found there.

28

WHEN NICOLAS WOKE UP BEFORE DAWN, HE COULDN'T REMEM-
ber having fallen asleep. He didn't recognize his surroundings
at first and thought he was in his own bedroom at home. He
was afraid, because while he was asleep, they'd closed the door
and turned out the light in the hall, breaking the promise they
made to him every evening. He whimpered, "Mama," almost
said it again louder, almost called out, but held back—and suddenly remembered everything. He lay for a moment without
moving, hoping that the night would last forever. Those condemned to die must hope so too. His eyes grew used to the
darkness, and he tried to think if there was anything hidden in
the room that could help him in some way or another. That
could stop the course of time, keep him out of reach, make
him disappear. But he saw nothing. Hiding underneath the bed

would be useless. Telephoning for help—but to whom? What would he say?

Going over to the window, he realized that it had bars on it. He had slept there for three nights without noticing them. Or had they just been installed, while he was asleep, to make sure he wouldn't escape? They seemed old, however, deeply embedded in the concrete. He just hadn't noticed them before.

No other way out except the door. He felt around inside the plastic bag, managed to put on his clothes. Getting into the jacket, he heard the familiar, sinister rustling of the flier with René's picture on it. He searched the desk drawers for money to help him run away but found nothing. Quietly, he opened the door and slipped out.

A light was on in the room below, faintly illuminating the top of the stairs, where once again Nicolas waited, motionless. Patrick and Marie-Ange were already up. They were talking quite softly, but the chalet was so quiet that Nicolas could hear them by leaning forward.

"One cube," said Marie-Ange, and a spoon clinked in a cup.

"Somehow," Patrick continued, "the kids will find out in no time. And then if the people in the village learn he's here, in the state they're in, you just can't tell what they'd be capable of doing."

"But it's not his fault," said Marie-Ange softly. She sighed heavily and murmured, "How awful, God, how awful . . ."

Nicolas heard a sob, then Patrick saying, "You know, it's atrocious what happened to René, but I think I feel even sorrier for him. Can you imagine having to deal with that? What kind of a life will he have?"

There was a silence; then Marie-Ange, still sobbing and stirring her spoon around, said, "It's a good thing it's you taking him back. You think you'll tell him?"

"No," replied Patrick in a hollow voice. "That—I just can't."

"Who will, then?"

"I don't know. His mother. She must have been expecting something like this to happen one day. His father already had some trouble, two years ago. It wasn't as bad, but still, it was ugly stuff."

More silence, sobbing; then, "I'm going to go wake him up. We have to leave."

Patrick found Nicolas standing at the top of the stairs, fully dressed, and tried to tell from his face whether he'd overheard them or not. But you couldn't tell a thing from Nicolas's face, and anyway, what difference did it make?

When they came back downstairs again, Marie-Ange set her cup on the table, dabbed at her red eyes with a wadded-up tissue, and, without a word, hugged Nicolas tightly. She also gave Patrick a little kiss, on the corner of his mouth, and then the two travelers left. It was still dark out. Everyone else was asleep in the chalet. Their feet sank into freshly fallen snow. Clouds of vapor puffed from their mouths, an almost opaque whiteness against the black of the fir trees. When they reached the car, Patrick asked Nicolas to hold his small travel kit while he brushed snow off the windows with his bare hands and wrestled with the wipers, which had frozen to the windshield. When he'd finished and had unlocked the car, Nicolas began to get into the front seat, where he'd ridden before, but Patrick said no. They were going to be driving on the highway, where police patrol cars watched out for such things.

29

"YOU WANT SOME MUSIC?" ASKED PATRICK. NICOLAS SAID HE'D
like that. Keeping one hand on the steering wheel, Patrick
flipped through the cassettes in the carrying case. Nicolas wondered if he was going to play the same tape they'd listened to
the day they'd gone shopping, but Patrick selected a different
one, something slower and softer. Accompanied only by a gui-
tar, the voice was almost plaintive, and even without understanding the English words, you could guess the song was about
a winter journey on snowy roads edged with sleep. Nicolas
stretched out on the backseat, using a frayed old blanket as a
pillow. The blanket smelled of dog, and Nicolas almost asked
Patrick if he had one at home, and where home was, and what
it was like where he lived, but he didn't want to seem as if he
was trying to make conversation, so he kept quiet. Patrick was
probably dreading his questions, and Nicolas decided not to

ask any. Since he was lying with his head behind the passenger's seat, he could look up and see Patrick concentrating on his driving. The end of his ponytail lay across one shoulder. Nicolas had noticed his hands on the steering wheel: tanned and muscular, exactly the hands that Nicolas would have liked to have when he grew up, but now he knew that was impossible. The heater was set on high, to keep the windows from fogging. Nicolas had curled up, tucking his hands between his thighs, and he realized to his astonishment that he could doze, allowing himself to be lulled to sleep—as though he were feverish—by the heat, the serene and wistful music, the soothing hum of the defroster. Before the drive to the chalet, he'd counted the miles on his father's map: two hundred and sixty. He and Patrick hadn't gone even fifteen yet. As long as he stayed inside the car, he was safe.

When he woke up, they were already on the highway. The snow was all gone, but the sky was white. Patrick hadn't put in another tape, probably to avoid disturbing Nicolas's sleep. He'd turned off the defroster. He was sitting up straight, concentrating on the road ahead, with his ponytail still draped over one shoulder as if he hadn't moved the whole time. Although he had certainly noticed when Nicolas sat up, Patrick hadn't said anything. Only after a few minutes did he force himself to ask, in what was meant to be a jolly tone, "Did you have a nice nap?" Nicolas answered yes, and then silence fell again. Nicolas kept an eye out for signs along the highway that would show how far it still was to the town where he lived. A hundred and twenty miles. They were almost halfway there. Nicolas reproached himself for having let the first half of the trip slip by so fast while he was asleep. He had the feeling that things would now start happening more and more quickly.

Patrick moved over into the right lane, slowed, and got off at an Esso station. Nicolas remembered Shell's prize coupons and suddenly began to cry, quietly, without sobbing. Tears trickled down his cheeks. Patrick would never have known if he hadn't stopped the car in front of the pumps at that instant and turned around. Nicolas couldn't stop weeping; he looked down, away from Patrick, who stayed twisted sideways in his seat for a moment, gazing at him without a word. "Nicolas," he sighed, one more time. That was the only thing left to do—say a name over and over, with love and despair. René's parents must have been doing that, too, at night, lying in the bed where they would never sleep peacefully, ever again—and the parents of the child buried alive by the botched anesthesia . . .

"Come on, Nicolas," said Patrick finally. "We'll have something to eat. You didn't have any breakfast, you must be hungry." Nicolas wasn't hungry and suspected Patrick wasn't either, but after the gas tank had been filled, he followed Patrick into the restaurant.

Near the entrance was a newspaper rack, before which Patrick had a moment of panic. He tried to distract Nicolas and block his view of it, but although Nicolas pretended not to notice, he still caught a glimpse of the photo and the word "fiend" in the headline half hidden by the fold in the newspaper. Patrick quickly dragged him over to the vending machine and made certain that they could leave by another door. He got himself a coffee, bought an orange juice and a *pain au chocolat* for Nicolas, then led him over to the corner by the rest rooms, where there were three gray plastic tables. They were sticky and cluttered with empty paper cups. Patrick politely said hello to the only person sitting there, a blond woman drinking coffee. She returned his greeting and gave Nicolas a smile that pierced him to the heart.

Her fur coat, which gleamed as if covered with dew, was open over a blue dress of some precious, shimmering material. The wisps of blond hair that had escaped from her loose chignon seemed to invite a caress. She stood out against the grimy drabness of the place with her air of wealth, luxury, and above all, gentleness—a gentleness that was enveloping, magical, almost unbearable. She was beautiful. Precious, gentle, and beautiful. She calmly surveyed her dreary surroundings and the parking lot outside, and when her gaze fell on Nicolas again, she smiled at him once more, with a smile that was neither distracted nor forced, but personally meant for him, bathing the whole of him in the celestial tenderness that surrounded her like a halo. Her blue silk dress, cut rather low, revealed the beginning of her breasts, and a bizarre thought struck Nicolas: everything inside her body—her internal organs, her intestines, the blood flowing in her veins—had to be as pristine and luminous as her smile. He remembered the Blue Fairy in *Pinocchio*. With her, there would be nothing more to fear. She could, if she wanted, make the horror disappear, make what had happened go away, and if she knew, she would want to, that was certain.

Patrick stood up, saying he was going to the bathroom for a minute. Nicolas realized that his fate would be decided in that minute. He had to speak to the fairy. Tell her to save him, to take him away with her to where she was going. He wouldn't have to explain; he was sure she'd understand. One sentence would be enough: "Please save me, take me with you." She would be astonished for a moment, but studying him attentively, with the care, the sweetness that touched your soul and made you want to cry, she would see that he was telling the truth, that only she could work the miracle. "Come," she would say, taking him by the hand. They would hurry to her car, leaving the highway at the next exit. They would drive a long time, sitting side by side. As she drove, she would smile at him, saying soothingly that it was over now. They would go far, far away, to where she lived a life as precious, gentle, and beautiful as she was, and she would let him stay with her always, out of danger, at peace.

Nicolas opened his mouth, but no sound came out. He had to attract her attention, to send her his message with his eyes, at least. She had to look at him, see his mute supplication— that would be enough: she would understand. Yes, yes, she would understand. She would know how to sense the anguish within a little boy encountered by chance at a rest stop, and she would know that she alone could set him free. But she wasn't looking at him anymore, she was looking outside, watching a man dressed in black who was striding toward them across the parking lot. Almost choking on the silence that caught in his throat, Nicolas saw the man come closer, push open the glass door. Bending a loving face over the woman, he kissed her on the neck, near the wisps of hair from her chignon. She smiled up at him with her heavenly smile. Now she had eyes only for him. Never in his life had Nicolas ever hated anyone so much, not even Hodkann.

"It's fixed," the man said. "We can go."

The fairy rose and left with him. As she closed the door behind her, she gave Nicolas a little wave, then turned away. The man slipped his arm around her shoulders to keep her warm, and Nicolas watched them walk to their car, drive off, disappear. Underneath the table his fingers were knotted together, hopelessly entangled, and he saw a kind of red-and-blue string lying on the ground between his feet, among the empty sugar packets and the cigarette butts. The bracelet had fallen off. He tried to remember the wish he'd made when Patrick had tied it on him, a week earlier, but he couldn't. Perhaps he'd hesitated so long, trying to choose the one that would best protect him from life's endless dangers, that he'd never made any wish at all.

30

FOR THE REST OF THE TRIP, NICOLAS WONDERED WHAT HIS LAST words had been. A short reply to Patrick in the car, most likely. He'd decided not to speak, not ever again. It was the only protection he could think of just then: not one more word. They'd never get anything else out of him. He would become a block of silence, a smooth, slick surface that would repel unhappiness and misfortune. Others would speak to him if they liked, if they dared, and he wouldn't answer them. Wouldn't hear them. He wouldn't hear what his mother would tell him, whether it was the truth or lies; it would probably be lies. She would say that his father had had an accident during his sales trip, that for some reason or other they couldn't visit him in the hospital. Or else that he was dead but that they wouldn't be going to his funeral or to pay their respects at his grave. They'd move to yet another town, perhaps they'd change their name, hoping to elude the hostility and shame that would dog them from then on, but it would be no concern of his anymore: he was going to keep silent, forever.

When they reached the outskirts of the town, Patrick reread the address that had been written down for him on a scrap of paper and asked Nicolas if he knew how to get to his house. The boy didn't reply. Patrick asked again, trying to catch Nicolas's eye in the rearview mirror, but Nicolas looked away, and Patrick gave up. He stopped and got directions from a policeman. Then they drove through the neighborhood in the rain. When they arrived at the street where Nicolas lived, it went in the wrong direction, so Patrick had to go all the way around the block, but he found an empty space right in front of the door. It took him two tries to get the car lined up properly along the curb. He opened the door for Nicolas to get out, then reached for his hand, as though Nicolas were a little child, but didn't speak, didn't say his name. Patrick's face had lost all expression.

Realizing that Nicolas was not going to help him, Patrick checked the names over the mailboxes in the narrow entrance hall of the apartment building. They waited for the elevator without a word. The sliding doors closed with a hiss. Patrick hesitated for an unusually long time before pushing the button. He was still holding Nicolas's hand, holding it very tightly. In the smoked-glass mirror on the elevator wall, Nicolas saw that he was crying. The box enclosing them seemed to sink into the ground, then rose with a shudder. The cable creaked. Nicolas hoped that the elevator would stop between floors and that they would stay there for all eternity. Or else that once it got high enough, it would break loose, plunging into a dark well that would swallow them up.

Nicolas's floor was a long, windowless corridor lined with doors, and his was all the way at the end. The light switch cast a dim glow along the hall. Patrick didn't turn it on. They walked down the corridor together, quite slowly. Nicolas remembered what Patrick had said that morning. "What kind of a life will he have?" They reached the door, behind which not a sound could be heard. Patrick raised his hand, hesitated even longer than he had in the elevator, and finally rang the doorbell. Gently, he withdrew his other hand from the child's grasp. There was nothing more he could do for him now. The carpet inside the apartment muffled the sound of footsteps, but Nicolas knew that the door would open, that in an instant his life would begin, and that in this life, for him, there would be no forgiveness.

The Mustache

Translated by
Lanie Goodman

For Caroline Kruse

1

WHAT WOULD YOU SAY IF I SHAVED OFF MY MUSTACHE?" AGNES, who was on the living room couch flipping through a magazine, laughed and replied, "That might be a good idea."

He smiled. Small islands of shaving cream sprinkled with little black hairs were floating on the water's surface in the bathtub, where he had been lingering. His beard was heavy and grew back quickly, which meant he had to shave twice a day if he didn't want to have five o'clock shadow. Upon waking, before his shower, he quickly performed this task in front of the mirror, as a series of mechanical gestures, without ceremony. In the evening this unpleasant chore became a moment for relaxation, he'd be careful to use the shower to run the bathwater, so the steam wouldn't cloud the mirrors surrounding the tub. He'd prepare a drink, kept within arm's reach, then lavishly spread the shaving cream on his chin, going back and forth with the razor, making sure not to come too close to his mustache, which he would later trim with a scissors.

For better or for worse, this evening rite had an important place in his daily equilibrium, like the one and only cigarette he allowed himself after lunch, ever since he'd stopped smoking. Since the end of his adolescence, the calm pleasure that he drew from this ritual hadn't changed; his work schedule had even accentuated it, and when Agnes affectionately made fun of the sacred aspect of his shaving sessions, he answered that they were, in fact, his form of Zen exercise. It was the only time he had left for meditation, self-knowledge, and the spiritual world, given his trivial but consuming activities as a young, urban professional. "Yuppie," Agnes would chide, tenderly mocking him.

He'd finished, for the time being. With half-closed eyes and all of his muscles relaxed, he scrutinized his face in the mirror. It amused him to exaggerate his expression of misty beatitude, then to change his look into efficient and determined virility. A trace of shaving cream stuck to the corner of his mustache. He'd only talked about shaving it off as a joke, the way he sometimes talked about cutting his hair—usually fairly long and combed back—very short. "Very short? How disgusting." Agnes inevitably protested. "Besides, with your mustache and leather jacket, you'd look like a fag."

"But I could also cut off my mustache."

"I like you better with it," she concluded. Actually she'd never known him without one. They had been married for five years.

"I'm going downstairs to pick up a few things at the super-
market," she said, sticking her head through the half-opened
bathroom door. "We have to leave in about a half hour, so don't
take all day."

He heard the swish of fabric from the jacket she was slipping
on, the jingle of the key ring being swept up from the coffee
table, the front door open, then close again. She could have
turned on the answering machine, he thought, so I won't have
to get out of the bathtub dripping wet if the phone rings. He
took a gulp of whiskey, turned the thick square glass around in
his hand, and enjoyed the tinkling of the ice cubes—what was
left of them. Soon he would get out, dry off, get dressed . . .

In five minutes, he compromised, taking pleasure in this little respite. He pictured Agnes making her way toward the su-
permarket, her heels clicking on the sidewalk, then patiently
waiting on line in front of the cashier, without letting any of this
trekking around affect her good mood or the vivacity of her
gaze. She was always noticing bizarre little details, not necessarily strange in their own right, but she knew how to make use
of them in the stories she invented. He smiled again. And what
if, when she came back upstairs, he surprised her by actually
shaving off his mustache? She'd declared five minutes ago that
it might be a good idea. But she couldn't have taken his question seriously, not any more than usual. She liked him with a
mustache, and besides, so did he, although after all this time he
was no longer accustomed to a clean-shaven face; there was really no way of knowing. In any event, if they didn't like his new
look, he could always let his mustache grow back. It would take

ten to fifteen days, and at least he would have had the experience of seeing himself differently. Besides, Agnes was always changing her hairstyle without giving him any warning. He complained about it, made fun of her, and then as soon as he started to get used to it, she grew tired of it and appeared with a new haircut. Wasn't it his turn? It would be amusing.

He laughed to himself, like a child about to play a prank. Reaching out, he put the empty glass down on the vanity and picked up a pair of scissors for the major part of his work. It immediately occurred to him that this clump of hair might clog the bathtub drain. All it took was a handful of hair and then what a production, you had to pour one of those cleaning products down the drain that would stink for hours. He took the toothbrush glass, which he placed on the bathtub rim; then precariously poised, he leaned toward the mirror and went about trimming off the bulk of his mustache. The hair fell to the bottom of the glass in compact little tufts, which were very black against the whitish tartar deposit. He worked slowly, to avoid nicking himself. A moment later, he looked up and inspected his handiwork.

While he was at it, clowning around, he could have stopped right there, leaving his upper lip decorated with this patchy vegetation, thriving in parts, sparse in others. As a child he'd never understood why male adults didn't make use of the comic potential of their facial hair. For instance, why should a man who'd decided to sacrifice his beard necessarily do it in one fell swoop, instead of granting his friends and acquaintances, just for a day or two, the hilarious spectacle of one clean-shaven

cheek and the other bearded, one half of a mustache, or side-
burns shaped like Mickey Mouse ears. It would only take one
stroke of the razor for this buffoonery to be corrected, after
everyone had been thoroughly amused. Strange how the desire
for this kind of joke had diminished with age, precisely when it
had become possible. Given the same chance, he yielded to
what was commonly accepted, and couldn't picture himself
going to dinner in this half-mown state at Serge and Veronique's, even though they were old friends who didn't stand on
ceremony. Petit-bourgeois prejudice, he sighed, and continued
to snip away until the bottom of the toothbrush glass was full.
That done, he could begin work with the razor.

He had to hurry; Agnes would be returning any minute. The
suprise would be spoiled if he hadn't finished in time. With the
joyous haste of someone wrapping a present at the last minute,
he applied the shaving cream to the patch cleared of its undergrowth. The razor made a grating sound. He grimaced, but he
hadn't cut himself. Fresh flecks of foam, speckled with black
hairs, many more than before, fell into the bathtub. He started
in again and soon his upper lip was even smoother than his
cheeks. Nice work.

He'd taken his watch off for his bath, even though it was waterproof. According to his own estimation, the operation hadn't
lasted more than six or seven minutes. While he was putting on
the finishing touches, he avoided looking in the mirror in order
to delay the surprise, so he could see himself the way Agnes
would soon be seeing him.

He looked up. Not great. The tan he'd gotten from skiing at

Easter hadn't quite worn off. In place of his mustache was a cutout rectangle of unpleasant pallor that looked fake, tacked on: a false absence of a mustache, he thought. The perverse high spirits that had made him do it hadn't quite lifted, but he already regretted his act a little. In ten days, he said to himself, the damage would be repaired. Still, he could have spared himself this silliness by doing it right before a vacation instead of afterward. That way he'd have an even tan and it would grow back more discreetly. Fewer people would know about it.

He shook his head. It didn't really matter; he wasn't going to make a big deal of it. And at least the experiment would have been worth it, to prove that he really looked better with a mustache.

Supporting himself on the rim, he got up and removed the stopper from the bathtub, which started to drain noisily while he wrapped himself in a towel. He was shaking a little. In front of the sink, he rubbed his cheeks with aftershave, hesitant to touch the milky spot left by his mustache. When he finally decided to go ahead and do it, the stinging made him wince. His skin hadn't come into contact with the open air in almost ten years.

He looked away from the mirror. Agnes wouldn't be long. Suddenly he discovered that he was worried about her reaction, as though he'd cheated on her and was on his way home after having spent the night out. He went into the living room, where he'd laid out the clothes he was planning to wear that night, and slipped them on hastily. Out of nervousness he pulled too hard on a shoelace, which broke. He cursed under his breath, and a vehement gurgling let him know that the bathtub had finished draining. He returned to the bathroom in his stocking feet, and contact with the wet tile floor made his toes curl up. He rinsed the inside of the bathtub until the remainder of the shaving cream—and most of all, the hair—had completely disappeared. He was about to begin scrubbing it with the cleanser that was stored under the sink, to save Agnes the trouble. But he changed his mind; he'd be behaving like an anxious criminal trying to eliminate any trace of his offense, not like an obliging husband. Instead, he emptied the glass containing the clipped hair into the white steel waste can, then rinsed it carefully, without scraping off the layer of tartar. He rinsed the scissors, as well, wiping them afterward so that they wouldn't rust. The childishness of this camouflage made him smile. What good was it to clean the implements of crime when the cadaver was as plain as the nose on his face?

Before returning into the living room, he glanced around the bathroom, avoiding his reflection in the mirror. Then he put on a bossa nova record from the '50s and sat down on the sofa with the distressing feeling that he was in a dentist's waiting room. He didn't know if he wanted Agnes to get back right away, or if he wanted her to be delayed, which would leave him a moment's respite to reason with himself, to put his act into proportion. It was a joke, or at worst, an unfortunate initiative; she would laugh along with him. Or else she'd proclaim herself horrified, which would also be funny.

The doorbell rang. He didn't move. A few seconds passed, then the key felt for the lock. From the sofa, where he hadn't budged, he saw Agnes push the door open with her foot and enter the hall, her arms loaded with shopping bags. Trying to gain time, he almost shouted, "Close the door! Don't look!" He spotted his shoes on the carpet and quickly leaned over them, as if the task of putting them on could occupy him for a long time, and prevent him from showing her his face.

"You could have opened the door," Agnes said without reproach. He was frozen in this position as she passed. But instead of entering the living room, she went straight toward the kitchen. Straining his ears from down the hall, he listened to the slight buzzing of the refrigerator as she opened it, and the crumpling of the paper bags as she took out her purchases. Then he heard her approaching footsteps.

"What are you doing?"

"I broke my shoelace," he muttered without looking up.

"So change your shoes."

She laughed and plopped down onto the sofa beside him. Sitting on the edge, his torso stiffly bent over his shoes, he took in the minute detail of their stitching without realizing what it was, and remained paralyzed by the absurdity of the situation. He must stay calm if he was to play out this joke, greet Agnes and reveal himself while making fun of her surprise. If that failed, make fun of her disapproval, but not curl himself into a ball, hoping to delay the moment that she'd see him as long as possible. He had to snap out of it quickly, get back on track. Perhaps encouraged by the slick undulations of the saxophone on the record, he stood up brusquely, turned his back to her, and walked toward the hall to the shoe closet.

"If you really insist on wearing those," she called to him, "you can always make a knot in the shoelace until you get another pair."

"No. That's okay," he answered, and he took out a pair of moccasins, forcing his feet into them as he stood in the hallway. At least there was no problem about shoelaces. He took a deep breath, touched his face, pausing on the spot where his mustache used to be. It was less startling to the touch than to the eye; Agnes would just have to stroke it a lot. He forced a smile, surprised to find that he could even manage it, shut the closet door, jamming it with the piece of cardboard that kept it from swinging open, and returned to the living room, his neck a bit stiff, his face unprotected and smiling. Agnes had turned off the stereo and was putting the record back into its sleeve.

"We should probably get going now," she said, turning toward him before gently lowering the cover of the turntable. The red light went out, although he couldn't recall having seen her push the button.

On the way down to the basement garage, she checked her makeup in the elevator mirror, then looked at him with an air of approval; but clearly this approval was directed toward his suit, not the metamorphosis, which she still hadn't commented upon. He held her gaze, opened his mouth then shut it again, not knowing what to say. During the ride in the car, he remained silent, considering a number of opening phrases, but none of them seemed satisfactory. It was up to her to speak first, and in fact, she was speaking, recounting an anecdote about an author at the publishing house where she worked, but he was hardly listening to her, unable to interpret her attitude, supplying only minimal answers. Soon they approached the Odéon, where Serge and Veronique lived, and where, as usual, it turned out to be nearly impossible to park. The traffic jam obliged him to circle three times around the same block, but gave him a pretext to vent his bad mood, hitting the steering wheel with his fist, screaming, "Shit!" to a guy honking his horn who couldn't hear him. Agnes made fun of him. Realizing he was being unpleasant, he offered to drop her off while he continued to look for a place to park. She accepted, got out near Serge and Veronique's building, crossed the street, then, as if she'd suddenly changed her mind, marched back to where he was waiting for the light to turn green. He rolled down his window, comforted by the thought that with a few tender words, she would stop teasing him; she only wanted to remind him of the automatic code to get into the building. He leaned out the window to detain her, but she was already on her way, tossing him a wink from over her shoulder that could have meant "see you in a few minutes" or "I love you," or just about anything. He shifted gears, perplexed and annoyed, feeling a strong urge for a cigarette. Why was she pretending not to have noticed anything? Was it so that she could retaliate with her own surprise to the one he'd arranged for her? But that was precisely what was so strange: she hadn't seemed surprised at all, not even for a second to regain her composure and put on a straight face. He had really studied her expression during that moment when she first saw him, as she was putting the record back into its sleeve: no raising of the eyebrows, no fleeting look, nothing, as if she'd had all the time in the world to prepare herself for the scene that awaited her. Of course, one could claim that he'd warned her, she'd even said laughingly that it would be a good idea. But that had obviously been in jest, a false answer to what was still, to his way of thinking, a false question. It was impossible to imagine that she'd taken him seriously, that she'd gone to do her errands and said to herself, He's in the middle of shaving off his mustache. When I see him, I'll have to pretend as if it were nothing. On the other hand, her sangfroid was even less believable if she hadn't been expecting it. In any case, he decided, hats off to her. Nice job.

Despite the traffic, his irritation subsided, and consequently, his malaise. Agnes's lack of reaction, or rather the speed of her reaction, betrayed the intimate complicity that bound them, their game of trying to outdo each other and get the last word, a bantering improvisation that was to be congratulated rather than sulked over. Trying to outfox him, that was just like her, that was just like *them*, and he now felt impatient, not to elucidate a misunderstanding, but to revel in this almost telepathic connection with her and share it with their friends. Serge and Veronique were going to laugh, first at his new look, then at the practical joke Agnes and played on him, they'd laugh at his nervous irritation, which he planned to acknowledge, sparing no details, making himself look as if he were in a fog, and ridiculously grouchy, playing tit for tat.

Unless . . . unless his opponent, who never ran out of ideas, was one step ahead of him and intended to let Serge and Veronique in on it, insisting that they behave in the same way. He was the one, without a doubt, who'd suggested that she go upstairs alone. If he hadn't done that, she might have suggested it herself. Or, just as he did, it was only now that she'd seen how to make use of this head start. Actually, that's what he hoped, delighted to be pursuing a game in which the humor and the challenge now seemed obvious to him. He'd be disappointed if she hadn't thought of it, but of course, she must have, it was too good a chance. He imagined her in the middle of coaching Serge and Veronique at that moment, Veronique chortling with laughter, on the verge of hysteria from trying to act natural. She didn't have Agnes's acting talent—far from it—neither her aplomb nor her inclination for practical jokes. She'd give herself away instantly.

The prospect of this gag, the pleasure that he was deriving from figuring out its possible developments and snags, dissipated the uneasiness he'd felt a moment ago. Stepping back, he was surprised by his own confusion, and reproached himself for his bad mood—but no, not really, it fit right into the game. In retrospect, it almost seemed as if he'd feigned that as well. He rubbed his face, craned his neck so that he could see it in the rearview mirror. Fine, it wasn't exactly smashing, that mushroom-colored upper lip in the middle of his tan, but they would all joke about it, and besides, the white part would tan, the tan part would fade, especially if he were to let his mustache grow back. The only reason to fret, if he was intent on finding one, was that the guy in the car behind him had just taken the space that he'd passed because he was too busy staring at himself to notice.

Serge and Veronique were in rare form. No supporting glances, no ostentatious display of discretion, they looked him straight in the eye, just as usual. Yet he provoked them. Using the pretext of wanting to help, he managed to get Veronique alone in the kitchen and test her by complimenting her on how well she looked. She returned the compliment. Yes, he had gotten a nice tan. Yes, the weather had been beautiful. You look great—you always do. So do you. During dinner the four of them talked about skiing, work, mutual friends, new films, so naturally that the joke began to lose its novelty, like those near-perfect pastiches that look so much like the original that they generate more respect than gaiety. The game was played so well that the pleasure he'd anticipated was spoiled; he almost resented Veronique, whom he considered the weak link in the plot, and who wouldn't give in. No one was taking up the increasingly bigger hints he was dropping about the "smooth" socialism imposed by the Fabius government or the mustache that Marcel Duchamp drew on the Mona Lisa. Despite the implicit tension that this impeccably crafted joke produced as the evening wore on, he felt sad, like a child who, during a family dinner held in honor of his prize for an outstanding achievement, wants the conversation to center only on this, and suffers because once he has been congratulated, the adults don't constantly refer back to it but speak of other things.

Thanks to the wine, he found himself forgetting for just a minute that he'd shaved his mustache, that the others were pretending not to have noticed, and when he realized this, he took a look in the mirror above the fireplace to persuade himself that he hadn't been dreaming, that this phenomenon, apparently forgotten by everyone else, persisted nevertheless, as well as the practical joke in which he was the consenting victim. This persistence surprised him all the more, when after dinner, Serge, a bit smashed, got into an argument with Veronique for some trivial reason that he, for that matter, had missed entirely. These kinds of arguments often took place between their hosts; no one paid any attention to them. Veronique could be ill-tempered, and Agnes, who had known her forever, was obviously amused by her furious shoulder shrugging; when she withdrew into the kitchen, Agnes accompanied her to throw more fuel on the fire. But this domestic squabble made him forget their act of indifference about the cut-off mustache, which was in itself comprehensible, but became more bizarre once the incident was over. The tension wasn't quite reabsorbed, since Veronique was annoyed and becoming detached from the group. It seemed logical that she would ostentatiously disengage herself from a joke whose circumstance was based on a mutual agreement. But she didn't. He looked for a way to push her into revealing a pact that in her anger, she might have completely forgotten about, but what he found was merely rude, and it would have put an awkward end to a gag whose brilliant denouement might have been planned by Agnes. Veronique was making it obvious that she'd had enough and wished they'd go, so that they could quarrel in private. It became clear, however, that there would be no denouement, that the gag had stopped right there, that it wouldn't be commented on by its players, who then would have congratulated one another and laughed wholeheartedly, as he had hoped. His childish disappointment increased; his irritation returned. Even if he found a clever way to get them to put their cards on the table, now there was hardly a chance of its coming out into the open. It had already been delayed far too long, and couldn't be met by anything other than a warmed-over playfulness, proving that the pleasure that one might have taken from acting in this farce had long since dropped by the wayside, and had been replaced by an unfeigned indifference that was frustrating for him.

In the car, Agnes didn't go into it any further. She regretted, no doubt, that her joke had gone on to the point where the whole gang had tacitly agreed not to revive it. But she didn't show regret, cheerfully commenting on the dinner, on Veronique's pigheaded temperament, ridiculing as she always did. And though he didn't expect her to show confusion, this refusal to bring up, even incidentally, the evening's incident seemed almost aggressive to him, as if, to top it off, she bore him a grudge because he'd been sucked into her joke. He hated to be angry with Agnes, wanted to be able to love her unreservedly, no matter how brief or ephemeral that reserve was; and in fact, the love that they had for each other went hand in hand with a sense of humor for private jokes that generally sufficed to take the sting out of their conflicts. Since it was such a harmless whim, a little bit of distance should have warded off any irritation. Despite all that, Agnes's attitude annoyed him, and even stirred up an inexplicable anxiety, an unsettling impression of being in the wrong, which he'd felt at once when he'd left the bathroom that evening. Obviously it was ridiculous, he could very well play this game for five more minutes if it amused Agnes, but he was going to end up being angry at her. He could feel it already, so why not stop? Because it was up to her to make the first move, and too bad if, having waited so long, there was nothing left for her to say but a banal, "You know, it doesn't look too bad," provided she said it in a nice way. Even if she thought it looked lousy, the point was to say it. Apparently she didn't want to. Stubborn as a mule, he thought.

For the last two minutes she'd been silent, and was looking straight ahead with a sulky little pout, as if she were reproaching him for his lack of attention. He adored the way her brow set obstinately under her bangs, rendering her instantly childish. His displeasure abruptly vanished, swept away by a wave of compassion that was slightly condescending, like an adult who gives in to a child's whim, showing that he who yields first is the smartest.

At a red light, he leaned toward her and brushed his lips around the contours of her face. As she tossed her head back to offer him her neck, he noticed that she was smiling, and thought about saying, "You won." He preferred to rub his smooth upper lip against her skin, pressing his nose against her neck as he worked up from her collarbone to her earlobe, and murmured, "It looks different, doesn't it?"

She sighed gently, putting her hand on his thigh as he moved away with regret, to go from neutral into first gear. Once they'd crossed the intersection, she asked in a whisper, "What looks different?"

He pursed his lips, refusing to let impatience get the better of him. "Give me a break."

"What do you mean, 'give me a break'?"

"Please . . ." he implored comically.

"But what's the matter?"

Turning toward him, she stared at him with such confident, tender, and slightly worried curiosity that he was afraid that if she kept it up he'd really be upset with her. He had made the first move, surrendered completely. She should understand that it didn't amuse him anymore, that he wanted to discuss it calmly. He forced himself to continue in the tone of an adult trying to reason with a stubborn little girl, and declared emphatically, "The best jokes are the shortest ones."

"What joke?"

"Stop it." He cut her off with a brusqueness that he instantly regretted. He began again, more gently, "That's enough."

"What's wrong?"

"Please stop, I'm asking you to stop it."

He was no longer smiling, and neither was she.

"Okay. Stop," she said. "Right now. Here."

He realized that she was referring to the car, veered sharply toward the bus lane, and turned off the engine, to give more weight to his order to get the whole thing over with. But she spoke first. "Tell me."

She seemed so disconcerted, shocked even, that he wondered for a second whether she wasn't being sincere, if it were possible that for some incredible reason she hadn't noticed anything. But not one incredible reason would do, it was even grotesque to ask himself that question, let alone to ask it of her.

"You haven't noticed anything?" he demanded nonetheless.

"No. No, I haven't noticed anything and you're going to explain to me right now what I was supposed to have noticed."

That takes the cake, he thought—that determined, almost menacing tone from a woman who is about to make a scene and is certain that she's in the right. It would be better to let it go. She'd get tired, just like children do when you stop paying attention to them. However, she was no longer using her childish tone. He hesitated and sighed, "Nothing," and moved his hand toward the ignition. She held him back.

"No," she ordered. "Tell me."

But he didn't know what to say. It suddenly seemed difficult and vaguely obscene to drive the nail in harder, to utter those few words that Agnes, prompted by some crazy notion, absolutely wanted him to say.

"Oh c'mon, my mustache," he blurted out, slurring the syllables.

There. He had said it.

"Your mustache?"

She raised her eyebrows in a perfect imitation of amazement. He could have applauded or slapped her.

"I beg of you, stop it," he repeated.

"You stop it yourself!" She was almost shouting. "What is this story about a mustache?"

He took her hand roughly, brought it to his lips, and applied her tense, slightly stiff fingers to the spot where his mustache had been. Just at that moment, they were blinded by the headlights of a bus approaching behind them. He let go of her hand, started the car, and swerved back into the middle of the boulevard.

"That bus runs late," he observed stupidly to interrupt the conversation, thinking at the same time that they had left Serge and Veronique's early, and that the way things were going, any attempt to break this off was useless. Agnes, who clung to center stage, was already back into her role.

"I would like you to explain this to me. You want to grow a mustache, is that it?"

"Now come on, for God's sake, touch this!" he shouted, taking back her hand and pressing it once again on his mouth. "I just shaved it, can't you feel it? Can't you see it?"

She withdrew her hand with a short little laugh that he didn't recognize, mocking and humorless.

"You shave every day, don't you? Twice a day."

"Shit. Cut it out."

"This joke is getting monotonous," she observed dryly.

"Your specialty, right?"

She didn't answer and he thought that he'd made his point. He accelerated, determined not to speak until she put a stop to this whole idiotic business. He who yields first is the smartest, he repeated to himself, but the sentence had lost the nuance of an affectionate scolding; the syllables pounded heavily in his head with a kind of infuriating idiocy.

Agnes kept silent, and when he stole a glance at her, the confused look on her face struck him as nasty. He had never seen her like this, hateful and frightened. She had never acted out a farce with such vehemence. Not one false move, a work of art, and why? Why do this?

They remained silent during the rest of the ride home, in the elevator as well, and even once they'd entered the bedroom, where they undressed in their own separate corners without looking at each other. From the bathroom, where he was brushing his teeth, he heard her laugh in a certain way that invited a question, but he didn't ask it. But by the sound of this laugh, which was not ill-tempered but almost a guffaw, he guessed that she was backing down. And when he came back into the room, she was already in bed, smiling at him with a look of sly modesty. This expression, remorseful and sure of being forgiven, rendered the one he had unexpectedly seen in the car almost inconceivable. She was sorry; of course, he would be generous with her.

"In my opinion," she said, "Serge and Veronique have already made up. Maybe we could do the same."

"That's a nice idea," he answered, smiling back at her, and he slipped into bed, took her into his arms, both relieved that she'd surrendered and worried about his modest victory. Pressed against him with her eyes already closed, she gave a small moan of pleasure and squeezed his shoulder, as if to signal that she was sleepy. He turned out the light.

"Are you asleep?" he said a little while later.

She answered at once, in a soft but distinct whisper. "No."

"What are you thinking about?"

She laughed softly as she had before when she was climbing into bed.

"About your mustache, of course."

There was a moment of silence. A truck passed by in the street, making the windows rattle. Then she continued, hesitantly. "You know, before, in the car . . ."

"Yes?"

"It's funny, but I got the impression that if you kept it up, I would have been scared."

Silence. His eyes were wide open, surely hers were as well.

"I was scared," she murmured.

He swallowed with difficulty. "But you're the one who kept it up."

"Please," she implored, clasping his hand as tightly as possible. "It scares me, I assure you."

"Well, then don't start again," he said, putting his arms around her, with the apprehensive hope of stopping her wheels from turning, which he felt were all ready to be reset into motion. She felt it too, fiercely broke away from his embrace and turned on the light.

"You're the one who's starting all over," she cried. "Don't ever do it again!"

He saw that she was crying, her expression had caved in, her back was convulsed with shivers. It was impossible to fake that, he thought, panic-stricken; it wasn't possible that she was being insincere. It was also impossible that she was sincere, because if that were the case, she was going crazy. He grabbed her by the shoulders, overcome by trembling and by the contraction of her muscles. Her bangs hid her eyes; he pushed them aside, exposing her forehead, took her face into his hands, ready to do anything to stop the pain. She stammered, "What's this story about a mustache?"

"Agnes," he murmured, "Agnes, I shaved it off. It's not important, it'll grow back. Look at me, Agnes. What's going on?"

He repeated every word gently, almost crooning as he caressed her, but she moved away again, with the same wide-eyed stare she had had in the car; it was the same thing all over again.

"You know very well that you never had a mustache. Stop it, please." She was screaming. "Please. It's ridiculous, please, you're scaring me, stop it. Why are you doing this?" Her voice trailed off in a whisper.

Overwhelmed, he didn't answer. What could he say to her? To stop this farce and go back to a cross fire of misunderstandings? What was going on? He thought of the disconcerting jokes she sometimes made, like the story about the walled-off door. Suddenly he remembered the dinner at Serge and Veronique's, and their obstinate pretending not to see anything different. What had she said to them, and why? What was she after?

He and Agnes often had the same ideas at the same time; it rarely failed. And the second she opened her mouth, he realized that whoever asked the question first would gain back the advantage.

Her move.

"If you'd shaved off your mustache, Serge and Veronique would have noticed, right?"

Hopeless. He sighed. "You told them to make believe that they didn't."

She stared at him, her pupils dilated, her mouth wide open, visibly as horrified as if he were threatening her with a razor.

"You're crazy," she hissed. "Absolutely crazy."

He closed his eyes, squeezing his lids shut so tightly that it hurt, in the absurd hope that when he opened them again, Agnes would be asleep, the nightmare would be over. He heard her stir, push the sheets aside. She was getting up. And if she were crazy, if she started to hallucinate, what should he do? Play her game, utter pacifying words, rock her in his arms and say, "Yes, you're right, I never had a mustache, I was just kidding. Forgive me"? Or prove to her that she was delirious? The water was running in the bathroom. When he opened his eyes, she was coming toward the bed with a glass in her hand. She'd slipped on a T-shirt and seemed calmer.

"Listen," she said, "let's call Serge and Veronique."

This time, once again, she was one step ahead, securing her advantage by making a fairly reasonable offer that put him on the defensive. And if she'd persuaded them to contribute to the hoax, if they had persevered during the entire dinner, nothing could guarantee that they wouldn't keep it up on the phone. But why? Why? He didn't understand.

"At this hour?" he asked, aware that it was a mistake to bring up a conventional and futile pretext, just to avoid an ordeal that he foresaw as dangerous.

"I don't see any other solution." Her voice had suddenly regained its confidence. She reached for the telephone.

"It won't prove a thing," he murmured. "If you've already warned them."

The words barely out of his mouth, he regretted this defeatist precaution, and worried that he should be taking the initiative. He grabbed hold of the phone. Sitting on the edge of the bed, Agnes let him, without a word of protest. After dialing the number, he counted four rings, and then someone picked it up. He recognized Veronique's voice, heavy with sleep.

"It's me," he said abruptly. "Sorry to wake you, but there's something I want to ask you. Do you remember what I look like? You saw me tonight, right?"

"Huh?" Veronique grunted.

"You didn't notice anything?"

"What?"

"You didn't notice that I don't have a mustache anymore?"

"Are you bullshitting me, or what?"

Agnes, who was listening in, made a gesture that clearly meant, You see? and said impatiently, "Let me speak to her." He held out the receiver, rejecting her offer that he listen in, to show her what small importance he attached to a test that was rigged, anyhow.

"Veronique?" Agnes said. There was a pause, and then she went on, "That's exactly what I'm asking you. Listen. Suppose

172

I'd made you swear, no matter what happened, that he never had a mustache? Are you following me?"

She waved the receiver in his direction, as if ordering him to come and listen in. Furious at himself, he obeyed.

"Fine," she continued. "If I have asked you to do that, now disregard it and answer me truthfully. Yes or no, have you ever seen him with a mustache?"

"No, obviously not. And besides—" Veronique broke off and they heard Serge's voice behind the static in the background, then a kind of aside with a hand over the receiver.

Finally, Serge took the phone. "You seem to be having a lot of fun," he said, "but we're trying to get some sleep. G'bye."

He looked at her, bewildered.

"You told them."

"Call whomever you want. Carine, Paul, Bernard, somebody from your office, anyone."

She got up, took the address book from the night table and threw it onto the bed. He realized that by picking it up, leafing through it, and looking for someone else to call he'd be admitting his defeat, even if it was absurd, impossible. Something had been thrown out of kilter tonight, something that obliged him to give proof of the evidence, and his proof was not convincing. Agnes had falsified it. Right now he was suspicious of the telephone, anticipating without actually being able to imagine the methods of a conspiracy in which he was a part—a gigantic hoax, not the least bit funny. While he rejected the wild hypothesis that Agnes might have called every person in his address book, using any sort of pretext to make them swear that whatever she said, even if she urged them to retract it, he had never worn a mustache, he sensed that by calling Carine, Bernard, Jerome, Samira, he would get the same answer. He'd have to refuse this ordeal, abandon this fruitless terrain, and move on to another where he would have the advantage, a possibility of control.

"Listen," he said. "We must have some photos somewhere. Yeah, like the ones from Java."

Getting out of bed, he rummaged through the desk drawer and took out a pile of photos from their last vacation. They both appeared in a good number of them.

"So?" he said, handing her one.

She glanced at it, looked up at him, and gave it back. He gazed at it. It was him all right, dressed in a batik shirt, his hair stuck to his forehead with sweat, smiling and mustached.

"So?" he repeated.

She, in turn, closed her eyes, reopened them, and answered in a weary voice. "What do you want to prove?"

Again he wanted to say, "Stop it," wanted to reason with her, but he remembered, suddenly exhausted himself, that it would start all over again, back to square one. He who was smarter would be the first to stop. Might as well surrender, wait for it to pass.

"Okay," he said, letting the photo fall onto the carpet.

"Let's go to sleep," said Agnes.

From a little brass box that was kept on the night table, she took out a packet of sleeping pills, swallowed one, and gave him one with a glass of water. He got back into bed, turned out the light. They didn't touch each other. A little later, under the covers, she lightly grazed the back of his hand, and for a few seconds he stroked hers with his fingertips. He forced a smile in the dark. With his mind at rest, gliding toward sleep, he couldn't really begrudge her. Sure, she came on strong, but that was her way and he loved her like that, a little wacky, like when she'd call up a friend and say, "So what's going on? . . . Well, you know, your door . . . Yes, your door . . . What, didn't you see it? . . . I promise you, your door downstairs has been replaced by a wall of bricks . . . No, the door's gone . . . Yes, I swear to you, I'm in the phone booth on the corner . . . Yes, bricks . . ." And so on, until her friend, incredulous but troubled nevertheless, would go down to the entrance of her building, go back upstairs, then call Agnes and say, "Oh, that's very funny!" "Very funny," he murmured softly to himself, and they fell asleep.

2

HE WOKE UP AT ELEVEN THE NEXT MORNING WITH A HEAVY HEAD
and a tongue coated from sleeping pills. Agnes had left him a
note under the alarm clock. "See you tonight. I love you." The
photos of Java were lying there, scattered on the rug by the foot
of the bed. He picked one up and studied it. He and Agnes,
dressed in light colors, pressed close together in a pedicab. The
driver behind them was grinning, his teeth reddened by betel.
He tried to remember who had taken the picture, probably
someone passing by who'd obliged their request. Every time he
had handed over his camera to a stranger, he had had the vague
fear that they'd take off with it as fast as they could, but it had
never happened. He touched his face, which seemed swollen
from his heavy sleep. His fingertips lingered on his chin, the familiar stubble, but he hesitated to venture toward the upper lip.
Then, when he finally decided to go through with it, he was not

at all surprised. He hadn't for a moment imagined that he'd dreamed up last night. However much his upper lip felt like his cheek, the feeling was unpleasant to him. He looked back at the photo of the pedicab, then got up and went into the bathroom. Since he had awakened late, he was going to take his time, allow himself the luxury of a bath instead of his usual morning shower.

While the water was running, he called the office to tell them he'd be there in the early afternoon. Strangely enough, this posed less of a problem than he had thought; they were backed up and would be working late that night. He almost questioned Samira about his mustache, but changed his mind. Enough of this childishness.

He shaved in front of the sink, not in the bathtub, taking care not to touch the newly grown mustache hair, which he would definitely allow to grow back. It was already obvious that he didn't like himself without it.

In the bathtub, he contemplated the situation. Without truly holding a grudge, he couldn't entirely understand Agnes's stubbornness, her persistence in this prank when, quite honestly, the humor was gone after five minutes. Of course, as he had told her himself, these weird jokes were her specialty. Even disregarding that business about the walled-up door, which he actually found a bit morbid, he'd always been surprised by the way she could lie.

Like everyone else, Agnes would occasionally tell little white lies, to excuse herself from a dinner, or from not being able to finish her work on time. But instead of saying, for instance, that she was sick or that her car just broke down, or that she had misplaced her appointment book, she offered convincing testimony, totally blown out of proportion, using obvious falsehoods rather than giving phony but believable reasons. If a friend was waiting for her phone call all afternoon, she wouldn't say that she'd forgotten, that the line was busy, or that no one was home, which after all might lead one to think that the phone was out of order. Instead, staring him straight in the face, she'd assure this friend that she had in fact called him, that they had in fact spoken, which he knew to be blatantly untrue, and would cause him to wonder if for some mysterious reason, a stranger had passed himself off as someone else. Or she, in turn, might accuse this friend of lying, which implicitly Agnes never failed to do, banking on the improbability of her explanation as proof of her sincerity. Why in the world did she have to invent such ridiculous excuses? Such tactics bewildered people, and what's more, she'd boast about them after the fact, telling everyone she could. But if one of the victims reminded her of these confessions, she'd answer yes, she did it often, but not this time. No, she swore she hadn't—she wasn't lying. She kept it up so convincingly that one was forced either to believe her or at least to make a grumbling compromise. Otherwise the discussion might drag on endlessly, and she'd never let up.

Last winter they'd spent a week with Serge and Veronique in their country house, where the heating system was pretty antiquated. The rooms maintained a reasonable temperature only if every radiator was on low, otherwise the fuses would blow. Agnes, who was easily chilled, had obviously turned up the radiator in their room to its maximum, and naturally, the fuses had blown. This had not discouraged her. But after three consecutive power outages, after three lectures in which Serge had pointed out the necessity of sacrificing a bit of her own comfort for the sake of the group, she seemed to have finally resigned herself to it. They had all spent a peaceful evening in the big common room, an evening marred by no other incident, even after Agnes, who was the first to go to bed, had left. Everyone had expected to be sleeping in a comfortably heated room, which explained the general consternation when it was discovered that the radiators were off and the rooms were freezing cold. There was no doubt in anyone's mind, the writing was on the wall. After convincing her weekend companions that she could be trusted, Agnes had tyrannically turned off everyone else's heat so that she could turn on her own full blast. Triumphantly reposing in her sweatbox, she never for a second imagined that her furious victims would be coming to wake her up and demand an explanation. Until the very end, against all evidence, she pleaded not guilty, indignant that she should be suspected of such foul play. "So who did it?" Veronique kept repeating, exasperated. "I don't know, but it wasn't me," said Agnes, and she wouldn't give in. Later they ended up laughing about it and so did she, but without ever admitting to it, without ever providing an alternate explanation, such as the boiler wasn't working, or a burglar might have broken in and played with the radiator dials.

Looking at these facts objectively, the business about his mustache seemed neither more nor less surprising than that story or the one about the bricks. The difference lay in the fact that they'd both pushed it too far, that he'd gone along with her to the point of hostility, and that this time he was also the victim. Usually, he became a silent accomplice to her irrefutable dishonesty, for which he would show an affectionate indulgence, even admiration. Curious, he thought, that during the five years they'd lived together she'd never inflicted this treatment on him, as if, in her eyes, he were off limits.

Not that strange, actually. He knew quite well that there were two Agnes: the brilliant, sociable one, who was always performing, whose sudden whims and unpredictable behavior came off as seductively natural and made him proud of her, even if he wouldn't admit it; the other one, known only to him, was fragile and anxious, jealous too, capable of bursting into tears over nothing, then curling up in his arms while he consoled her. She had another voice, a hesitant, almost affected one, that would have annoyed him in public, but that, during their private moments together, revealed an unsettling lack of inhibition.

As he thought about it, in bathwater that was now turning cold, he understood with displeasure what had bothered him the most during their fight the night before. For the first time Agnes had thrown one of her society-game acts into their protected sphere. Even worse, in order to give her act more credibility, she'd used the tone of voice and posturing usually reserved for the realm of taboo, in which, theoretically, no acting was allowed. By violating their implicit agreement, she'd treated him like a stranger. She reversed the roles in his disfavor with every bit of virtuosity she'd acquired playing this game, in an almost hateful way. He remembered her anguished face, her tears. She'd really seemed frightened. With total conviction, she'd really accused him of persecuting her, of deliberately scaring her for no reason. That was just it, for no reason. . . . Why had she done it? What was she trying to punish him for? Not for having shaved off his mustache, for God's sake. He hadn't cheated on her; in no way had he betrayed her. Searching his conscience did nothing to reassure him, since it implied that she was penalizing him for a mistake that he wasn't even aware he'd made. Unless she wanted to torture him gratuitously, or more likely, hadn't realized what she was doing. For that matter, he himself hadn't actually realized it until now, after a good night's sleep. He had to make allowances for that slightly perverse sense of giddiness that one must feel when manipulating somebody else. He'd have to make it spin around faster and faster to the point when equilibrium was restored. Then he'd say, "That was fun, wasn't it?" But really, even under the pretense of a farce, she had gone too far in securing her position against him by involving Serge and Veronique. That they agreed to participate, had played their roles the way she'd asked—well, it was understandable. They thought they were lending themselves to a game among themselves, one of those private jokes that they were accustomed to playing, and not the first serious skirmish in a kind of conjugal guerrilla warfare. No, he shouldn't really blow it out of proportion. They'd had a little too much to drink. It was all over now; she wouldn't bring it up anymore. But all the same, without any exaggeration, it hurt—it was a betrayal, the very first. Her distraught expression from the night before flashed in front of his eyes, her theatrical tears, as real as real could be, they'd caused a rift in their mutual trust. Here I go, he thought. I'm exaggerating again. Got to stop.

He stepped out of the tub, shook himself off, and decided to forget the whole incident. He promised himself that he wouldn't reproach her, even if there were cause to do so. No, there wouldn't be any cause. The case was closed. They wouldn't speak of it again.

But as he dressed, it occurred to him that he'd been really stupid, not only by entering into the game, but by lacking a certain presence of mind during the telephone call. Agnes had maneuvered it so that she'd been the first to call Serge and Veronique, and then, objecting that she hadn't been able to coach them, continued her bluff by suggesting that he call anyone he please, anyone at all. And like an imbecile, he'd had the impression that on that particular night, through some twist of fate, everyone would disavow his claim, when in fact, she positively could not have warned anyone but Serge and Veronique. From the moment Agnes had seen him with the shaved mustache, right before they left for dinner, they hadn't left each other's side for more than ten minutes, just the time for him to park. She had taken advantage of this delay to let Serge and Veronique in on it, but it was out of the question that she'd also gone through the entire phone book of all their friends to give them instructions. He'd been had. Especially now that this morning, if she wanted to, she'd had all the time in the world to get everyone that they knew, one by one, on her side. No sooner did the idea dawn on him, than it made him smile: the simple fact of catching her at her own game, of imagining her weaving a telephonic conspiracy all for the sake of a stale joke . . . Well, he'd talk to her about it, she'd laugh about it too, and maybe through this amiable approach, without having to put the blame on her, she might just understand that what she considered an innocent prank had managed to affect him. No, better yet, if she didn't lose face, however small it was, he wouldn't tell her, he wouldn't speak of it again. It was over.

When he arrived at his office, he realized that it wasn't over at all. Hunched over their sketches, Jerome and Samira looked up when they heard him come in, but had no reaction. Jerome beckoned him over, and a minute later, the three of them were dividing up the work, since their client wanted the project ready for him by next Monday, and they were still way behind. They were going to have to make a real effort.

"I have a dinner tonight," Samira explained, "but I'll manage to get back here afterward." He looked her straight in the eye. She smiled, playfully mussed up his hair, and added, "Hey, you don't look so hot. You must be doing crazy things to your body." Jerome left the room, and then the telephone rang. She grabbed the receiver, and he suddenly found himself alone, feeling like an idiot, his fingers groping at the sides of his nose.

He took a seat in front of his drafting table and started to examine the drawings, which he kept from rolling up with the palm of his hand. He put the corners under some ashtrays and pin trays, and began to work. He answered the phone several times, his mind elsewhere; with all the precise thoughts floating around in his head, he was incapable of formulating a coherent hypothesis as functional and harmless as the community center that they were overtaking. Had Agnes called them too? Ridiculous, especially since he couldn't imagine that Jerome or Samira, who were bogged down with work, would allow anyone to explain the roles that they'd have to play in an idiotic joke. Unless, strictly out of necessity, they might have said, "All right," and wouldn't have given it another thought, but upon his arrival, would surely have shown their surprise. Was it simply that they didn't notice anything? His frequent trips to the bathroom during the course of the afternoon, his lingering stance in front of the mirror assured him that even if they were distracted, even if they were myopic—which besides they weren't—these people with whom he'd worked every day for the last two years, whom he often saw socially outside the office, could not possibly be unaware of the change in his appearance. But the sheer absurdity of having to ask the question prevented him from doing so.

Around eight o'clock he called Agnes to say that he'd be coming home late. "Are you okay?" she asked.

"Yeah, I'm fine. Up to my ears with work, but I'm fine. See you later."

Except for a fifteen-minute chat with Jerome about the plans, he hardly spoke. The rest of the time they stayed riveted to their drawing tables, one smoking like a fiend, the other persistently stroking his upper lip. The absence of tobacco was

more oppressive than usual. Once his one and only daily cigarette had been smoked, the one reserved for the lunch he hadn't
eaten, he had to reason with himself. He knew all too well the
cycle that had given rise to his former resolutions: First, you ask
for a puff from someone nearby, then once in a while an entire
cigarette, then Jerome comes into the office with an extra pack,
and says with a wink, "Help yourself, but stop bugging me," and
by the end of the week, he'd be back to buying his own. Now,
after two months of abstinence, he could see the light at the
end of the tunnel, although the pessimists always say that it
takes three years before you can consider the battle won. All the
same, a cigarette would calm his nerves, would help him con-
centrate on his work. He thought about it just as much as he
thought about his mustache and the prank that they were playing on him, and associated the sensation of the filter between
his lips and the taste of smoke with the solution of the banal
mystery that obsessed him. All at once he felt a revived interest in the plans spread before him. He finally asked Jerome for
a cigarette, who was too absorbed even to joke about it and
merely held out the pack. Of course, he reaped none of the
benefits he'd hoped to gain. His mind continued to wander.

A little before eleven, Samira, who had disappeared to go to
her dinner, called to ask if they'd open the door in ten minutes.
The office looked out onto the courtyard of the building, and
the lobby door, which had no intercom, was locked after eight
o'clock. He remembered the story about the bricks. Seizing the
opportunity, he went out to stretch his legs and wait for Samira
downstairs. It was raining, and the little café that sold ciga-

rettes on the other side of the street was about to close. He walked across, slipped beneath the half-lowered iron gate, and asked for some cigarettes. For Jerome, of course, who'd soon be running out of them. The owner, who was counting the money in the cash register, greeted him with a brief nod of recognition. He stole a glance in the mirror between the bottles lined up on the shelves, and smiled wearily at himself. The owner of the café, who happened to look up at that moment, automatically smiled back as he handed him the change.

In the street, he smoked another cigarette, furious at himself. He crushed it under his foot when he saw Samira approaching. She was brandishing a bottle of vodka, which she'd just bought. "I think we're going to need it," she said.

Past the main door, he reached for the hallway switch, but something was out of order; the light would not go on. They entered the courtyard, in full view of the lit window through which one could see Jerome hunched over his architect's lamp, and he took Samira by the arm.

"Wait."

She stopped without turning toward him. Maybe she thought that he wanted to kiss her. He could have put his hands on her shoulders, brought his lips to her neck; she probably wouldn't have offered any resistance.

"Did Agnes call you?" he asked hesitantly.

"Agnes? No. Why?"

She swung around and looked at him with amazement.

"Are you all right? What's the matter?"

"Samira . . ."

He took a deep breath, searching for the right words.

"If Agnes called you, I beg of you, please tell me. It's important."

She shook her head.

"Are you having problems with Agnes? You have a strange look on your face."

"You haven't noticed anything?"

"Yes, that you have a strange look on your face."

He was going to force himself to ask her that question, no matter how ridiculous it might seem. Samira had come a bit closer, attentive, already sympathetic; it was difficult to believe she was acting. He would have liked to tell them all to stop it, that he'd had enough. He sat down on the stoop of the building with his head in his hands. He heard the swish of her raincoat, and the creak of the wooden stairs as she sat down next to him. "What in the world is the matter?" she said. He stood up and dusted himself off.

"It'll pass. I think I'll go back in."

"Don't say anything to Jerome," he said before pushing open the office door, and he moved aside to let her in first.

He went to get his coat, said that he didn't feel well, that he'd come back tomorrow to finish. Jerome grumbled something, not really listening. He shook his hand, kissed Samira good-bye, gave her shoulder a strong squeeze to show that she shouldn't worry about him, that it was just a passing moment, and he left.

He found himself in the deserted street, the café now closed. He slipped his hand into his jacket pocket and discovered the cigarettes he'd bought for Jerome, hesitated over whether or not to return to the office and give them to him, and didn't.

Agnes had waited up for him and was watching an old movie on the late show. "How're you doing?" she said. "Fine," he answered, and sat down beside her on the sofa. The film had started almost an hour ago, and she summarized the beginning in an amused, lazy tone that he thought was affected. Cary Grant was playing the role of an enterprising doctor who falls in love with a pregnant young woman, prevents her from committing suicide, restores her desire to live, and marries her. But the other doctors in the city where he practices, jealous of his success, begin a campaign against him, digging up certain questionable episodes from his past that would bar him from medical practice. It was hard to tell whether or not these suspicions were founded, which rendered his idyllic love affair with the young lady slightly suspect. One wondered if he really loved her, or if he were only marrying her so he could use her in some kind of scheme. At any rate, the two plots didn't seem to have much to do with each other. He followed them with a kind of dazed attention, certain, without succumbing to the desire to verify it, that Agnes was watching him out of the corner of her eye. Before long, there was a scene of the trial in which Cary Grant's secret was revealed. From what he understood, they were reproaching him for having practiced medicine in a neighboring town, where in order to allay the suspicions of its inhabitants concerning his profession, he passed himself off as a butcher, until one of his clients, whom he'd treated while pretending to sell her steaks, discovered his medical diploma, was appalled by his deception, and he had to leave town under the threat of being lynched. "That's wild," Agnes squealed with delight, when he defended himself by explaining that he sold the meat at cost, and made absolutely no profit from this paramedical practice. Cary Grant also had a sidekick, an old guy with very slow gestures who followed him everywhere without saying a word, even into the operating room. It added a bizarre touch to the melodrama, like one of those horror films in which the mad scientist—although Cary Grant hardly resembled a mad scientist—is followed around by a grimacing hunchback who limps along in the pouring rain carrying stolen cadavers back to the morgue. This assistant proved all the more mysterious when, accused of being a murderer, he calmly recounted in full detail that he'd once had a friend and a girlfriend, but that he'd realized that his friend was actually his girlfriend's boyfriend, so they'd fought over it. When he was spotted on his way back to town alone, covered with blood, and his friend's body was nowhere to be found, he'd been sentenced to fifteen years in prison. "But they never found the body?" exclaimed the judge. "Yes," the assistant answered politely. "I found it myself, fifteen years later, when I got out of prison. It was in the window of a restaurant where he was having some soup, split pea, I think. I asked him why he'd never told anyone that he was alive, and since his answer didn't satisfy me, I beat him to death, figuring that I'd already paid for it, so it was only fair that

I finish him off. But the jury didn't agree, and this time, I was hanged." Hanged, then more or less resuscitated by Cary Grant. Absolved by this touching explanation, as well as by the nonprofit aspect of his meat business, Cary Grant winds up modestly triumphant by the end of the film, energetically conducting a joyous orchestra of hospital nurses. The words "The End" appeared, accompanied by the applause of the concert audience. Then the television announcer came on to bid everyone a good night.

They remained there, sitting side by side on the sofa, their eyes glued to the empty screen. Agnes switched to another channel, but there was nothing else on. The movie left a curious impression, particularly because he'd missed the beginning. It appeared to be composed of various elements that didn't fit together: the realistic and sentimental story of the child bride and smiling doctor clashed with the one about crazy townspeople who want to lynch their butcher when they find out he was a doctor, or people who commit murders after having served the sentence that penalized them. It almost seemed to him that instead of watching the movie, they had both gradually made it up without consulting each other. Or maybe each of them had strived to undermine the other one's work, the way you'd go about making a *cadavre exquis*, hoping that yours will be a failure just to irritate the other participants. That was probably the way it was, he reflected, when screenwriters tried to work together, having a showdown until one of the partners danced. The static was still buzzing on the set, which was all there was for the rest of the night. He wished they had a VCR so they could keep watching.

"Well," Agnes finally said, as she pushed the button on the remote control, making the static disappear, "I'm going to bed."

He remained on the sofa for a while as she got undressed and vanished into the bathroom. He hadn't shaved that evening, hadn't eaten a thing all day. His palms were clammy. On top of it all, he had smoked three cigarettes. But it seemed as though everything was back to normal, that they wouldn't mention his mustache anymore, and in the long run, it was better that way.

Agnes walked across the living room, naked. "Are you coming to bed?" she asked from the bedroom. "I'm getting sleepy." Why, in spite of everything, wouldn't she explain herself? If she had called all their friends during the day, there had to be some reason, a collective trick, something like a surprise party, only it wasn't his birthday. During the movie he'd felt as if she'd been watching him, and now she was calmly going to bed. "I'm coming," he answered, but took his turn in the bathroom. He grabbed his toothbrush, put it down again, sat on the edge of the bathtub and looked around. He broke off his gaze at the small metal waste can under the sink, and raised the lid with the tip of his foot. Empty, except for a piece of cotton that Agnes must have used to remove her makeup. Obviously she had gotten rid of all evidence. He made his way into the kitchen, looking for a full trash bag, but there wasn't any.

"Did you take out the garbage?" he shouted. Try as he might

to seem innocent and natural, his question would inevitably sound somewhat odd.

No answer. He went back into the living room and repeated his question.

"Yes. Thanks. Don't worry about it," Agnes replied languorously, as if she were already asleep. Turning on his heels, he walked toward the front door, which he discreetly closed behind him. He then went all the way down to the lobby, to the corner under the stairs where the trash cans were. They were also empty. The concierge must have already put the bags out onto the sidewalk. Yes. In fact, he'd noticed it on his way back from the office.

They were still there. He started to rummage through them, searching for the bag that might be theirs. He ripped open several of the blue plastic ones with his nails. Curious how easy it was to recognize one's own trash, he thought, unearthing bottles of liquid yogurt, crumpled frozen-food wrappers—the trash of rich people, of the bohemian rich who rarely dined at home. This discovery prompted a vague feeling of sociological security, of belonging in his niche, redeemable and recognizable. He emptied everything onto the sidewalk with a kind of glee. He quickly found the smaller bag that they used for the bathroom waste can, picked out cotton swabs, two Tampaxes, an old tube of toothpaste, another one for skin lotion, and some used razor blades. And there it was, his hair. Lots of it, but scattered all over, not exactly as he'd hoped. He'd imagined a nice compact tuft, something like a mustache, holding together all by itself. He gathered as much of it as possible and collected it in the palm of his hand. When he'd amassed a little mound, less than he thought he'd shaved off, he went back upstairs. He entered the room without a sound, his cupped hand outstretched. Sitting down on the bed next to Agnes, who was apparently asleep, he switched on the night-table lamp. She moaned softly. Then, since he was shaking her shoulders, she blinked open her eyes and grimaced when she saw his open palm thrust in front of her face.

"And this," he said harshly, "what do you call this?"

She leaned up onto her elbow, now squinting under the bright light.

"What going on? What's that in your hand?"

"Hair," he said, holding back a contemptuous laugh.

"Oh no! You're not going to start that again."

"The hair from my mustache," he continued. "You can look at it."

"You're crazy."

She'd said it calmly, as though it were a simple fact. Not a trace of last night's hysteria. For a split second, he thought that she was right. Through the eyes of any stranger who might take them by surprise, he looked like a lunatic, bent over his wife, practically rubbing her nose in a handful of hair that he'd dug out of the garbage. But what did it matter, he had the evidence.

"And what is that supposed to prove?" she asked, now completely awake. "That you had a mustache, is that it?"

"That's right."

She pondered a moment, then looking straight into his eyes, said gently but firmly, "You'd better go see a psychiatrist."

"For God's sake, you're the one who should go to a psychiatrist."

He was pacing back and forth in the room with his fist clenched around the tuft of hair. "You're the one who goes and calls everyone so that they'll make believe that they don't know anything about it! Who let Serge and Veronique in on it? And Samira? And Jerome?" He was going to add, "And the owner of the café across from the office," but held it back.

"Do you realize what you're saying?" Agnes asked soberly.

Yes, he realized all right. It didn't make sense, of course. But nothing made any sense.

"So what do you call this?" he repeated, opening up his hand again, as if he were trying to convince himself. "What do you think this is?"

"Hair," she replied. Then she sighed. "Hair from your mustache. What do you want me to say? Let me go to sleep now."

He slammed the door, stood for a moment in the middle of the living room, and looked at the hair. Then he lay down on the sofa. He removed the pack of cigarettes he'd bought for Jerome from his pocket, pulled the cigarettes out one by one, so that he could put the hair inside it. Afterward he smoked a cigarette, watching the rings of smoke, but it had no taste. He undressed mechanically and tossed his clothes onto the carpet, went to get a blanket from the hall closet, and tried to get to sleep by letting his mind go blank.

It was the first time that they wouldn't be sleeping together. Their quarrels, whenever they had any, took place in bed. Like their lovemaking. There was hardly any difference. This noc-

turnal separation troubled him even more than the hostile dishonesty that Agnes had been displaying. He wondered whether
she would come and join him to make peace, snuggle up in his
arms, reassure him and let herself be reassured by him. He'd tell
her, "It's over. It's over now." He'd keep repeating it until they
both fell asleep, and it would really be all over. Unable to sleep,
he imagined the scenario. First he'd hear the sound of the bedroom door opening very softly, her footsteps on the carpet coming closer and closer to the sofa. Then she'd appear within his
field of vision, would kneel down right in front of his face, and
he'd reach out his hand to caress her breasts and stroke the
nape of her neck. She'd lie down next to him and repeat, "It's
over now." He rehearsed all this, going back to the beginning
with the sound of the door. He could almost hear her steps
treading on the carpet. He would have liked to kiss her toes, her
heels, her calves, kiss her all over. In this version, he even rose
to meet her in the pale light of the window. They were standing face to face, naked, soon to be pressed close together, and
it was all over. Or instead, he was already up, waiting for her
near the door. He could even go himself to join her—strange
that he hadn't thought of it before. He would get up . . . No, he
couldn't. If he did that it would start up again, he'd think about
the pack of cigarettes he'd emptied, he'd ask questions, they'd
never find a way out. But if she came to him, what difference
would it make? The pack full of hair would still be there on the
coffee table, proof of the grotesque scene that she'd forced him
into. They would definitely have to talk it over one more time.
And if they didn't ever speak of it again, never, if he decided to

agree, I never had a mustache. Does that make you happy? No, not that either, he shouldn't say that. Nothing should be said anymore, he wouldn't mention it, she wouldn't either. She would just come and lie down beside him, warm and close. He rehearsed the scene again, varied it, felt her body, and that's exactly what happened. He wasn't surprised; she'd thought and desired the same thing as he, just at the same time, everything was back to normal. The door opened very softly, her heels grazed the carpet. Now he heard the ticking of the alarm clock. It was the only sound in the room, along with the sound of their own shallow breathing, which finally mingled into one when she knelt down in front of the sofa and brushed her lips against his, began to breathe harder when he felt for her breasts, glided his hands along her waist, her lips, on her buttocks, between her legs, and her breathing became a gentle moan. She swept his shoulder with her hair, kissed his shoulder, bit his shoulder, he felt her saliva and her tears running down his shoulder, and he was crying as well. He pulled her up into his arms so that she was stretched out, tangling her legs with his, spreading them and drew her breasts into his mouth, sitting up arching her back, moving her belly toward his mouth as he kissed it, kissing the insides of her thighs, the flesh that connected her thighs with her vagina, he thrust in his tongue, pushing it in as deeply as he could, pulled out a moment to suck on her lips, thrust it in again with joy at hearing her moan above him, raising her arms to spread wider, throwing them behind her back to take his cock in her hands, gliding it back and forth between her fingers as he sucked her, made her scream, he too was screaming in her, certain that she could hear him, that his cry vibrated inside her like the vocal cords in her throat, and his mouth could never be anywhere else, would never be anywhere else no matter what happened, he repeated it to himself, mouth inside her, nose inside her, forehead inside her, ears open to the cries that escaped from her mouth, and she was crying, "It's you, it's you," saying it over and over, making him repeat it along with her, inside her, louder and louder, it was him, it was her, and while they screamed, he wanted to see her scream it, his hands left her hips, went up toward her face, he brushed her hair aside, looked at her in the shadows, on top of him, her eyes open, he took her by her shoulders, spun her around, her back against his stomach, his mouth inside her, her hair falling around his braced legs, the two of them forming a bridge, stretching further and further, arching higher and higher over the sofa in the dark, and they tumbled onto the floor repeating, "it's you," rolled over, on their knees now, face to face, their outstretched hands caressing each other's cheeks, touching the contours, tears streaming onto their hands, on their cheeks, she says "come," draws him near, inside her, they pull at each other's hair, bite each other as they fuck, together inside her, biting the words between their teeth that shine in the dark: "you, it's you, it will always be you," they said nothing else, always in the same tone, it was the only thing to say, they would have said it even silently, their eyes were open even wider than their mouths, to recognize each other, to be sure, sure of being sure and that they both were sure, sure of being there, nowhere else, never anywhere else, never anyone else again, "only you,

you, it's really you," they continued saying it softer now, a long time after they'd climaxed, joined together dripping with sweat, until, sighing, smiling and loving him all the while, she reached out, groping for the pack of cigarettes and he held back her hand and said no.

Without asking for an explanation, she docilely withdrew her hand. Then they talked, holding each other tight under the covers, until morning. She wasn't putting him on, she said, but he already knew it. She swore to it, and he replied that there was no reason to swear, that he was sure she wasn't, even if this type of thing had become a habit with her. A habit, yes, but not with him, not like that, not this time, he had to believe her, that she believed him. Of course they believed each other, they really did believe each other, but what were they supposed to believe? That he'd gone mad? That she'd gone mad? They held each other closer as they dared to say this, licking each other, they knew that they shouldn't stop making love, touching each other, or else they might no longer believe each other, or be able to talk about it. The next morning, if they separated, there was the risk that it would start all over, it could only start all over. They'd break down, it was inevitable, they'd doubt each other again. She says at first, all this seemed impossible, but that it was, perhaps, something that sometimes happened. But to whom? To no one, he didn't know anyone, had never heard of anyone to whom this had happened, believing one had a mustache and not having one. Or else, she corrected, believing that the man who one loves doesn't have one, when he actually does. No, that was unheard of. But it wasn't madness, they weren't crazy, it must be a passing state of mind, a kind of hallucination, maybe the beginning of a nervous breakdown. I'll go see a psychiatrist, she said. Why you? If someone is nuts, he replied, it's me. Why? Because everyone else thinks the same thing, they also believe I've never had a mustache, so I'm the one who's deranged. We'll both go, she said, giving him a kiss, maybe it's just something that happens all the time. You think so? No. Neither do I. I love you. And they kept on repeating that they loved each other, believed each other, trusted each other, even if it was impossible, what else could one say?

3

THE NEXT MORNING, WHILE HE WAS MAKING COFFEE, HE THREW
out the pack of cigarettes with the shaved hair inside. Standing
naked in the kitchen, watching the hiccuping coffeepot, he was
afraid that he'd later regret it, having sacrificed his only piece
of evidence if the trial ever resumed, if they no longer agreed to
face this together. He was also afraid to think about whether
she'd made love to him, reassured him, pressed him close to her
last night just to regain his trust. Had she pushed him into it?
But he must not begin to think like that, it was crazy, especially
with Agnes.

As they drank their coffee in the living room, now flooded
with daylight, they avoided the subject, and talked about the
film from the night before. Around eleven o'clock he had to
leave for the office, even though it was a Saturday. The project
was supposed to be ready by Monday, and Jerome and Samira

were waiting for him. When he was halfway out the door, he quickly said to Agnes that they should think about this psychiatrist business, despite the difficulty he had in pronouncing the word. She replied that she'd take care of it, in the same tone she might have used to announce that she was going to order Chinese food from the restaurant downstairs.

"You're letting yourself go," Jerome said, noticing that he hadn't shaved. He didn't answer, simply smiled. Besides this remark and some absentminded banter from Samira when he asked her for a cigarette, the first part of the day went by without any major incident. If things were actually what they seemed, he was suffering from hallucinations, maybe on the verge of a nervous breakdown. It would be better not to tell anyone, to avoid encouraging sympathetic whispers behind his back like, "Poor guy, he's going off the deep end . . ." The whole business would be settled, he was sure of it, as long as it didn't get spread around, didn't follow him into the office, wasn't heard among the clients—his reputation as a sick person, a reputation he'd have a hard time getting rid of afterward. So he guarded himself from committing any sort of blunder.

Samira seemed to have forgotten his strange behavior the night before. At worst, she'd attribute it to a marital conflict; he'd been right not to push it any further, not to ask her the fatal question, although at the time, he'd reproached himself for his cowardice. In a way, he'd gotten out of it nicely. His delirium, if it was delirium, had remained discreet, since the incomprehensible disagreement was based on a past event. Unless he brought it up, which he kept himself from doing, nothing in his present appearance would give him away.

Looking at himself in the mirror, touching his face, he saw that his upper lip was adorned with stubble, that of a man who hadn't shaved, not yet a mustache, and maybe it was disagreeable, but apparently acknowledged by everyone, which reassured him. He even started to think that the entire affair might well stop right there. It wouldn't be necessary to see a psychiatrist. With regard to his ex-mustache, it would suffice to adopt what appeared to be the general opinion, and to speak of it no more. Of course, the general opinion wasn't very well represented. If he counted the number of witnesses involved, there was Agnes, Serge and Veronique, Jerome and Samira, plus a few people with whom he'd inevitably crossed paths during the last forty-eight hours, and to whom his face was familiar. He forced himself to count them as well. There was the owner of the café across the street, the office courier who had been there twice the night before, a neighbor from his building whom he'd met in the elevator. Not one of them had made any comment. Nevertheless, he reasoned, if he himself had run into someone he hardly knew and noticed that he'd shaved off his mustache, would he go and talk about it as if it were a federal case? Certainly not, and whether one attributed it to dignified reserve or lack of attention, the silence of these passersby was not the least bit surprising.

As he worked, gnawing on the tip of his pen, he fought against the temptation to test at least one person who knew him very well, to ask the question one last time before putting it aside, or rather before putting it in the hands of a psychiatrist. Because the problem would come up again no matter what the answer might be. If the guinea pig responded by saying no, he'd never worn a mustache, that would not only confirm that he was going mad, but what's more, it would bring this madness to the attention of one more person. Whereas up until now, only Agnes had really been aware of it. If the person replied that, of course, he had always known him with a mustache, what a silly question, and in that case, Agnes was obviously guilty. Or maybe crazy. No—guilty, since she'd had to talk the others into participating. Which all came back to the same thing, since that kind of guilt, a joke pushed that far, so methodically, to the point of conspiracy, implied a form of madness. Whether he found the proof of his own delirium, or Agnes's, there was nothing to be gained from it anyway, only an unpleasant certitude in either case. And actually beside the point. All he had to do was look at the picture in his identity papers to verify that he had a great big thick black mustache. Anybody consulted on this matter couldn't help but confirm it with his own eyes. And thus contradict Agnes. Thus prove that she was crazy or that she was trying to make him crazy. But hypothetically, let's say he was the one who'd gone mad, to the point where he'd plastered an imaginary mustache onto ten years of his life and onto his identity photo. That would mean that Agnes, on her end, adhered to exactly the same kind of reasoning, that she thought he was a lunatic, a pervert, or both. In spite of which, in spite of her extravagant scene about the hair recovered from the trash, she had come to him on the sofa, had assured him of her

love, her trust, once and for all, which meant that she deserved
to be trusted back, right? Right, but inevitably the trust could
only be reciprocal if one or the other was lying or raving mad.
Well, he knew for a fact that it wasn't him. So it was Agnes,
hence their lovemaking last night had been just another trick.
But if, for some extraordinary reason, that wasn't the case, then
she'd been heroic, sublime in her love. He should rise to her
level. But . . .

But come to think of it, where did the difficulty lie? In the
risk that the arbitrator might let himself be won over by the op-
posing party? To get around that, all it would take would be to
address the first person who came along, a passerby in the street
whom Agnes positively could not have circumvented. Which
would, at the same time, diminish the other problem: how to
deal with the embarrassing nature of the question? If put to a
friend or a working acquaintance, it would make him look like
a nutcase. To a stranger as well, but that was of no consequence.
The whole idea was to choose someone whom he'd never see
again. He grabbed his jacket and said that he was going out for
some air.

It was three in the afternoon. The sun was shining, the stores
were closed. One might have thought it was summer, or at least
a Sunday. He always felt as if it were a holiday when he worked
in the office on weekends, like when he didn't go to work on a
weekday. His profession allowed for this kind of flexibility,
which made him appreciate the loose and carefree nature of his
life, and at that moment, given his lighthearted mood, he

found it strange that such a bizarre thing could endanger his equilibrium. His jacket thrown over his shoulders, he walked slowly down the nearly deserted Rue Oberkampf, where he finally crossed paths with a little old man who was carrying a straw basket spilling over with leeks. He smiled, imagining the man's bewildered expression if he were to ask him politely to please look at his identity papers and tell him whether or not he was wearing a mustache in the picture. He'd think that he was being made fun of, maybe he'd even be shocked. Or else, if he didn't take it badly, he'd answer what he supposed was a joke with another one. That too was a risk not to be underestimated. He wondered how he himself would react under the same circumstances, realizing uneasily that he would undoubtedly say the first thing that came to mind, being at a loss for a witty reply. Well, it was true, how could anyone answer that sort of question with something *funny?* "But of course, it's Brigitte Bardot!"? Ha ha. Actually, the best solution would be to clearly explain his problem, but he couldn't imagine himself doing it. Or he could speak to someone, who because of vocation or profession, was not supposed to joke around. A cop, for example. But if the one he happened to ask was in a lousy mood, he might very well find himself at the local precinct for verbal assault. As a matter of fact, while he was at it, why not a priest? He could go to a confessional and say, "Father, I have sinned, but that's not the issue. I was only wondering if you could take a look at this photo through the wooden slats. . . ." "You're completely off your rocker, my son." No, if he really wanted an earnest listener for these kinds of questions, there was no get-

ting around it, it would have to be a psychiatrist. Since that was
the case, he'd go see one soon: Agnes would take care of it. All
he really wanted was to somehow prepare himself for the visit,
so that he'd know which leg to stand on.

Thirsty, he turned toward a café that was open on the Boulevard Voltaire, then changed his mind. He was positive that if
he went inside, he'd never ask the question. He'd be better
off staying outside. That way he could quickly escape from
the person he'd be speaking to, whatever the outcome of his
attempt.

He sat down on a bench facing the sidewalk, hoping that
someone would sit down beside him and engage him in a conversation. But nobody came. A blind man was groping around
for the traffic signal button that regulated the lights on the
boulevard, and he wondered how he did it, how he knew
whether it was red or green. Probably by the sound of the cars,
but since very few were passing by, he might be fooled. He got
up, cautiously touched the blind man's arm, and offered to
help him cross. "That's very nice of you," said the young man—
for it was indeed a young man, with green-tinted glasses, a
white cane, a khaki polo shirt buttoned all the way up—"but
I'm staying here on the sidewalk." He let go of his arm, and
walked away thinking that he could have asked him, at least he
wouldn't run the risk of being deceived by what he saw. Another
idea occurred to him, which made him smile. Aha, he thought,
already realizing what he was going to do. Only problem: he
didn't have a white cane. But after all, some blind people disdained them, probably out of vanity. Fearing that his eyes might

give him away, he remembered that he had a pair of sunglasses
in his pocket and put them on. Ray-Bans. He doubted if he'd
ever seen them worn by a blind person, but in a certain way, it
was logical for a blind man to refuse the servitude of a white
cane, or to wear glasses as a decorative pretext. He took a few
more steps toward the boulevard, intentionally hesitant, his
hands slightly in front of him, his chin held very high, and
forced his eyes closed. Two cars passed, a motorcycle started up
its engine a fair distance away, then another sound approached
him. Half opening his eyes, he had to cheat a little to identify
it. A young woman pushing a baby carriage was advancing toward him. He closed his eyes again, making certain that the
real blind man was no longer around, determined not to open
them again until it was all over, not to burst out laughing either,
and he proceeded tentatively, so that he'd walk right into what
he presumed was the path of the young mother. He bumped
into the carriage with his foot, said, "Excuse me, sir," and moving his hand forward until he felt the plastic material of the
hood, politely asked, "Would you do me a little favor, please?"
The young woman took a while to answer. Maybe, in spite of his
calculated blunder, she hadn't figured out that he was blind.
"Of course," she finally said, swerving the carriage a bit so it
wouldn't run over his foot, but also to continue on in her direction. His eyes still closed, he kept his hand on the hood, and
began to walk alongside. He decided to take the plunge. "Well,
you see," he said, "as you can tell, I'm blind. Five minutes ago,
I found what I think is an identity card, or a driver's license. I
wonder if it belongs to a pedestrian who might have lost it, or

to my friend who I was with a while ago. I might have put it in my pocket by mistake. If you wouldn't mind, could you describe the face on this picture, so that I know what I'm dealing with and can act accordingly?" He fell silent, began rummaging around in his pocket, still flustered, suddenly aware that something was off in his explanation. "Of course," the young woman repeated, nevertheless. He fumbled as he held out the card in her direction. He felt her take it from him, but they kept on walking; she was probably pushing the carriage with just one hand. The child inside must have been sleeping, for it wasn't making any noise. Or else there was no child. He took a gulp, fighting the temptation to open his eyes.

"Sir, you've made a mistake," the young woman finally said. "This must be your identity card. In any case, that's you in the picture." He should have realized it, he knew very well that his strategy was faulty, she could see that it was him. But there was nothing strange in that, it was quite possible to have made a mistake. The only thing was, he wasn't wearing sunglasses in the picture. Did identity cards have to mention the word "blind"?

"Are you sure?" he asked. "Does the man in the picture have a mustache?"

"Of course," the young woman said once again, and he felt her slipping the rectangle of folded cardboard between his outstretched fingers. "Well," he insisted, putting all his cards on the table, "I don't have one!"

"Yes, you do."

He started to tremble, and opened his eyes without thinking. The young woman continued to push the empty carriage, without even looking at him. She wasn't as young as he'd thought from far away. "Are you really sure," he quavered, "that in this photograph I have a mustache? Look again." He waved the identity card in front of her nose to incite her to answer, but she jerked her hand away and suddenly screamed, "That's enough! If you keep it up, I'm going to call the police!" He made a hasty retreat and crossed while the light was green. A car came to a screeching halt to avoid hitting him; from behind, he heard the driver shouting, but he kept on running all the way to the Place de la République, went into a café, and collapsed into a booth, out of breath.

The waiter gave him an inquiring look. He ordered coffee. Slowly he came to his senses and digested the news. Because of his difficulty in carrying it out, what had begun as a harmless joke had proved to be a conclusive experiment. He forced himself to reconstruct the exact content of the confrontation. When he'd protested that he didn't have a mustache, the woman with the baby carriage had said it wasn't so. He'd been unable to tell whether she was referring to the photo or to him as well, since he'd been standing right in front of her. But maybe she considered a mustache to be the black fuzz that during the last two days had started to grow in on his upper lip. Maybe she didn't see that well. Or maybe he'd dreamed it, he'd never shaved off his mustache, it was still there, nice and thick, in spite of the testimony of his trembling fingers, of his eyes that, when he abruptly whirled around toward the mirror behind the booth, registered a strangely somber, greenish image.

He then discovered from the reflection that he was still wearing his sunglasses, took them off, and examined himself in the now normal daylight. It was him all right, unshaven, still shaking, but him. Therefore . . .

He clenched his fists, closed his eyes as hard as he could to turn his mind off, to escape this bouncing back and forth between two hypotheses, which he'd already replayed fifty times over and which lead nowhere, except from one to the other and back again, without an emergency exit to return to normal life. It was already starting again, he couldn't stop himself from gauging the advantage he had just won, the proof that he had to confuse . . . To confuse whom? Agnes? But why Agnes? Why was she doing this? No reason in the world could justify such a thing. It was both absurd and irreparable. No reason, except that madness doesn't need a reason, or rather, it has its own reason, and it was precisely because he wasn't crazy that this reason escaped him. And Serge and Veronique, he thought angrily, who had encouraged his delirium! Bunch of irresponsible jerks! He was going to have to tell them off, warn them, insist that they never do this kind of idiotic thing again, unless they wanted to see him wind up in a padded cell.

He vacillated between anger and a nauseating tenderness for Agnes, poor Agnes, his wife, Agnes, totally fragile, delicately put together, a sly fox, with a fine line between an active mind and the irrationality that had begun to consume her. In retrospect, the warning signs had made themselves clear: her flamboyant dishonesty, her excessive appetite for paradoxes, the stories on the phone, the brick walls, the radiators, the double personality, so sure of herself during the day, in the presence of a third person, and sobbing in his arms at night, like a child. He should have interpreted these warning signs earlier, this exaggerated brilliance, and now it was too late, she was falling in too deep. No, maybe it wasn't too late. Through the power of his love, patience, and tact, he'd tear her away from her demons, row with all his strength to get her to shore. He'd hit her if he had to, for the sake of love, just like you'd knock out a struggling swimmer to keep him from drowning. A wave of tenderness swept over him, facilitating this sudden burst of terrible and disturbing metaphors, which reminded him of his lack of foresight and his responsibility. He saw now that last night had been her desperate call for help. In a state of confusion, she'd understood her condition. When she'd mentioned a psychiatrist, it was to oblige him to take her there. Caught in the net of madness, she was struggling, trying to make him comprehend. For the last two days she'd made up this whole farce, this absurd business about his mustache, like someone who was screaming and making faces behind a soundproof opaque window, to get his attention, to call for help. Unless, without really having understood, he'd heard her cry when he'd made love to her, when he'd reassured her of his support, that he'd be there, always, and he'd always help her to be herself. He'd have to continue to behave that way, solid as a rock so she could lean on him. He couldn't let himself be thrown off track and get involved in her craziness; otherwise, it would be a lost cause.

He bought a pack of cigarettes and smoked one, casting aside self-reproach, which would have been ridiculous given the situation, and began to establish a course of action. First, it was up to him to call a psychiatrist. Because of course, when she'd flung out the idea like a bottle in the ocean, what she was really counting on, by offering to take care of it, was her ability to outwit him. She was undoubtedly deluding herself; psychiatrists wouldn't fall for that kind of stuff, like other people, like Serge and Veronique. And besides, having thought about it, it would be wiser to let her go ahead. Her maneuver itself was enough to betray her. A specialist would understand what he was going through much better after listening to her ranting and raving. He imagined him jotting down Agnes's explanations on his pad. "You see, my husband thought that he had a mustache until last Thursday, and it's not true." That alone should alert him, and persuade him that she was the one who was suffering from—from what, exactly? He didn't know anything about mental illness, and wondered again what this thing was called, if it was curable. . . . He remembered that basically, there were neuroses and psychoses, that the second one was more serious, but other than that . . . Whatever it was, he'd have to prepare a small dossier for the shrink, who later on would be able to shed some light on it: photographs of himself, that was no problem, maybe the testimony of a third party concerning Agnes's personality, her mood swings. But first he'd let her take the initiative. It was the simplest thing to do.

Next, speaking of third parties, he'd warn their friends. It was a necessary evil, to avoid Serge and Veronique's clowning around from happening again. It would be hard to find just the right balance of firmness and discretion. He mustn't overly alarm them, so that Agnes wouldn't feel as if she were being treated like a sick person. But he'd also have to make them understand the gravity of the situation. He'd contact them all, including her own personal friends, her colleagues at work, and he'd keep them away from her as best he could. It was atrocious, really, to make phone calls behind her back, but he had no choice.

As for him, at least in the immediate future, he'd be better off if he went along with her point of view, to avoid new conflicts, maybe a catastrophe. He was going to go straight home to take her out to dinner, as if nothing had happened, not mention the mustache ever again, and if she mentioned it, he'd admit that he'd had a hallucination, that it was over. He'd procrastinate, appease her. Not too much, though; not so she'd conclude that the visit to the psychiatrist was no longer necessary. He'd insist that he himself be treated, making it into a simple matter, but then again, it would be fairly difficult to make a visit to a psychiatrist seem ordinary. He'd ask her to accompany him. It almost seemed logical; she wouldn't suspect a thing. Or else she'd know that he knew. It would probably have to wait until Monday, but definitely on Monday, first thing.

He paid for his coffee, and went downstairs in the brasserie to call the office. It was out of the question to go back there today or tomorrow, too bad about the gymnasium project, and too bad about the presentation to their client on Monday. Jerome began to protest, "Shit, this is no time for that," but he cut him off sharply. "I suppose," he said, "that you realize Agnes hasn't been feeling well, so listen to me. I don't give a fuck about the gymnasium, I don't give a fuck about the office, I don't give a fuck about you, and I intend to take care of her. Got that?" and he hung up. He'd call back tomorrow to apologize, he'd lecture Jerome and Samira without blaming them too much for their complicity, which was excusable, after all. They couldn't have known, as he himself had almost been sucked into it. Now he was in a rush to get home, to make sure that Agnes was still there. He thought from now on he could never stop being afraid for her, and while it worried him, he was strangely exalted by this prospect.

When he arrived, a little before five o'clock, Agnes had just gotten home and was paging through some galleys, listening to a program on the radio about the origins of the tango. She told him that she'd had lunch in the gardens of the Bagatelle with Michel Servier, one of her friends whom he hardly knew, and she gaily described the throng that had crowded into the out-door restaurant, eager to take advantage of the first days of good weather. She had him admire the slight sunburn of her forearms. Too bad, he said, that she'd already had lunch out-side, he'd been thinking of going to dinner at Le Jardin de la Paresse, in the Parc de Montsouris. He was afraid that this sug-gestion might surprise her, since they generally preferred not to go out on Saturday night, but she only remarked that it might be a little too cool to eat outside on the terrace. By the same token, she really liked the interior part of the restaurant. In other words, sold!

They spent the rest of the afternoon peacefully. She read on the sofa listening to the tangos, he leafed through *Le Monde* and *Libération*, the newspapers he'd purposely bought on his way home, with the vague idea that this would make him appear relaxed, would give him an air of composure. Behind his nonchalantly unfolded paper, he felt just like a private detective spying on the pretty woman whose husband had hired him to watch her. In order to dispel this impression, he burst out laughing several times, and upon her request, read the personals from *Libération* out loud, where for the third consecutive week, young homosexual wants to meet, for friendship and more, man between the ages of sixty and eighty, portly, bald, and distinguished, bearing a resemblance to Raymond Barre, Alain Poher, or René Coty. They wondered whether the recurrence of this ad meant that the young man had a hard time finding someone to fit the bill, or if, on the contrary, he enjoyed an abundant weekly consummation of important and pudgy officials, their paunches stuffed into pin-striped suits. Checkered, added Agnes.

During all this, three people telephoned, and he answered each call. The third was Veronique, who didn't mention his late phone call the night before. Agnes's presence prevented him from telling her what he had on his mind. Agnes motioned that she wanted to get on the line, and invited Serge and Veronique to dinner the following evening. He reflected that he'd have to call them beforehand, which he'd counted on doing anyway. Not for one moment did they bring up the question of a psychiatrist.

As night was falling, they made their way to the Jardin de la
Paresse, where they arrived a bit early for their reservation.
While they waited, they took a walk in the Parc de Montsouris.
Sprinklers covered the lawn with a fine mist; a sudden breeze,
carrying off the spray, showered Agnes's dress, and he put his
arms around her shoulders and kissed her for a long time, bending over to caress her bare legs, which had little drops of cold
water running down them. She laughed. Holding her close,
cheek to cheek, he squeezed his eyes shut, opened his mouth
as if he wanted to scream. He was drowning in the love he had
for her, and the fear that she was suffering, and when they broke
away from each other, he caught an unexpected glimpse of sad-
ness in her eyes, which upset him. Hand in hand, they went
back into the restaurant, stopping several times to kiss.

The dinner was lively, surprisingly relaxed. They talked about
everything and nothing in particular. Agnes was being witty,
even sarcastic, but with a tinge of childlike abandon that distinguished this particular brilliance from the one she reserved
for others. Yet he could hardly eat; his throat was tight from the
way they interacted. Their tender, easy manner suggested, to
him, the spectacle of a couple putting on a brave front. The
woman knows that she's doomed, and that the man she loves
knows it too, and is intent on not letting anything show, ever,
not even at night, awake in his arms, certain that he too is not
asleep and that like her, he's struggling to fight back tears. And
just as such a woman would make it a point of honor to prove
that the word "cancer" didn't frighten her, Agnes, as she stroked

his cheek, then his upper lip, murmured, "It's growing back, isn't it?" He restrained her hand in his own, held it against his face, retracing with his own fingers the path her fingers had taken, as when, hand over hand, they would both caress his cock and he'd think, Yes, it's growing, it's back again.

A while later, as they joked about the coy pretentiousness of the menu, and took turns inventing even more pretentious names for various dishes, she blurted out that she hadn't yet called a psychiatrist. He was on the verge of suggesting a *chiffonnade* of freshly hooked red mullet, and for the garnish, hesitated between a wild mushroom sauce "*à ma façon*" and a tender bed of spinach steamed in succulent marrow, and had to make an effort not to drop his fork. She didn't know any psychiatrists, she continued, but thought that Jerome, because of his wife . . . Without dwelling on the fact that he'd also had the same idea, he interpreted her suggestion as a sign of renewed lucidity. By proposing that he take the initiative, since Jerome was more or less his friend, she was intimating that she'd understood his suspicions, had perhaps decided against pursuing her dead-end intrigues with a psychiatrist, and accepted that he take care of it. He squeezed her hand again and promised he'd call Jerome right away.

Picking up the check that was folded between the bill, the waiter asked for identification, which irritated him. When it was returned to him, Agnes said what he had been hoping she wouldn't say: "Let me see it."

He held it out to her, fighting back the thought that she

was abusing her status as an incurable just a tiny bit. She attentively examined the photo, then shook her head as a sign of indulgent disapproval.

"What?"

"Try something better the next time, darling," she said, licking her index finger and gliding it across the photograph. Then she turned it toward him, showing him a small black spot, licked it again, held it near his face, and tried to slip it between his lips. He brusquely shoved her hand away, as he had done before to the woman with the baby carriage.

"If you ask me," she said, "it's Magic Marker. Good quality, too, it's hardly coming off. You know it's against the law to tamper with your identity card? But wait a minute."

Without letting go of the card, she rummaged through her purse and took out a little metal box with a razor blade inside.

"Don't," he said.

It was her turn to push his hand away, and she started to scrape off the mustache on the picture. Paralyzed, he watched her do it, removing from his upside-down face fine black particles, scraping until the space between his nose and his mouth had become, not gray, like the rest of the photo, but a grainy slashed-up white.

"There," she concluded, "you're legal."

Overwhelmed, he took his card back. She'd scratched off his mustache from the surface of the picture, also a bit of his nose, a strip of his mouth, and of course, it didn't prove a thing about the face in the picture before it had been mutilated. He almost said something, but remembered his decision to play her game; he wouldn't contradict her, at least until Monday. It was already a miracle that she'd seen a mustache there, although admittedly she suspected him of having drawn it in with a felt pen. In a way it was even better, better than getting back to the subject of the psychiatrist; that would have meant she was mimicking his own attitude. At least she accepted giving herself away, destroying the symmetry that might lead one to believe that she was of sound mind, that she was the temporizer, the peacemaker. . . .

And, as usual, as if she'd been reading his mind, she took his hand and said, "I'm sorry. It was wrong of me."

"Let's go."

In the car, they remained silent. For a moment she lightly caressed the back of his neck, and repeated in a barely audible voice, "I'm sorry." He relaxed his neck into the palm of her hand, but not one sound would come out of his mouth. He was tormented with the idea that maybe she'd mutilated or destroyed all of their photos, all of the tangible proof aside from the confirmation of their friends, still a delicate subject. If she hadn't already done it, he'd better hurry and put the pictures in a safe place, if for no other purpose than for the psychiatrist's dossier. He sensed that, after a brief setback, she was trying to recapture her advantage. She was preparing an offensive to put him back into the position of the accused, the position of someone who has to furnish proof, and if she was playing so ingenuously, if she was exposing her ploy, it meant that she'd covered her tracks, already gotten her hands on that very proof.

Even though it was probably already too late, he wished he'd been the first one to get home to the apartment, that he hadn't left her there all alone. He'd been crazy to stay out for so long. There was still hope. When they arrived in front of their building, before he went to park the car in the underground lot, if she expressed the desire to go up there ahead of him, then he could say no. You stay here. He'd keep her there by force if he had to. But she said nothing, went down to the parking lot with him, which meant that the damage had already been done. Remember, she's crazy, he kept repeating to himself. Don't hold it against her, love her that way, help her to pull herself out of this. . . .

At the front door of the apartment, he had to rationalize letting her go in first. Having paid tribute to gallantry, he gave up trying to pretend he wasn't looking for something, and after having scanned the shelves, the coffee table, the top of the chest, he opened one by one the desk drawers, which crackled with the sound of dry wood when he roughly pushed them back into place.

"Where are the pictures from Java?"

She'd followed him, standing there right in front of him, staring. Never, even during lovemaking, had he ever seen her look so discomposed.

"From Java?"

"Yeah, from Java. I feel like looking at the pictures from Java. No reason," he added without any hope that she'd believe him.

She came toward him, cradled his face in her hands, a gesture that she must have, that he must have, performed a thousand times, that she now wanted to instill with conviction, with earnest prayer, cast off the dead weight of its routine quality.

"My love," she murmured. Her lips were trembling, as if her jaw were about to unhinge. "My love, I swear to you, there are no pictures of Java. We've never been to Java."

He'd expected this, he realized. It had to come to this as well. Now she was sobbing, as she had the night before, and the night before that, and the next day—it would never end. The same scene every night, the lovemaking and the reconciliation every night, trying to forget it all in the tender calm of their bodies, a forced smile the next morning, and every night it would start all over, because they couldn't just pretend it was nothing. Weary, he only wished he could speed up the process, plunge into the night, hold her in his arms—and he was already holding her, could wipe away her tears, soothe her shoulders; he was sick with love and grief. From the racking sobs of her body, he knew she wasn't lying. Tonight she really believed that they'd never been to Java, and she was in too much pain to manage to hide it from him. Well, all right, they'd never been there. All right, he'd never had a mustache. All right, he'd faked his picture. Anything was all right, providing she'd calm down, stop crying, even for a moment. They were asking each other's forgiveness, both ready to sacrifice everything, to deny the evidence, to buy themselves some time at any price, but she was still crying, still shaking, and behind her, on the wall, as he kissed her hair, he spied the large woven blanket they'd brought back from Java. Too bad for the blanket, too bad for Java, too bad for everything, stop, stop, stop, my love, he repeated again, gently, as always.

The telephone rang, the answering machine came on. They listened to Agnes's poised, almost-laughing voice rolling on the message, when all the while she was weeping in his arms, then after the beep, Jerome's voice saying, "What's going on? Would you mind explaining it to me? Call me back." He hung up. Agnes broke away, and went to curl up on the sofa.

"You think I'm going crazy, right?" she murmured.

"I think," he said, kneeling down to her level, "that there's something wrong and we'll find out what it is."

"But you think it's me. Admit it."

A moment of silence.

"You or me or something else," he answered without conviction. "Anyway, we'll find out what it is. Just pretend it's like when you're stoned, it wears off after a while."

She was crying more quietly, taking in little gasps.

"I know it was wrong of me, before, in the restaurant."

"I would have done the same thing. I don't blame you for it." He wondered if she was thinking, Thank God for that! but she only said, "I want to go to sleep," and got up. Then she straightened her clothes, went into the bedroom, came back with a packet of sleeping pills, and once again, like the night before last, handed him two tablets.

"I'd rather be alone," she added.

His eyes followed her out the room, and the moment she closed the door, a horrible idea occurred to him: that the other night they'd made love for the last time. At the same time he was suddenly afraid that she'd kept the other sleeping pills to swallow them all. He wanted to go get them. She might think the same thing of him, but too bad. He knocked on the door, entered without waiting for an answer, and grabbed the packet of pills on the night table. She was lying on the bed, still dressed. Watching him, she guessed right away, smiled, said, "Being careful, huh?" then added, "You know, I'm afraid we're going to need them tomorrow too." He wished he could sit down on the side of the bed and prolong this intimacy a while longer, but understood it was useless and went out, closing the door behind him.

Quietly he began to dig around the living room in search of photographs that Agnes might have overlooked. Considering how stupid it was to have left her alone all day, he had few illusions about what he might find. Moreover, he'd been forbidden any access to the bedroom where she was sleeping—if she was sleeping. After a while, he was convinced that the vacation photos of Java, of their other vacations, of their wedding, the entire wealth of pictures and memories accumulated during five years of living together, had disappeared, or at best, been hidden but more likely destroyed. Of course, certain objects remained as proof: the woven blanket from Java, some trinket that he'd bought her, actually everything in the room had a link to their past, the past that she seemed to want to erase. But he knew very well that this sort of evidence didn't have the same importance. With an object, you could also claim that you'd never seen it before, whereas a photo is irrefutable. Not even irrefutable, since Agnes's absurd strategy consisted of refuting the proof, of saying white when everyone else sees black, without even making the effort to paint that pending evidence white. Obviously, this position was insufferable. But the problem wasn't to confuse Agnes, it was to help her get well. It wasn't enough to work on symptoms, to confront her with the proof. One would have to get at the root of the evil, which was no doubt deeply buried and had branched out, perhaps for years, eating away at the mind of the woman he loved. He remembered a documentary he'd once seen by chance on TV about a little town in the southwest of France that made most of its income from housing the mentally ill. It wasn't at all, as he'd first thought, some modern psychiatric experiment that aimed to reintegrate these sick people into daily life; it was just a simple economic measure. A day in the hospital for the average mental patient was costing the Social Security too much, and the citizens of this village needed the money, so they were allocated a very modest sum, something like six hundred francs a month, to shelter a couple of incurable but harmless mental cases, in little houses, shacks sort of, where they were brought soup at mealtimes. They also made sure—this was their main concern—that the patients took their medicine, and they managed to make a small profit off their living expenses. The mental patients seemed calm, and their hosts not at all displeased with this rental income, which had the distinct advantage of arriving on the first of each month, without fail, with no risk of ever running dry, since the tenants would remain there until they died. Each patient kept busy with various activities. For

twenty years one of them wrote the same pompous and mean-
ingless sentence again and again, another rocked plastic dolls to
sleep, changing their diapers every two hours, and claimed to be
happy. . . . It's horrible, he had thought while watching the documentary, but of course in the same way that the famine in
Ethiopia is horrible. He never thought he'd be picturing Agnes
sitting on the steps of a garden shack, repeating in a soft voice
that her husband had never had a mustache, as the years
passed, still repeating it, going from middle age to becoming an
old woman. He imagined her, God knows why, dressed like a little girl. Eventually he would detach himself from her, his love
would be transformed into pity, into remorse. Naturally she
wouldn't be sent to one of these villages for needy mental patients; he'd find her the most luxurious of institutions. But it
wouldn't make any difference. As time passed, indifference
would set in. She would become a burden, a weight on his conscience that he could never entirely appease with the belief
that, after all, he'd done his best, gone to see her every month,
paid for her expenses every month. When she finally died, without admitting it, he'd be relieved. . . . He couldn't rid himself
of this image of Agnes as an old woman, muttering softly to herself in a little girl's dress. Oh no, no, he thought with a knot in
his throat. No, of course it wasn't that serious, not that extreme. They'd treat her, she'd pull through. At one point,
Jerome's ex-wife had gone from bouts of anorexia to nervous
breakdowns, and she'd certainly come out of it okay. Strange,
though, that after having been through it himself, Jerome
hadn't caught on earlier, at the time of the conspiratorial phone

call that Agnes must have made, or even before that, way before. Maybe, to protect himself, he refused to acknowledge this kind of thing. In any case, he'd have to call him and explain everything, ask his advice. Get him to recommend a good psychiatrist, the one who'd gotten Sylvie out of her mess.

The smartest thing to do would be to go downstairs right away, call from a phone booth to avoid the risk of Agnes's overhearing the conversation. On the other hand, he hated to leave her alone, even for five minutes. Unraveling the cord, he carried the phone into the kitchen, intending to whisper. Besides, he wouldn't have been able to utter certain words out loud. He dialed the number and let it ring for a long time. Jerome was out, or he'd unplugged the phone. He hung up cautiously and thought, Tomorrow, wondering when, since he'd decided not to stray too far from Agnes. Actually, the best solution was to take advantage of the fact that she was asleep. It would take less time to carry out his plan.

He went back into the living room, dragging the phone with him, sat down on the sofa, more distressed than ever, unable to figure out what to do next. You don't call a psychiatrist on a Saturday in the middle of the night, and the emergency hot line would be no help. No, it would have to wait until Monday, and the prospect of what might happen between now and then was alarming, as if Agnes's madness, after a long period of gestation, were accelerating rapidly. It might expand its growth in a matter of hours, like a kaleidoscopic show of water lilies ceaselessly doubling in volume. He took his altered identity card out of his wallet, disturbed by the idea that this was the only photo that he had of himself. No, not really. She must at least have spared his passport, and he could always resort to asking his friends for pictures in which he might appear. There should be lots of those around.

As if counting sheep, he began to form a list of pictures of himself that might be in circulation and readily accessible. As he lit a cigarette, the last one of the pack he'd bought that afternoon, he remembered an incident that had taken place three days ago on the Pont Neuf. Inadvertently he'd walked right into a picture, at the precise moment that a Japanese tourist, who was taking a photo of his wife in front of Notre Dame, clicked the button of his camera. Ordinarily he was careful to avoid this kind of faux pas, waiting for the picture to be taken before he passed, or else slipping behind the photographer's back. Once he'd even gone so far as to stop himself from entering the field of vision of a pair of binoculars. On the Pont Neuf he'd apologized, the Japanese tourist had gestured that it didn't matter, and now he really would like to have this accidental photograph in his possession, or others taken throughout the years in which he happened to appear but wasn't the focal point, as though the coincidental aspect of his presence would make it more authentic. But especially the one taken either last Wednesday or Thursday by the Japanese tourist, when he'd still probably had his mustache. . . . He could always run an ad in a Tokyo newspaper, he thought gloomily. It would be more practical to content himself with the pictures that his friends had taken, that his parents still had in their possession, copies or negatives that institutions must retain in duplicate from their laboratories. But immediate access would be impossible. Tonight he could only contemplate the Fotomat picture on his identity card that had been scratched with a razor, licked to make the imaginary traces of black felt pen disappear.

Abandoning this train of thought, he furrowed his brow. Then licking his finger, he wiped it across the picture, onto the darkest spot, which corresponded to the shoulders of his jacket. His finger had remained clean. Obviously, he reflected, photographs don't perspire. But the experiment denounced Agnes's premeditation, which he hadn't realized at the time: knowing full well that scraping it with a razor meant absolutely nothing, she had prefaced it with the wet finger test, seemingly more conclusive, and to make it so, she must have stained her finger with a black marker beforehand.

She's mad, he murmured, completely mad. A perverse madness, even spiteful. And it wasn't her fault, he must help her. Even if she tried to gouge out his eyes, in real life, not in a picture, he'd have to protect himself and protect her at the same time. That's what was so horrible, not so much that she wanted to obliterate the past, his mustache, or Java, but that all of her maneuvers were directed against him, calculated, aimed at setting him against her so that he couldn't possibly, wouldn't ever want to come to her aid. So that he'd eventually abandon her, discouraged. Racing through his mind was the metaphor of the lifeguard who, for the sake of the swimmer bent on suicide, knocks him out. But it didn't comfort him as much as it had this afternoon in the café. He wondered whether she was really asleep. He hadn't seen her take any sleeping pills. He tiptoed toward the bedroom door, and making sure that it didn't creak, opened it. He was fighting back an atrocious image, even more atrocious than the one of a little old lady dressed like a doll: Agnes sitting cross-legged on the bed, awake, having anticipated his every move, waiting for him with a triumphantly demonic smile, drool seeping from her lips, like the possessed little girl in *The Exorcist*. But she seemed to be sleeping peacefully. He drew nearer to the body curled up under the covers, the body of the woman he loved, fearing that she might suddenly snap open her eyes, on the lookout.

No.

He stood there for several minutes and looked at her in the dim light shining in from the living room, then went out again, not yet reassured. He spent the night lying on the sofa, his hands folded behind his head, and did not sleep. He mentally rehearsed his thwarted plans of the afternoon, deciding to stick to them despite this evening's mounting fever. He'd play Agnes's game, he'd call Jerome without her knowing, he'd call a psychiatrist. This calmed him down a bit, as he imagined how he would circumvent the difficulties of carrying out this plan, how, without leaving her alone, he would seclude himself to make his phone calls. At one point, the red light on the answering machine, which they'd forgotten to check upon arriving home, attracted his attention. He listened to the messages, the sound turned very low, his ear pressed against the speaker. Jerome, apparently worried; then his father, who as he did every week reminded them about lunch the next day; a press agent who wanted to speak to Agnes; Jerome again—the time they hadn't picked up. He wrote down the name of the press agent and erased the messages. He dozed off a little before dawn, conscious of the fact that he'd hardly slept for the past two days, that he hadn't shaved, not even his beard, and that he'd have to be in good shape to face whatever came next.

4

THE TELEPHONE RANG JUST AT THE POINT IN HIS DREAM WHEN HE
was asking himself whether it was pronounced *mus*tache or
mus*tache*. Someone who he couldn't quite identify answered
that you could say it both ways, like *chauf*feur or chauf*feur*,
then burst out laughing, which made him think that it was exactly the type of thing a shrink would say, who would then immediately launch into some nonsense about castration. Given
these coinciding thoughts, he wasn't surprised to hear Jerome's
voice on the other end of the line, and instantly regained his
lucidity.

"So, are you going to explain to me what's going on?"

"Hold on a second."

To prevent Agnes from overhearing, he thought he'd close
the bedroom door, which was open, but as he glanced around,
he discovered that she was no longer there. Not in the kitchen,

not in the bathroom, not in the john, all of which he had hastily inspected.

"Agnes isn't at your house, by any chance?" he asked, picking up the receiver again.

"No. Why?"

He hesitated for a moment between running out to find her, no matter where she was, and taking advantage of her absence to speak to Jerome. He decided on the second alternative, convinced that he had to do it quickly, so that he wouldn't be taken by surprise when she came back. If she came back, if she wasn't dead, or hiding in a closet, spying on him.

"Listen," he said, startled by the clarity of his own voice, "Agnes really isn't doing so well. Do you know of a good psychiatrist?"

Silence on the other end, then, "Yes, I think so. What's the matter with her?"

"She called you yesterday, didn't she? The day before yesterday?"

"No," said Jerome.

He paused. "She didn't call you to tell you—"

"To tell me what?"

"To tell you—" he took the plunge, "that I'd never had a mustache."

Another silence.

"I don't understand," Jerome finally said.

Again, silence.

"Let's get this straight," he tried once more. "You must have noticed that I shaved my mustache."

Strangely enough, the fact that he'd pronounced it this way, with the accent on the last syllable, alarmed him. Jerome laughed softly, just like in the dream.

"Neither one, not your *mus*tache nor your mus*tache*. Is that what the trouble is?"

He clung to the arm of the sofa. The scheme was back into full swing, he had to stop it, shoot it down at any cost. For that, he'd have to stay cool.

"Yeah, that's it," he managed to say. "Are you at the office?"

"Well, actually . . ."

"Ask Samira, then."

"Samira went to the café for some coffee, but I assure you, I can tell you myself. And as for you, I'd like some explanation."

"You swear to me that Agnes or someone else didn't put you up to this?"

"You mean that you had a mustache?"

"No, that I *never* had one. Listen, Jerome, whatever she said to you, you've got to tell me. It's important. I know it seems absurd, but it's no joke."

"Forgive me if I'm having a hard time believing you, but if it makes you happy, I solemnly swear that Agnes did not call me and that you do not have a mustache. No, you do, a little, since yesterday. I even commented on it." He dropped his joking manner, his voice became gentler. "If I'm getting this straight, you and Agnes are both convinced that you had a mustache. Is that it?"

"Only me," he admitted, almost glad to let himself go, to respond to questions like a schoolboy to a teacher who knows the answers and will correct him if he makes a mistake.

"And Agnes?"

"Agnes says no."

He thought about bringing up Java, but Jerome replied, "Look, if you're really not kidding . . ."

"I'm not kidding."

"Then I think there's actually something screwy going on. But not with Agnes. You've been working hard lately—"

"You too."

"Me too, but as far as I can tell, I haven't had any hallucinations that I know of. I think you're going through some kind of, maybe not depression, but a transitional period, and you should really see a psychiatrist. I can recommend one for you. How's Agnes taking it?"

"Agnes . . ."

He heard the key turning in the front-door lock.

"I think she just got home," he said hurriedly. "I'll call you back."

"No, let me speak to her," Jerome ordered. But he'd hung up.

"I bought some croissants," Agnes said as she entered. "It's beautiful outside. Who was that?"

She'd heard him hanging up.

"No one," he mumbled, without looking at her. The telephone started to ring again. He wanted to answer it, but she beat him to it. He knew it was Jerome.

"Yes," said Agnes. "Yes, glad you called. . . . No. . . . I know. . . . Yes, yes, I know. . . ."

She was smiling at him as she spoke, as if everything were back to normal. When he motioned that he wanted to listen in, she firmly covered the receiver with her hand and said to him, "Could you go get me something to write with?"

He obeyed, brought over a pad and pen that she grabbed from him after giving his hand a little squeeze.

"Yes," she continued. "What did you say? . . . Sylvain who? . . . Yeah, I'm writing it down."

With the receiver tucked underneath her chin, she wrote on the pad, *Sylvain Kalenka.* "With two K's?" Then, a phone number.

"Today? . . . Even on a Sunday? . . . All right. Jerome, you've been a great help. Thanks. I'll call you back."

She hung up. And now, what next? he thought.

"I'm going to make some coffee," she announced.

He followed her into the kitchen and watched her, leaning against the doorframe. Her movements were precise, efficient. The sun shone on the tile floor.

"So, is it me?" he finally said, looking down.

"Yes, I think so."

She wasn't able to conceal her relief. As if now, ever since Jerome's phone call, everything had become clear, everything was going to be all right. He was crazy, that's all there was to it, and he would be treated. And in a way, he was relieved by this as well, the prospect of letting go, of putting himself in the hands of Agnes, Jerome, the psychiatrist Sylvain Kalenka, whom he'd forgive in advance for his intelligent airs, his remarks on the pronunciation of mustache, chauffeur, and castration complexes.

The coffeepot was perking. She threw the filter into the garbage, which had been emptied the night before, then set the cups on the tray he brought in from the living room. The grease had already seeped through the bag of croissants onto the coffee table.

But, he thought, if this was the case, why did Jerome's mediation assume so much importance for her? During the last two days of his delirium she should have known what to believe. She couldn't have been conscious of the doubts that explained in his own case, the troubling, contradictory attitudes of Jerome and Samira, and the woman with the baby carriage. She should have been sure from the very beginning, and should have adhered to one type of behavior. Yet she'd changed it. Of course, so had he, but he was crazy. If a madman starts to deny the evidence, it's up to him to furnish the proof of whatever it is that he's maintaining, and since he has none, to attack those who contradict him, to act impulsively. Whereas the normal reaction of a sane listener would be to object—with perseverance and conviction—to the evidence that had been so easily gathered. To confront him with a third party, to show him photographs. But ever since the late-night phone call to Veronique and the moment when Jerome, acting on his own initiative, had interfered, apparently she'd consulted no one. And instead of making use of them, she'd hidden the photos. Really now, whether he was crazy or not, he'd stuck to the same story. But not Agnes. Perhaps it was precisely his madness that made him think that way. . . .

She held out a cup of coffee to him, which he put back down on the tray without adding sugar.

"The photos," he said.

"What photos?"

She took a sip of coffee, slowly, looking at him from over the curved rim of the cup.

"The ones from Java."

"We've never been there."

"So then where's this from, huh?"

He pointed to the blanket on the wall. He remembered every detail of the long bargaining session in the village, the pleasure she'd displayed when they'd finally completed the deal, and even the few Indonesian words that they'd picked up during the trip: *Selamat, siang, selamat sore, terimah kasih.* . . . But of course, madmen were known to rant deliriously in tongues they didn't even know.

She answered in an even voice, as if she were reciting a lesson, as if he'd already asked her the same question five minutes ago.

"It was Michael who brought it back for us."

"What about the other photos?"

"You really want to see them?"

She shook her head, as if reproaching herself for acquiescing to such childishness, but got up, went into the bedroom, and came back with a heap of color prints, which she placed on the floor, near the tray. At least she hadn't destroyed them. He went through them one by one, without making the slightest effort to remember the places or the circumstances under which the pictures had been taken: in the country, at Agnes's parents' house, in Guadeloupe. . . . The ones from Java were, of course, missing, but in every single one he was wearing a mustache. He held one out to her.

"All I want to hear you say is that I don't have a mustache in this picture. Then I'll stop."

She sighed.

"Say it," he insisted. "So that at least it's clear."

"No, you don't have a mustache in that picture."

"Or in any of the others?"

"Or in any of the others."

"Fine."

He rested his head on the back of the sofa and closed his eyes. It was, in fact, clear; all he could do now was be treated. And in one sense he understood that she'd hidden the photos to avoid the danger of his opening fresh wounds. In her position . . . But only the night before, he'd been in her position, certain that she was the one who was sick, and not him. And during all this time, even now, she still clung to exactly the same arguments: He's crazy but I love him, I'll help him pull through. Recalling his own agony, he felt sorry for her. And also felt that he was loved, with a kind of violent passion.

"If you'd rather that we didn't go to lunch at your parents' . . ." she said softly.

"I'd rather not. You're right," he replied, without opening his eyes.

"I'll go call them."

He heard her pick up the phone and speak to his mother. He admired her lively tone, which he knew she was faking, even if she was relieved that the suspense was over. She said that he had a ton of work to finish by the next day, that he'd be spending the day at the office, that he'd undoubtedly call her from there. He thought that his mother might possibly call the office, for no reason, just to say hello, and that he should warn Jerome, or ask Agnes to do it. No, that was pointless. Jerome already had enough presence of mind not to botch things up. He wondered what they all thought—Jerome, Samira, Serge, Veronique—about what had happened to him. The fewer people who knew about it, the better it would be for everyone. He'd have to try to prevent the story from spreading, and establish a stopgap measure: he'd already thought of that.

He remembered that Agnes had invited Serge and Veronique over that evening. In spite of the bizarre phone call, they probably knew nothing. The prospect of dinner, having to constantly check himself so that they wouldn't get suspicious, appalled him even more.

"While you're at it," he said, "don't you want to cancel with Serge and Veronique? I'd prefer it."

No answer. He repeated his request, certain that she wouldn't protest. In his state, the need for solitude was perfectly natural. Agnes was standing behind him, near the sofa;

the neutrality of her voice alerted him, as her silence wore on, he understood.

"Cancel with whom?"

Everything was falling apart. He made an effort to articulate, emphasizing each syllable.

"Serge and Veronique Scheffer, our friends. Who you invited for dinner tonight. With whom we had dinner on Thursday, when all of this started. Serge works for the Environmental Commission. Veronique is studying languages at the Institute of Oriental Languages. They have a country house in Burgundy—we go there all the time. One time you even vandalized their radiators. They're our best friends," he finished, all in one breath.

She knelt down in front of him, her hands on her knees, and began to swing her head from left to right, in a bizarre mechanical gesture of denial. All the while, she was saying "No," murmuring at first, then louder and louder. He thought she was going to have a nervous breakdown, and fought the impulse to slap her, but she calmed down and was now just biting her lips, staring at the carpet.

"You don't know Serge and Veronique, is that what you're telling me?"

She shook her head.

"So who were we with last Thursday night?"

"With each other, just you and me," she stammered. "We went to the movies. . . ."

"What did we see?"

"*Péril en la Demeure.*"

"Where?"

"In Montparnasse. I don't remember which movie theater."

She was stubbornly twirling the spoon in her empty cup. Carried away by the detective-story logic of his questions, he nearly asked her to produce the ticket stubs, but of course, nobody keeps ticket stubs to movies, not even during the film—no one ever checks them. One should always hold on to everything, never overlook the slightest bit of evidence. Like that animist tribe, in the village where they'd bought the blanket. The tradition was disappearing, but they'd been told that once upon a time, the inhabitants fastidiously collected their fingernail clippings, their excrement, their hair—their facial and body hair as well—everything that was a part of them and that would allow them to enter the gates of paradise in one whole and unmutilated piece.

Tracing the movie wouldn't get him very far. He was sure that he'd never seen *Péril en la Demeure*, he'd only expressed the desire to see it, eventually, on the basis of its good reviews. He already sensed that from this moment on, everything would accelerate, that any question he might ask, even if it wasn't a question, any remark referring to a shared past might cause his world to collapse even more. He would lose his friends, his job, his daily routine . . . and he was tortured by his hesitation: would it be better to pursue this investigation, to discover the entire range of the disaster, or to react like an ostrich, to keep silent and say nothing more that would undermine him further.

"What do I do for a living?" he ventured.

"You're an architect."

At least that was resolved.

"So does Jerome exist or not? He phoned before, to give the psychiatrist's address, right?"

"Yes," she admitted. "Doctor Kalenka."

"And you," he continued, encouraged by this success, "you work in publicity at Belin Editions, right?"

"Yes."

"Your name is Agnes, right?"

"Yes."

She smiled, brushing her bangs out of her eyes.

"You phoned my parents ten minutes ago to say we wouldn't be going to lunch, right?"

He sensed her hesitation.

"I phoned your mother, yes."

"But we were supposed to have lunch at my parents', like we do every Sunday, isn't that right?"

"Your father died," she said, "last year."

For a moment he was struck dumb, his mouth wide open, surprised that the tears wouldn't come, the sudden catastrophe was of a totally different nature. This time his new loss of memory, however horrifying, troubled him less than the news of his father's death and the realization that he'd never see him again—that, in fact, he hadn't seen him for an entire year. Yet he remembered lunch last Sunday. And even his voice, the night before, on the answering machine. Which he'd then erased.

"I'm sorry," Agnes murmured, timidly placing her hand on his shoulder. "I feel bad too." He didn't know whether she felt bad because of his father's death, because of the suffocating grief that he felt, or because of what was happening right then between them. He shivered, so that she'd take away her hand; her touch suddenly exasperated him. He would have liked her to retract what she'd said, as if she had killed his father by saying it. A few minutes ago he was still alive.

"Before," he scolded her, "you said, 'At your parents' house,' not 'At your mother's.' "

She answered, "No" very softly, shook her head once more, and it seemed to him that the list of possible gestures had become monstrously limited between the two of them: shaking one's head, closing one's eyes, wiping one's brow. . . . They were ordinary gestures, but they kept repeating themselves, shutting out all the others, just like the walls in a room that gradually close in to the point of imprisoning its occupant, crushing him in a vise. And the movement accelerated. Serge and Veronique, the vacation in Java, which Agnes, the night before last, still remembered, had disappeared in twenty-four hours. Now it only took a few minutes to engulf his father, before he could turn around, without even the space of a night, of a brief absence, to separate the moment when Agnes, he was positive, had said, "Your parents." "Do you want me to call you parents?" from the moment that his father had been wiped off the face of the earth. This atrocity had happened right in front of his eyes, he couldn't do a thing about it, and she would start all over again. He would have liked to ask her more questions, even repeat the ones that had reassured him a few minutes ago, but he no longer dared to, convinced that he'd lose these winnings if he speculated on them again, that he would no longer be an architect, that Agnes would no longer be Agnes, she'd tell him to call her Martine or Sophie, she wouldn't be his wife, he wouldn't know what he was doing here. He mustn't ask another thing, he'd resist the temptation of this roller coaster until the psychiatrist arrived. Just to survive. He wouldn't telephone his mother, wouldn't attempt to verify anything anymore, nor interfere with a cross-examination that the doctor would take care of himself. It was his job to dig around in his past, sum it all up. Right now he was overwhelmed with fatigue and a kind of discouraged resignation. He got up, could barely stand on his own two feet.

"I'm going to try to get some sleep. Please, call that psychiatrist."

He went into the room and closed the door behind him. Inexplicably he was obsessed by the feeling that the number of possible gestures was gradually being reduced. It seemed as if he'd already done this before. Of course he had—he'd passed from the living room to the bedroom hundreds, thousands of times, but it wasn't the same, it hadn't been like this merry-go-round spinning madly out of control, tossing him back and forth so that he couldn't get off, couldn't breathe. By secluding himself, he also figured that he'd be giving Agnes some elbow-room. She could call Jerome or even the psychiatrist Sylvain Kalenka without feeling that she was being watched. She could organize a friendly conspiracy to save him. Meanwhile he had to get some sleep, to recuperate, to recover a bit of lucidity so that he could begin his examination under the best possible conditions. For a few hours he'd let go of everything, not think about it anymore. He'd sleep. Agnes would wake him gently when it was time for his appointment, just as when he was young, and shivering with fever, he'd been driven to the doctor, wrapped in a blanket, half unconscious. Although he was only a general practitioner, the family doctor had, on several occasions, surgically separated Siamese twins. This bizarre specialty had won him the esteem of his father, who always referred to the doctor as "a real big shot." The sound of his father's voice rang in his ears; he remembered certain phrases he'd recently heard, and the very idea that these phrases could only have been pronounced in his deranged mind made him wince. He wasn't even able to cry. He gulped down a sleeping pill without any water, then half of another to be sure he'd sleep. Then he took off his clothes, stretched out naked on the bed, which still had the imprint of Agnes's body. He sunk his head into the pillow and murmured Agnes's name several times.

The sun filtered in through the venetian blinds. There wasn't a sound, except for a very distant one of a washing machine somewhere in the building. The slow and gentle spinning of laundry that could be seen through a little round window was a soothing image. In the same way, he too would have liked to wash and thoroughly squeeze dry his own sick brain. Just as he'd done the night before, Agnes certainly would not leave the apartment. She'd watch over him, taking care not to trouble his sleep. He would have liked a little noise in the background, to establish her presence, and since he didn't hear a thing, he suddenly feared that she'd gone or that she, too, no longer existed. Then there would be nothing left. Anxious, he got up and opened the door a little. She was sitting upright on the living room sofa, her eyes glued to the VCR in front of her. She turned her head at the creaking of the door, and he saw that she was crying. "Please," he said, "don't disappear. Not you." She only replied, "No. Go to sleep," without giving it any particular emphasis. It was better that way. He closed the door again and went back to lie down.

He'd sleep now, not think. Or, if he really had to think about something in order to fall asleep, he could say to himself that he'd soon, very soon, be in the hands of science, that they'd know what was wrong with him. What would Doctor Kalenka look like? The traditional stereotype was the soulful-looking middle-aged doctor, bearded and shrewd, with a harsh Central European accent, and since stereotypes were surely false or at least outdated, he imagined him completely the opposite: well built, frank, resembling a newscaster or rather a young cop, the way they look these days—beat-up sport coat or leather jacket, a woven tie. Simply imagining the details of his appearance would help him fall asleep. But just what was he? A psychiatrist? A psychoanalyst? A psychologist? Knowing that psychoanalysts weren't necessarily doctors, he hoped that Sylvain Kalenka would be a psychiatrist. In a case such as his, he couldn't run the risk of its being some guy who would make him talk, make him recount his childhood for the next two years as he shook his head and pretended to find it interesting. He needed someone who believed in a more substantial cure, an efficient go-getter with a degree who would say without hesitation after fifteen minutes, "Okay, that's it, this is what your sickness is called, this is the medicine to treat it, I know all about it, you're not the first." Reassuring words, partial or temporary amnesia, a nervous breakdown, a decalcification, all danced in his head, where his father's respectful "a real big shot" was still resonating. And Jerome certainly wouldn't have recommended a charlatan, a small-time operator. But if he were such a big shot, was it at all possible that Doctor Kalenka wouldn't be disconcerted by a patient who was convinced that he'd had a mustache for the last ten years, that he'd spent his vacation in Java, that his father was still alive, that his friends were named such and such, while his wife patiently explained that it wasn't so, that he'd always been clean-shaven, that they'd never gone to Java, that his father had died last year, and that he'd been terribly affected by it. Perhaps it would even be necessary to check there for the source of his problem, a delayed reaction, all the more violent because it had been incubating for so long.

He chuckled nervously, seized with the classic apprehension of a patient who, while in the doctor's waiting room, is afraid that all the symptoms he is about to report will disappear. And what if, right in front of Doctor Kalenka, everything returned to normal, what if he suddenly remembered that he'd never had a mustache, that he'd buried his father last year? And what if, on the contrary, while examining the photos, Kalenka said that he was right, seeing the mustache and deciding that he was crazy because he'd sided with Agnes, and had admitted to an error in judgment that would have only taken a simple glance to dispel? Then his father would still be alive, he could call him and explain what had happened to Agnes. Right now, he was feebly debating whether it might be dangerous to cling to this dream, if the pleasure it provided would help him fall asleep. Where was all his passivity coming from? From declarations by Agnes and Jerome? As he thought about it, he felt twinges of a kind of excitement, like a detective confronted with an apparently insoluble enigma who suddenly discovers that, from the very beginning, he's approached it from the wrong angle, and that because of the abrupt change in his perspective he'll get warmer, he'll finally discover the key. Just what hypotheses had he actually investigated? First of all, that he was crazy. And he knew for a fact, even against all appearances, that it simply wasn't so. A sure sign of madness, of course; you could always say that, but no, no, his memories were far too exact. Therefore, his father was still alive, his friends did exist, and he had indeed shaved off his mustache. If all this were true, then the second hypothesis was: Agnes was crazy. Impossible, the others would never have played her game. In the beginning, perhaps, thinking it was a joke, but not afterward, not Jerome, when it had become clear that this business had gone beyond all innocent proportions.

Third: Agnes was really and truly playing a joke on him, pushing it to its extreme, confident that the others would participate. Same objection: they would have put a stop to it when they saw that it was turning sour. Besides, Jerome didn't joke about this kind of thing, because of Sylvie, and anyhow, since he was way behind in his work, it would be in his best interest for his partner to be at the office, not at home with a case of the jitters because he thought he was going crazy. There remained a fourth possibility that he hadn't considered until now. That it was something other than a joke, in really bad taste, something much more serious that had to be confronted, at least as a hypothesis: an organized plot against him, aimed at driving him crazy, to push him to suicide or get him locked up in a padded cell.

He sat up in bed, suddenly fearful that the sleeping pills would have an effect on him, after having hoped earlier that they would. He'd taken enough to kill a horse, had barely slept for forty-eight hours, hardly eaten, and felt extremely weak. Yet even though his thoughts were drifting in a sort of nebulous vein, they were becoming sharper, advancing like the edge of an X-Acto knife slicing through the fog, he could almost hear it scrape as it carved out his line of reasoning. Absurd, of course, unbelievable, as absurd and unbelievable as those thrillers in which the suspense covers up the flaws of the structure. Like *Les Diaboliques* or *Hush . . . Hush, Sweet Charlotte*, where the conspirators, who are meanwhile in the midst of staging their pseudo-supernatural apparitions, never stop reassuring their unfortunate victim with the words, "You're very tired, my dear. Get some rest. It'll pass." Exactly what they'd been telling him; or rather, what he'd been telling himself. And what if they'd banked on it, on the certitude that such an absurd and unbelievable idea only had a one-in-a-million chance of occurring to him? If he remembered correctly, *Les Diaboliques* had been based on a true story. Which proved that it wasn't so absurd, the idea had almost escaped him. He'd been about to fall asleep in a state of utter trust, giving in to the deception. But his eyes had been opened—he had to be guarded, not allow himself to be taken in. He'd have to calmly examine the problem, based on the assumption that there was only one explanation; however monstrous it was, it had to be the right one.

He went back over the list of his arguments. First and foremost, he wasn't crazy. Now, besides Serge and Veronique, who might have been told it was just a joke, besides Samira, who Jerome could have influenced, who was left? Agnes and Jerome. Jerome and Agnes. A classic combination: the husband, the wife, and the lover, no need to look any further. Objection: if they'd had an affair, he would have caught on, there would have been telltale signs. But not necessarily, since the whole plot depended on his blindness. A further objection: Agnes could have asked for a divorce. He would have suffered horribly, but she was a free woman. He couldn't have held her back, and he had no impending inheritance, nothing that would justify a desire to be his widow. But it was an objection that one could maintain for most crimes of passion, and people committed them nonetheless. The idea that Agnes, his wife, and Jerome, his best friend, were plotting against him could only be true at the expense of an insane reversal of thinking, but besides the fact that it had spread to great proportions, this reversal, once set into motion, explained everything. Given this variable, everything fell into place. In the first phase, Serge and Veronique had been unknowing accomplices, figuring that they were part of one of Agnes's typical jokes, and then they were eliminated. Not physically, of course, simply by preventing him from communicating with them in one way or another. Once he'd been psychologically conditioned, Jerome had entered the picture, remained there, had taken charge of everything, had insidiously cut him off from the others, while assuming the role of the devoted friend, always there when he needed him, giving him his undivided trust. And then, out of Jerome's sleeve, came Doctor Kalenka. Surely he wasn't a real psychiatrist who was part of their plot, but a second knife in his back, in charge of spreading even more confusion in his mind. Or else it was more likely, since you don't need fifty people to commit a perfect crime, that there was no Doctor Kalenka. Later on, perhaps tomorrow, Agnes would take him to an apartment, probably on one of the upper floors. There wouldn't be any metal sign on the door, maybe just a fake plaque for the sake of perfectionism, and the door would lead to a void, to a construction site. Jerome would be standing in the corner, would push him off the edge, and they'd conclude that he'd been going through a phase of depression, that he'd committed suicide. No, that wouldn't hold together; not enough people were aware of this supposed depression. They'd need many more witnesses to clear themselves, providing they were even suspected, but their entire strategy was aimed at warding off all possible witnesses. . . . This flaw in their reasoning irritated him. Then he realized that the goal wasn't really to make him appear crazy, it was actually to drive him crazy, and to get him locked up or else for him to commit suicide. When he thought of it that way, it made more sense. It was even foolproof. It would suffice that whenever they were alone, Agnes would consistently deny all of his mem-

ories and certitudes in order to provoke more relapses as she
pretended to be horrified, while Jerome helped her by inter-
vening at crucial psychological moments. No one was preventing him from communicating with anybody, it was he who,
panic-stricken, no longer dared. And if he did, if he called his father, or Serge and Veronique, if he went to see them, any confidence he might regain would be destroyed that very night by
Agnes. She would take him in her arms, softly repeat that his father was dead, and she'd have a fit of hysteria. Jerome, as if by
chance, would call just at that moment, would confirm it,
would tell him about the funeral, and it would be like the
woman with the baby carriage; it was pointless, as vain an effort
as the frenzied struggles of a fish beating its tail when caught
in a net. Even a confrontation, a dinner with Agnes and his father, for instance, would be of no use once they were alone,
back home in the apartment. He'd be constantly wondering
whether he was going insane, whether he was seeing ghosts,
whether they were lying to him and why. It was much more
subtle and straightforward than *Les Diaboliques*. A few days
later, this sapping of his spirit would bear fruit. He was already
restraining himself, rejecting even the easiest of verifications,
no longer daring to ask anything of anyone. In a few days, skillfully, without any violence, and even without any outside in-
terference, Agnes and Jerome would have really and truly
convinced him of his madness, and would have quietly driven
him crazy. And if he accused them, if he showed them that
he'd caught them in the act, that would be further proof. He
could already see their incredulous, dumbfounded faces. They

would let him do all the work, let him destroy himself. And given all this, now that he'd finally understood, it was up to him to take the initiative. Only a counterattack on their own ground remained. He'd work out a plan as twisted as theirs to snare them in their own trap.

Maybe he was a little ahead of himself in eliminating the risk of physical aggression. Their scheme was so sophisticated, they must have planned its course so well, that in the past five minutes that he'd guessed it, he might have missed a vital element. It was quite possible that the coup de grace was imminent, completely without warning, and it would be too late to discover the reasoning that would have warded it off. Two solutions remained. He could let it happen, behave as if he hadn't caught on, obediently follow Agnes to the so-called Doctor Kalenka, thereby taking a risk that was even more enormous than what he'd imagined. Or he could run away, upset their fragile house of cards, and assume a position of retreat. He felt lucid enough to realize that the lack of sleep, the sleeping pills, maybe even drugs that they'd slipped him, might possibly affect his judgment, his reflexes; thus the more prudent solution was the necessary choice. Just long enough to recover his energy, to figure out his plan of defense after a good night's sleep. That established, he was doubtlessly deluding himself by thinking that he'd take them by surprise. Again, the scheme was way too well rigged for them not to have foreseen the possibility of his escape. That was what was so frightening: to know that what he was only now discovering and not yet in full detail—was that they'd been programming him for days, weeks, maybe months: that they were prepared for anything. Therefore, the first priority was to make up for their head start, and it hardly mattered now if he screwed up their whole plan or if he'd only be choosing one of many possibilities. Thus, he'd make his escape. Right away, no matter how, no matter at what cost. All he had to do was walk across the living room and he'd be at the front door. He hadn't heard a sound since his retreat into the bedroom. Agnes must be alone; he would only have her to confront, and too bad if she suspected that he'd figured it all out.

He got up and staggered forward, his head bobbing on his shoulders like a puppet. He took a deep breath and dutifully put on his clothes. Underwear, socks, pants, shirt, jacket, and finally, shoes. Fortunately, he'd gotten undressed in the bedroom. He closed his eyes for a moment's concentration, feeling as though he were in a war movie, just about to leave his shelter and rush onto the battlefield under open fire. No point in trying to look relaxed and saying he was going out to buy cigarettes; it would be better to make a run for it.

He took another deep breath, then opened the door and ran blindly through the living room. He didn't catch sight of Agnes until he turned around to open the front door. Sitting on the sofa, she opened her mouth as if to cry out, but he was already on the landing, down the stairs, four at a time. His temples were throbbing. He could barely hear Agnes, who was leaning over the stairway calling him, screaming his name; he was already running through the hall, into the street. He had no car keys—too bad—he ran without stopping to the Duroc intersection, his heart pounding. People were sitting on the terraces of the cafés, carefree and calm—a typical springtime Sunday afternoon. He bounded down the stairs of the metro, jumped over the turnstile, kept running all the way to the platform, arriving just at the moment that a train was pulling in. He got on and got off two stops later, at La Motte-Picquet. Because of a cramp in his side that had just begun to take hold, he made his way back outside like a little old man, doubled over. He wondered whether Agnes had tried to run after him or if she'd immediately called Jerome. He sneered at the thought of her having to announce that there'd been a little hitch. But maybe she was sneering herself, declaring that everything had gone as planned.

Beneath the elevated metro, he looked around for a phone booth, fumbled in his jacket pocket for change, found both, and the cramp in his side went away. Miraculously the phone booth worked. He dialed his parents' number. Busy. He waited, dialed again, let it ring for a long time, but there was no answer. While he was waiting, he thought about calling the police. But he didn't have sufficient proof—they'd laugh in his face. Most of all, he wanted to see his father. Not to reassure himself that he was alive—that he knew—but simply to see him, speak to him. It was as if there'd been a plane crash and the victims had not yet been identified, but they'd announced his death by mistake. Then corrected the error. Since there was still no answer, he decided to go to Boulevard Emile-Augier. He checked to see if he had enough money on him to take a cab, went to the taxi stand at the intersection of Rue de Commerce, and collapsed onto the backseat. If his parents weren't home, he'd wait

on the landing until they got back. No, not on the landing.
Jerome and Agnes were probably deliberating. They knew he'd
probably go there, and they'd find it amusing to corner him. He
could already see the ambulance parked in front of the building, the strapping medics who would be told not to pay any attention to his protests; if they saw their prey trying to escape,
they might go all out, using every means to speed things up,
provoking such a mess that he'd find himself in a straitjacket
and soon become a real raving lunatic. Realistically, however,
there was little chance of their getting to his parents' house before he did. If his parents were out, he'd take refuge in a café by
the La Muette metro station. He'd keep calling them until they
picked up the receiver.

The taxi had crossed the Seine, was turning around the
Maison de Radio to get onto Rue de Boulainvilliers. He looked
at himself in the rearview mirror. His features were pale and
drawn; a three-day beard consumed his face. Two days, he corrected himself. For one who'd gone two days with no sleep
and loaded himself full of tranquilizers, he was holding up
pretty well.

"What number?" the taxi driver asked, having arrived at La
Muette.

"I'll tell you when to stop."

Shit, he thought, he couldn't remember which number. The
number of his parents' building, where he had spent his entire
childhood. This often happened with a friend, he could easily
find his way to a building without knowing the number, but in
the case of his parents . . . It was absurd. His fatigue, the sleep-

ing pills, the lapses of memory. The taxi drove slowly along the wide, curving boulevard, and farther down he recognized the iron gate surrounding the railroad tracks where a little train used to pass, and the tall, sandblasted bourgeois facades. They'd been black with soot during his childhood. He remembered the renovation, the scaffolds, the tarps, which, for a month, maybe more, had blocked the windows, depriving the tenants of their light, not an insignificant amenity, considering their social status.

Which floor? He couldn't remember the floor either.

"Stop," he said.

He paid and got out. His hands were clammy. Think. One thing was sure. His parents lived on the right side of Boulevard Emile-Augier, coming from the direction of La Muette, since there was no left side. The left side was called Boulevard Jules-Sandeau. And he also knew the code to the entry gate. He wished he could write it down, to be sure he wouldn't forget it, but he had nothing to write with and didn't dare stop a pedestrian. Anyway, no one was passing by. He strode up and down the sidewalk. You couldn't even claim that all the buildings looked alike. There were differences, even if they were all from the same period. It was impossible not to find the right one, the one he'd lived in for ten years, where he visited once a week. Besides, he was an architect. When he'd almost reached the Avenue Henri-Martin, he realized that, in any case, he'd gone too far and retraced his steps, trying to be more attentive.

Despite everything, he found himself back at La Muette. He entered a phone booth, and fortunately hadn't yet forgotten

the number. Just as he was dialing, an ambulance siren began
to wail close by. His hand stiffened around the receiver; no one
was home. And he knew his parents weren't listed in the phone
book, they were even somewhat proud about paying for that
service. Panicked, he began his search once again, went back
down the boulevard, stopping at every door. He didn't hear the
ambulance anymore, but the entry code, which he'd been repeating to himself for fear of mixing it up with the phone number, would do him no good. Nearly all the buildings had
identical panels: the first nine digits and two or three letters. In
his desperation he fiddled with several of them, rang for the
concierge, who told him to get lost, claiming there was no one
there by that name, his name, in the building, and he was back
on the Avenue Henri-Martin.

He resumed his course on the sidewalk across the street, a
pure waste of time; it wasn't even Boulevard Emile-Augier. He
passed a woman who looked like his mother, but it wasn't her
at all. Neither Jerome nor Agnes could be held responsible for
this catastrophic situation, only his fatigue—maybe the drugs
they'd given him as well—or else they had already totally succeeded. Now he was really going mad.

Back at La Muette, he sat down on a bench and forced himself to cry, hoping to calm his nerves, to recover a lucidity that
he felt was giving way. Here he was in the middle of Paris, in a
quiet neighborhood, on a spring afternoon, and they were trying to drive him crazy, kill him, and he had nowhere to go. He
had to get out of there quickly, before they arrived. He knew
that his confusion would be all that was needed to confirm

everything they'd claim, if they decided to have him locked up right away, without any further delay. And what if he beat them to it? If he went either to the cops or to the hospital and told them everything? But the prospect of having to tell all, to explain what, in the eyes of any sensible person would look like a bunch of nonsense, telephoning Agnes in front of the cop, asking her to come get him . . . No, it was impossible. Nowhere safe, no one to confide in. If he'd had a mistress, a double life . . . but his life was linked with Agnes's, his friends were her friends. She must have informed them all; to phone any one of them now would be giving himself away to his tormentors, throwing himself into the lion's den.

He had to escape, fast, leave behind his father, who was possibly on his deathbed (why did he think that?), get some rest. A hotel? That was dangerous too, they would investigate that possibility as well; he'd be taken away the next morning. More than that, he'd have to put a great distance and time between himself and this nightmare. Leave the city, the country. Yes, that was the only solution.

But how? He only had fifty francs on him, no checkbook, no passport, no credit cards. He'd have to get back to the apartment. He snickered. If he went to a hotel, one out of five hundred or a thousand hotels in Paris, he imagined he'd be throwing himself into the lion's den, but to return home—that was all right? It was ridiculous, except that . . . Except that they'd be waiting for him anywhere but there. They'd gone out to look for him, and he could just call to make sure they were out. In their position there was no way they wouldn't answer.

Well, it was pretty unlikely; it was a risk he'd have to take. He got up, wanting to make one last attempt to find his parents' building, but no, time was running out. He hailed a taxi and took it to the intersection at Duroc. The simplicity of his plan seemed brilliant; it almost made him laugh.

Having arrived at his destination, he hurried into the café on the corner, noticing en route that the crowd on the outdoor terrace had thinned. The afternoon was coming to a close; it was getting cooler. Standing at the bar, he asked if he could make a phone call. The waiter replied that the phone was reserved for customers only.

"So get me a coffee, the most disgusting kind you've got, and drink it to my health."

Shooting him a dirty look, the waiter handed him a token for the phone. He plunked a bill on the counter, and went downstairs, congratulating himself on his witticism, which seemed like a good test of his reflexes. It stunk in the booth. He looked up his number in the phone book, then dialed. Agnes answered immediately, but he'd already foreseen this. He wasn't going to let it disconcert him. On the contrary.

"It's me," he said.

"Where are you?"

"Near La Muette. At . . . at my mother's." He chuckled to himself—it was a good answer. "Come over right now."

"But you're crazy. You have an appointment in an hour with Doctor Kalenka on Avenue Maine."

"Precisely. Take the car and come and get me. I'll be at the café on the corner, at La Muette. I'll be waiting."

"But . . ."

She fell silent. He could hear her thinking on the other end of the line. Breathing, in any case.

"All right," she said. "But please, don't go away."

"No. I'll wait for you."

"I love you," she cried just as he was hanging up.

He murmured, "Bitch," slammed his fist against the side of the phone booth, then hurried upstairs and stood behind a pillar, where he wouldn't run the risk of being spotted from the outside and would be able to see the car go by. Because of the one-way streets, she couldn't avoid the intersection. Giving her time to go downstairs, he went back to the bar and asked for another token. He was a bit sorry that he'd been nasty to the waiter; if, by chance, he refused, it would seriously jeopardize his plan. But the waiter didn't even appear to recognize him, and clutching the token in his moist palm, he returned to his lookout post.

As he'd anticipated, he saw the car pass by and stop at the light. From where he was standing, despite the glare in the window, he recognized Agnes's profile, but he was unable to make out her expression. When she turned onto the Boulevard des Invalides, he went back downstairs, dialed the number again, let it ring, in vain. In her haste she'd forgotten to switch on the answering machine. And Jerome wasn't there either. At worst, if he really were there and not answering, he'd feel justified in punching him out.

He left the café, ran all the way home, thinking that two hours earlier he'd been running in exactly the opposite direction like a fugitive, and that now he had the situation under control. He'd maneuvered like a general to slip into enemy camp without taking any risks. No one was in the apartment. He ran over to the desk, opened the drawer that contained his passport, which he scooped up along with his credit cards: American Express, Visa, Diner's Club. He even found some cash. Agnes shouldn't have neglected these details, but that's the way it goes, he thought with satisfaction, the best-laid plans. . . . He wanted to leave a sarcastic note, "I've got your number" or something along those lines, but he couldn't figure out just how to say it. Next to the telephone he spied the beeper for the answering machine, stuffed it into his pocket, and left the apartment. Even before he'd reached the intersection, he found a taxi and asked to be driven to Roissy Airport. Everything was going fine, just like a meticulously planned holdup. He was no longer the slightest bit tired.

The traffic was flowing; they had no trouble getting onto the outside boulevard, then onto the highway. During the ride he took pleasure in dismissing any logical or probable obstacles that could prevent his departure. Even if Agnes and Jerome had guessed his intentions and had discovered the missing passport and credit cards, they would never stop him in time to prevent him from boarding the airplane. As far as transmitting his description to the airport police, that was a measure beyond their grasp. He almost regretted that he'd gotten off to such a good head start, depriving himself of the sight of their tiny silhouettes scurrying down the runway as the plane was taking off, and of the rage they'd feel at having allowed him to slip through their fingers. He wondered how long he would have to wait to leave, to get a seat on a flight whose destination was of no importance, as long as it was far away. The fact that he was arriving without luggage, asking for a ticket to any-where, gave him a kind of giddy sensation, an impression of supreme freedom that he thought could only happen to movie heroes, but it did little to affect the fear that in real life it was never that easy. But after all, why not? And this giddiness in-creased even more when the driver asked, "Roissy One or Two?" He felt rich with the power of cosmic choice, free to decide at will, right away, whether he'd rather take a flight to Asia or America. Actually, he didn't really know what parts of the world or what airlines corresponded to the various sections of the airport. But his ignorance was merely part of the normal order of things, he was not the least bit bothered, and said, at random, "Roissy Two, please." He sunk back into the seat with-out a care in the world.

After that, everything happened very quickly. He consulted the departure board. Leaving himself an hour, the time to buy a ticket, he had the choice among Brasilia, Bombay, Sydney, and Hong Kong. As if by magic, there was still a seat for Hong Kong, no visa was necessary, the woman behind the counter didn't seem taken aback, only said it might be a little tight for the baggage check-in. "No baggage!" he declared proudly, lift-ing up his arms, a trifle disappointed that she hadn't shown more surprise. The passport verification posed no problems, and the employee's indifferent gaze, as he glanced back and forth between the photo with him wearing a mustache and his face with the one starting to grow back, dispelled the last of his apprehensions: everything was in order. In less than a half an hour after his arrival at Roissy, he fell asleep in the departure terminal. A while later someone touched his shoulder and said it was time. He held out his boarding pass and stumbled into his seat, where minutes after he'd fastened his seat belt, he fell asleep once more.

5

SOMEONE TOUCHED HIS SHOULDER AGAIN, DURING THE STOPOVER at Bahrain. It took him a few seconds to remember where he was, his destination, what he was running away from. He followed in a daze the flow of weary passengers who were obliged to get off the plane because of some regulation or another and wait around in the terminal, even though they wouldn't be changing aircraft. It was a long corridor divided into a grid of brightly colored booths where duty-free items were sold, one side facing the airport runway, the other facing a vast expanse that was hard to distinguish in the dark because of the reflections in the window from the glare inside the terminal, but there was nothing to see but some low buildings near the horizon, probably part of the airport. Most of the men and women who were dozing on the benches were dressed in Arabic costume; they must have been waiting for a connecting flight. He sat off to the side, caught between the desire to go back to sleep, return to his seat like a zombie, sleep all the way to Hong Kong without asking himself any questions, and the vague feeling that he had to figure out his actual position; now that the excitement of his departure had died down, it wouldn't be that easy.

The idea of finding himself in Bahrain, in the Persian Gulf, fleeing a conspiracy mounted by Agnes, suddenly seemed so totally incongruous that his mind, still confused, was less inclined to examine the situation than to ponder its reality. He got up and went into the men's room, where he rinsed his face with cold water and stared at his reflection in the mirror. Another traveler came through the door behind him, and he hastily stuffed his passport back into his pocket. He'd taken it out to compare the picture with his face in the mirror. Then he returned to the terminal, walked around for a while to clear his head, zigzagging back and forth between the two rows of benches on either side of the duty-free boutiques. He pretended to look interested, examined the labels of ties, the electronic gadgets, until a salesgirl approached and said, "May I help you, sir?" and he quickly retreated. As he sat back down, he noticed an ashtray containing an empty pack of Marlboros that had been ripped open in a manner somehow familiar to him, although he had to make a considerable effort to recall what this shredded wrapper reminded him of. It came back to him. Two or three years ago, a rumor had been circulating in Paris, maybe elsewhere, he didn't know for sure, a rumor of completely mysterious origin, like the strange stories that crop up, are spread around, then disappear before you can ever find out who started them. And this particular rumor claimed that the Marlboro corporation was linked to the Ku Klux Klan and was secretly advertising it through certain distinguishing marks that were incorporated into the design of the pack. This could be evidenced first by calling attention to the lines that separated the red spaces from the white spaces, which formed three K's, one on the front, one on the back, one on the upper portion of the pack; also, at the bottom of the inside wrapping were two dots, one yellow, the other black, which meant, "Kill the niggers and the yellow." Whether it was true or not, this explanation briefly gave rise to a popular social pastime, and on café tables you would often see ripped-up packs of cigarettes, proving that someone had been taken in by it. These vestiges gradually became rarer, because the number of people in on the secret was so great that there was no one left to initiate, or people had grown tired of it, but mostly because it didn't always work. Agnes, who at the time never missed a chance to perform the demonstration, was even able to deduce from her increasingly numerous failures that the yellow and black dots were the unquestionable proof of the anecdote's authenticity. According to her, since the secret message had spread, the bosses at Marlboro had given up this form of circulation; now it was just a matter of discovering where it had been transferred. Out of boredom he scrutinized the package with no luck, then got up and went to buy a carton in the duty-free shop, which he paid for with his American Express card. He smoked a cigarette, then another. Facing his seat was a speckled planisphere of clocks, indicating the time in various parts of the world; Spain was missing, inexplicably replaced by a dark blue sea that extended from the Pyrenees to Gibraltar. It was 6:14 in Paris.

At 6:46, according to that same time zone, a woman's voice came over the buzzing loudspeakers, asking all passengers en route to Hong Kong to kindly board the aircraft. There was a shuffling of feet in the yellow light. A man awoke with a start and put on his sunglasses to hunt around for his boarding pass, which had slid beneath his seat. Back on the plane, a while later, the flickering lights faded from the outside window, and the cabin lights were turned off. The passengers wrapped themselves in red-and-green plaid blankets, which they had removed from their plastic wrappings. A few of them switched on their reading lamps. It was night all over the sky; he lay there awake. This was real.

6

THE PLANE LANDED IN HONG KONG, TOWARD LATE AFTERNOON. HE
remained in his seat while the passengers were restlessly moving about around him, grabbing their carry-on baggage as the
stewardess collected the plastic headphones that had been left
on the seats. He got off at last, with regret. He had become accustomed to the slow motion of life in the cabin. The regular
succession of meals, of films, of announcements over the loud-
speaker hadn't really dulled his mind, but at least offered him
no resistance, a bit like a room where you were expected to
bang your head repeatedly against the wall, which out of benevolence was padded with rubber. Smiling, he reflected on the
meaning of his thought, which had come to him quite naturally: in effect, he longed for a padded cell, without admitting
to himself or actually believing he was crazy, but simply to feel

protected. All that was over from now on; he was exposing himself to new territory.

A cloud of steam blurred the glass silhouettes of the buildings that rose behind the airport. Having no luggage, he was able to quickly pass through customs and passport control, and found himself in the arrivals terminal, surrounded by people who were running, pushing baggage carts, waving signs, vehemently pawing one another, talking loudly, some syllables guttural, some singing. Of course, he didn't understand a thing. He took off his jacket and threw it over his shoulder. What should he do now? Buy a return ticket? Call Agnes to ask her forgiveness? Leave the airport and walk straight ahead until something happened? He stood there for a moment in the rush, immobile. Then, as if these actions had been just as obligatory as landing procedures, as if they were a part of a series of gestures to be carried out one after the other, delaying the moment of having to make a decision, he went from counter to counter until he found American Express and procured himself the equivalent of five thousand francs in Hong Kong dollars. He put them in the pockets of his trousers, which were sticking to his legs. Then, following the advice of the employee whom he'd questioned in English, he went into the tourist bureau and reserved a room in a medium-priced hotel, chosen from the hotel brochure. He was given a coupon for the taxi ride, which turned out to be useful, since the driver spoke no English. The car turned into a maze of streets swarming with people, lined with skyscrapers that were already old and decrepit and covered with clotheslines and dripping air conditioners, to the point where

the little pools had formed on the broken, jackhammered side-
walks. Some of these buildings seemed to be in the process of
demolition without actually having been evacuated; others
were being built. There were barriers everywhere, fencing off
the construction sites, enormous bamboo scaffolds, concrete
mixers, pedestrians, and cars with their radios blaring, dodging
in between them, all to the rhythm of a mad traffic jam, like a
film that had been speeded up. The taxi finally emerged onto
a wider avenue and dropped him off in front of the King Hotel,
where he had made his reservation. The receptionist had him
fill out a form before he was taken up to his room on the eigh-
teenth floor. The cold from the air conditioner—a huge box
built into the damp walls—made him realize that he was
sweating profusely. He tried regulating it, and no sooner had he
turned the dial than it began to rattle, forcing out a powerful
surge of air. It finally shut down completely, so he could hear the
noise from the street. Behind the venetian blinds the window
was sealed shut. His forehead pressed against the pane, he
looked down at the traffic for a moment. Then as the heat returned he got undressed and took a shower, doggedly pushed
aside the plastic shower curtain, which kept sticking to him.
Wrapped in a towel, he went back into his room, stretched out
on the bed, and folded his arms behind his head.

There. Now what?

He could either remain there on the bed until all this passed,
but he knew it wouldn't pass, or he could return immediately
to the airport and sit on a bench until the next flight for Paris,
but he didn't feel up to it. Or he could decide that just as he

had needed a roof over his head, he now needed a change of
clothes, a toothbrush, a razor. He could go downstairs and buy
all that, and minutes later find himself in the same position,
lying on the bed, asking himself again, Now what?

Unaware of the passing time, he didn't budge until it started
to get dark. Then he decided that at least he'd call Agnes. There
was a phone in his room, but he could neither obtain a direct
line—he didn't know what the country code for France was,
anyhow—nor reach the front desk. He got dressed again, in
clothes smelling of perspiration, and went down into the lobby.
The receptionist, who spoke English, agreed to dial the number
for him, but after a fairly long time, she reemerged from the
office behind the desk and told him no one was answering.
Surprised that Agnes had gone out without turning on the answering machine, he insisted that she try again, but to no avail.
He went outside.

Nathan Road, the big, noisy avenue adjacent to his hotel,
was illuminated like the Champs-Elysées at Christmastime.
The traffic was flowing beneath arches of red lanterns with
dragons on them. He walked aimlessly in the dense and indifferent crowd; there was a slightly stale odor of steamed vegeta-
bles, and at times, dried fish. Farther down, the stores became
more luxurious. They mostly sold electronic equipment tax-
free, and a large number of tourists were doing their shopping.
He finally reached the end of the avenue, where there was a
large square that opened onto the bay. Extending along the
other side was a shimmering chaos of skyscrapers set against the
side of a mountain, its peak obscured by the night fog. He re-

membered the photographs he'd seen in magazines, and realized that this spectacular city was Hong Kong. So where was he?

He asked a European girl in shorts, an outdoorsy type who
must have been Dutch or Scandinavian, but who said nonetheless, "Here, Kowloon." The name was vaguely familiar to him;
he must have read about it somewhere. Looking at the map
that the girl had unfolded, he understood that one part of the
city was situated on the island facing him, the other on the
mainland, something like Manhattan and New York, and that
he'd chosen his hotel in the continental sector, Kowloon. A
ferry service linked the two banks; apparently people used it
like the metro. Joining the crowd, he headed toward the pier,
bought a ticket, waited until the ferry slid against the dock and
the passengers got off. He got on as soon as the attendant let
people through.

He enjoyed the ride so much that, once they'd arrived on the
other side, he decided not to disembark, but rather to set out
again in the opposite direction without leaving his seat. The attendant signaled that he had to get off. He obeyed but immediately purchased another ticket and went back out again. Now
familiar with the way things worked, he realized, after three
round trips, that instead of buying a ticket each time, it was
faster and more practical to slip a fifty-cent coin into the slot of
the automatic turnstile, and when he bought his last ticket,
he got change for an abundant supply of coins, enough so that
he wouldn't have to leave the boat until closing time, which he
hadn't even inquired about. He then discovered another characteristic of the ferry: its total reversibility. The front of the

boat became whatever direction you were going, the back was the one you were leaving behind, though out of the water, it would have been impossible to distinguish the prow from the stern. Even the backs of the seats slid in lateral grooves so that one could orient them toward the desired direction. With a flick of the wrist, people reversed them in order to sit facing the direction opposite that faced by the passengers who'd just left. When you were going toward Hong Kong, everybody, even the nose-behind-the-newspaper types, was facing Hong Kong, and the same thing went for Kowloon. He became aware of this custom, which later struck him as obvious, because of a particular incident: he had just climbed back aboard the boat and, for fun, returned to the same seat he'd left two minutes before. Looking up, he realized that he'd forgotten to turn the back of the seat, and was sitting alone, against the tide, facing all the other passengers. Moreover, they didn't seem to care at all, not even the trio of high school girls in white bobby socks whom he'd expected would burst out laughing. They looked at him with neither mockery nor animosity, as though he were part of the urban landscape of the approaching shore. He experienced a moment of embarrassment, but their general indifference gave him a feeling of tranquillity, and he stopped in the middle of turning it, remained where he was, and even laughed out loud. One, against all, the only person to maintain that he had a mustache, a father, and a memory that was being sabotaged. But here, apparently, this singularity went unnoticed. All that was asked of him was that he get off the ferry when it arrived at the dock; he was free to climb back on board once he'd paid.

Another idea occurred to him, crazy but intoxicating, that he could very well stay in Hong Kong, never to be heard from again. He'd never expect to hear from Agnes, from his parents, from Jerome. He'd just forget them, forget his profession and find anything to do to subsist here, or elsewhere for that matter, someplace where nobody knew him, where nobody cared about him, where they had no idea if he'd always worn a mustache. He'd turn over a new leaf, start from scratch, that old and useless catchphrase of all the embittered souls on this planet, he thought, except that his case was a little different. Supposing he went home, and instead of locking him up, they tacitly agreed to wipe the slate clean, to go back to the way things were before, both at the office and at home; maybe life would go on, but it would be distorted forever. Distorted not only by the memory of this episode, but above all, by the constant fear of its sequel, the risk of witnessing the horror rise up again in the middle of a conversation, an innocent allusion to shared memories, a person or an object. As soon as he saw Agnes go pale, bite her lips, noticed a long silence on her part, he'd know that was it, it was starting all over, his world was falling apart once again. Living that way, on a minefield, feeling one's way, always anticipating another explosion—no human being could possibly bear it.

He understood that this perspective was what had forced him to flee, much more so than the ridiculous theory about a plot against him. In his fever of the night before, he hadn't fully grasped it, but it was obvious: he had to disappear. Not necessarily from the world, but at least from the world that was his own, the one he knew and that knew him, since the conditions of life in that world were now undermined, corrupted under the influence of an incomprehensible monstrosity that one either refused to understand or confronted within the walls of an asylum. He was not crazy. The idea of an asylum made him shudder; escape was the only thing left. At each new crossing he became more and more elated, knowing he'd chosen the only possible way out, and that only because of a barely conscious but deep-rooted survival instinct had he dissuaded himself from buying a return ticket to Paris in the airport, throwing himself back into the lion's den. He no longer had a place among his own kind, he thought, conscious of striking a chord of heroic sentimentality that reinforced his determination, just like the saying that it is no use wiping off the table with a sponge when you have to change the tablecloth, or maybe even the table. Yet he already sensed that it would be difficult to maintain the exhilaration, which might fade all by itself once he'd gotten off the ferry. For the time being, the world consisted of this gentle rolling, of the shimmering dark water, of the groaning of steel cables, of the clicking gates that opened for loading and landing, of this regulated and unchangeable back-and-forth to which he'd succumbed, beyond reach in the soft evening breeze. But he couldn't spend the rest of his life going from Kowloon to Hong Kong, couldn't let it end with this image, like the Chaplin film where Charlie's chased by cops from two neighboring states and he ends up continuously duck-walking back and forth, across the border. There's a fadeout, then the words "The End" appear on the screen. But in real life there is no equivalent to this finale. Yet one could stop.

He'd been observing the powerful wake since they'd left the shore, leaning over the rails of the boat's temporary stern. His eyes followed the frothy curve all the way to the propeller, which he could almost hear vibrating below the boards of the deck. It would be easy just to fall in. In a few seconds he'd be torn to shreds by the whirring blades. No one would have time to intervene. The passengers on deck, few at this hour, would cry out, get excited, make the ferry stop, and at best, what would they find? Pieces of flesh mixed with garbage from the port, dead fish, crates, and ripped clothes. Maybe his answering-machine beeper, his passport, if they really looked. But then again, would they drag the whole bay of Hong Kong to identify some unknown tourist? Besides, if he wanted to do it in style, nothing was stopping him from destroying his passport before jumping, thereby eliminating any trace of his stay. No—he'd filled out a form at the hotel. It would, in fact, be easy to cross-check. Two days later the French consul in Hong Kong would have the privilege of announcing the accident to his family. He could imagine the whole telephone call perfectly; that is, if they still used the telephone to carry out that sort of painful task. And Agnes, on the other end of the line, her teeth clenched, her pupils dilated . . . But it would be less horrible for her to get it all at once than to wait weeks, months, years without hearing from him, and, given the circumstances, gradually forget him without ever knowing what had happened. The only thing she'd remember, for the rest of her life, was those three days of horror, the words she'd said on the phone during his last call to her, supposedly from La Muette. "I love you" she'd cried out before she hung up, and he'd thought, You little shit, you bitch. He'd hated her, even though she was being sincere, even though she loved him. . . . The memory of this last cry, doomed to remain unanswered, moved him to tears. Not daring to scream, he softly articulated, "I love you, Agnes, I love you, I love only you," and it was really true, even more true because he'd detested her, because he'd shown himself to be unworthy of the trust that she'd never failed to show for him. She, at least, had never given in. He would have done anything to hold her in his arms again, hold her close, tell her again and again, "It's you," hear the same from her lips and never again stop believing her. Whatever came to pass, no matter how improbable it seemed, even if she held a gun to his head, at the very moment she was about to pull the trigger, when his brains would splatter all over his broken skull, he'd think, She loves me. I love her. That's the only thing that is real.

Three days ago, or four, counting the time change, they had made love for the last time.

For perhaps the twentieth time, the ferry came up alongside the banks of Kowloon, and instead of getting off last, as he'd gotten in the habit of doing, he bounded onto the gangway, ready to take a taxi to the airport, to go home at once. But riding up the escalator, the feel of the fifty-cent piece he'd kept in his clenched fist for the next crossing suddenly made him slacken his pace. He turned the coin around with his fingers, hesitating whether to flip, heads or tails, when in fact, he'd already made his decision. In front of the turnstile once again, he slipped fifty cents into the slot and walked slowly down the escalator opposite the one he'd just clambered up. He waited patiently in front of the gate as the ferry emptied out. He couldn't go back, there was no use trying again. He'd cradle Agnes's face in his hands, caress her, and then? And then it would be the same, even more painful after the hope of forgiveness. Or maybe Agnes would watch him come toward her, and say, "Who are you?" He'd shout, "It's me, it's me. I love you," but the trouble would have gotten worse during his absence, she would no longer recognize him, wouldn't even remember that he'd ever existed.

During this crossing, he kept his eyes on the wake and began to cry. He cried for Agnes, for his father, for himself. He continued to ride back and forth. Once, out on the water, a strong sense of revolt made him promise himself he'd stop the next time around; he'd take a taxi, a plane, at least make a phone call. But at the landing, he took out another coin. Every now and then the attendant would give him a little wave, a token of his perplexed sympathy. He even went back to get more change, bought a Sprite, took a couple of sips, then let the bottle roll between his feet.

What he'd been afraid of had finally happened. When he landed on the Hong Kong side, there was a rusty lock on the loading gate. With a questioning and helpless gesture, he pointed to it, and the attendant replied, laughing, "Tomorrow, tomorrow," and held up seven fingers, probably the time they opened.

And now? he thought, sitting down on the damp steps of pier.

Well, he could always go back to his hotel, on the opposite shore. It would probably be easy to find a little boat that would serve as a taxi, but he didn't feel like taking one. He didn't feel like venturing into the city either, which loomed up behind him, the lights reflecting off the oily water of the bay. So, should he remain on the pier, wait until daybreak and take the ferry back? To start all over again the next day, and the day after? Despite the absurdity of this plan, no other came to mind, and he found himself considering the practical aspect, assessing his situation. If he stayed on the boat from seven o'clock to midnight, slept on the pier at night, how long could he hold out? The trip cost fifty cents, he made approximately four an hour, which meant two dollars an hour, times seventeen hours per day; that came to thirty-four dollars a day, and there might still be other expenses. Counting six dollars for food, hamburgers, soup, or a cheap bowl of noodles, he could get by with forty Hong Kong dollars a day, about forty francs if he'd gotten the exchange rate right. Multiplied by 365 days, 14,600 francs a year, not even 15,000, that was what he made per month in Paris, and it was barely twice the budget allocated for the care of the mentally ill in the southwest. All he'd have to do now and then was to draw out some more money with his credit cards, and at that rate he could prolong his stay indefinitely. Except that after a while the bank might wonder; Agnes had probably informed the credit-card agencies of his disappearance. It wouldn't take her long to find him.

He imagined her landing in Hong Kong, sick with worry, running into her on the ferry. He'd calmly explain to her that his life had become too painful, that he couldn't bear it under these conditions, and taking the ferry all day long was the only way to recover some peace of mind, and that if she loved him, the only thing she could do for him now was to relieve him of his credit cards, wire him the necessary sum of money, about fifteen thousand francs, to be put into an account at a local bank, which she would open for him, and then leave him alone. She would cry, kiss him, shake him, but she'd end up giving in. What else could they do? Every once in a while, frequently in the beginning and less often as time went on, she'd make a trip to Hong Kong, come and join him on his ferry, speak to him gently as she held his hand, avoid using certain words. Kowloon–Hong Kong, Hong Kong–Kowloon, eventually she would grow accustomed to seeing him live that way. Maybe she wouldn't come alone; maybe she would have begun a new life. She would explain everything to the man who'd come with her, who'd be discreetly waiting on the pier; she'd point out this bewildered-looking bum, who, for the regular ferry-goers had already become a kind of bizarre mascot, soon to be referred to in guidebooks as "The crazy Frenchman of the Star Ferry," and she'd say, "There he is. That's my husband." Or else she wouldn't tell anyone about it. Her friends would never know the reason for her solitary pilgrimages to Asia. And he, her husband, would be gently shaking his head. At the end of the day she'd try and persuade him to accompany her to the hotel, at least for one night, and he'd say no, gently; as always, he'd roll his mat out on the pier. He would never have gone beyond that point, the only part of the city he'd know was that short path from the loading dock to the bank where he'd go each month in order to renew his supply of coins. Of course it was absurd, he thought, but what else could a man who has gone through what I have possibly expect? Ultimately he preferred this to being shut away under lock and key, to madness supervised by some mediocre Doctor Kalenka and his horde of musclebound medics. He'd much rather live on the ferry than in the southwestern village where he would finally wind up, after a long road of sophisticated cures and top-notch institutions. Because, in the long run, that was what awaited him if he returned to France.

Yet he knew he was of sound mind; most crazy people were convinced of the same thing, nothing could make them change their minds, and he was aware that in the eyes of society a misadventure like his could only signify lunacy. But in reality, he now perceived that everything was more complicated. He wasn't crazy. Neither were Agnes, Jerome, or the others. It was just that the order of the world had been thrown out of whack, it was both abominable and discreet, it had passed unnoticed by everyone but him, which put him in the position of being the only witness to the crime, which consequently had to be fought. Besides, in his case, nothing suspicious was going on anymore, and for that matter, nothing was in its right order;

decidedly, rather than the padded cell, he'd take the monotonous, dreary, but voluntarily chosen reprieve of life on the ferry. Never go back, fight the temptation, remain in hiding like a witness that the Mafia is forced to eliminate. He should make Agnes understand this necessity. His disappearance was not a sudden whim, it was a vital obligation. From a distance, without trying to see him again, she would have to help him pull through this as best he could. She'd have to stop tracking him down, let him use his credit cards, and later on, send him money to guarantee his survival. Now, how would she welcome these kinds of instructions? And if he were in her place, how would he react? He bitterly admitted to himself that he would no doubt do anything possible to get her back home, against her will, entrust her to the best psychiatrists, and that was exactly what must not be done. She'd have to bend a little, understand. Sitting on the steps, across from the lights of Kowloon, the gigantic billboards for Toshiba, Siemens, TDK, Pepsi, Ricoh, Citizen, Sanyo, all of which he now knew by heart, the rhythms of their blinking on and off, he forced himself to compose sentences, find just the right tone to facilitate the superhuman effort of making his demands appear not as an additional proof of insanity, but on the contrary, a reasonable and thought-out reaction. The mustache, his father, Java, Serge and Veronique—none of that mattered anymore, there was no point going back to it. The only thing that counted now was the practical attitude he chose to adopt regarding this incurable confusion. She would have to understand; it would be hard, and she'd have to help him, but he'd also have to stick with it.

He couldn't underestimate the power of his disordered mind; he couldn't ignore that what he thought right now, he might no longer think in two days or even two hours. The absolute certainty of his convictions had only served in blinding him when he'd believed that Agnes and Jerome were guilty. He now realized he'd made a mistake, he could finally see things clearly, but soon, no point fooling himself, his thoughts would begin to waver back and forth, racing from one obstacle to another. Just the idea that he'd never again make love to Agnes set the infernal machine into motion, tempted him to forget about all his resolutions, to go home, to hold her in his arms and assume that life would go on.

He liked the ferry, it had pleased him at the very first because it provided a setting for his fluctuating moods. All he really needed was enough coins to go with the flow; he could hesitate, rebel against it, but not have to act on any of it. Now that he'd taken the only reasonable action, figured out how to escape to the ends of the earth, the trick was to stay there, not to budge, not to act, not to do anything but think about the to-and-fro movement. Outside the ferry that kept him in check, the world could not offer sufficient resistance to his passing whims. It should be possible to burn his bridges, put himself in a material or physical situation in which his return would be forever prohibited. For even if he were to throw away his credit cards, his passport, he could just walk into the consulate and soon be sent home to his country. Short of closing off those exists, nothing could insure that his determination wouldn't break down, that an even stronger tide of thoughts wouldn't carry off his present conviction and substitute another in its place; he might even find what he now considered to be a ludicrous idea, amusing. Nothing in the world could forewarn him of this inconstancy, not even the tranquil rhythms of the ferry rides, which he already sensed he'd get tired of. At least the madmen in the village or the ones in the asylums had as an ally the torpid effect of their medicine: it regulated their clocks, circumscribed their movements, like an inner ferry that would never stop its peaceful rounds back and forth in their sluggish brains. The machine never jammed, it ran on pills, tablets, daily capsules, even more reliable than the fifty-cent pieces because there was always someone there to administer them. He remembered the confession of one of the women in the village, naïvely explaining to the reporter that the advantage of these particular patients was that they were incurable, so one could hold on to them for life and scrape a modest fortune off the cost of their care until their deaths. He almost envied those madmen, completely freed of all responsibility, beyond reach.

Later, as the sky began to pale, there were sounds, hints of movement disturbing the nocturnal calm of the pier. He could see something stirring in the shadows. A man in shorts and a muscle shirt, a few yards away, stood out as a moving white blur, throwing his arms forward, backward, bending down, standing up. Others appeared. Everywhere along the pier, silhouettes gradually became more distinct, slowly gyrating, calmly, almost silently. He could hear deep and regular breathing, sometimes the cracking of a joint, a half-whispered phrase, promptly echoed by another, with an intonation that struck him as jovial. A little old man in a warm-up suit, who had just arrived nearby to do his exercises, flashed him a friendly smile and gestured for him to come join in. He got up and awkwardly went through the motions that the old man showed him. Two fat women, stifling their laughter, were busy touching their toes with their fingertips in an unhurried and graceful rhythm. Moments later it was his turn to laugh, and he made it understood to his exercise companions that he wasn't accustomed to this, that he'd have to stop. The old man said, "Good, good," one of the women mimed applause, and under their only slightly ironic gaze, he walked away.

He climbed up a stairway and soon found himself on a large concrete overpass, which opened onto an esplanade lined with benches. Everywhere gymnasts of all ages were leisurely going about their routines. He stretched out on one of the benches, his back turned to the bay. The loading dock of the ferry, visible from over the railing, was still locked. Overhead a small arbor of pale blue pipes framed a very tall building, whose windows looked like octagonal screws; a second unfinished building had been covered halfway up with mirrored windows. The upper floors were obscured by bamboo scaffolds and green tarps. In between these two blocks of concrete, cranes, and chunks of other buildings, the somber green mass of the Peak stood so high that when he looked up, he couldn't even see its top, which was lost in the shimmering fog. The sun was already beating down on the windows, on the metal sheets, on the pipes; a bustling uproar had started to rise from the port, and for the first time, the idea of being in Hong Kong filled him with a kind of excitement. He lay there for another half hour, watching the sun come up as it reflected off the city buildings. When he turned back toward the bay, he recognized his ferry slowly making its way between the cargo ships and the sampans. He observed its progression all the way up to the Kowloon loading dock, and watching it begin its return trip; felt as if he were already aboard. The resumption of the boat's activity inspired such a strong feeling of security that he caught himself thinking, Well, after all, I'm not in any hurry. He also thought that in the morning everything seemed more simple.

He got up and walked down the promenade, where the peaceful morning exercises had been replaced by the more disorganized and hurried movement of people who were rushing off to work. Yet despite the crush of the mob, every now and then some of the soberly dressed bureaucrats would stop in their tracks, put down their attaché cases, and take twenty to thirty seconds to stretch their arms, bend their knees, arch their backs, which induced a sudden calm. No one paid any attention to him. Weaving through the dense crowd, he came out onto a patio at the foot of a building under construction, the lower floors of which were completed and already housed offices. A bank. He smiled, remembering his plan to live on the ferry. Farther down, there was a post office, not yet open. He promised himself he'd come back there later to call Agnes. Then he changed his mind; perhaps a long letter would be best.

The overpass spanned a wide avenue that could not be reached any other way; he walked across, then went down to the crowded sidewalk. It was already very hot. The moment he realized this, the sweat on his back turned cold. He came to an abrupt halt, as if his feet were rooted to the red carpet that was rolled out on the sidewalk in front of the hotel, and perceived that its air-conditioning created a microclimate all the way out into the street. He slipped on his jacket and went inside. The lobby was freezing; it was suddenly another world. Leather chairs, smoked-glass tables, green plants, all surrounded by a loggia and expensive boutiques. The walls were decorated with bronze bas-reliefs that looked like a conglomeration of blown fuses, and a hideous fresco of vaguely Oriental design. There was a sign indicating the direction of several restaurants and a coffee shop. Buttoning his jacket, he decided he'd go have some breakfast.

He ate and drank with a hearty appetite, then requested something to write with. But once he had the piece of paper in front of him, contemplating the first sentence in his letter to Agnes, he recognized that his fears from the night before were grounded, grounded to such a degree that in retrospect they inspired a kind of incredulous disbelief. His plan to spend the rest of his life going back and forth from Kowloon to Hong Kong, his budgetary calculations, especially the fact of having considered this solution the only alternative to confinement in a southwestern village—predictably, all of this now seemed as ridiculous as the suspicion that Agnes had concocted a plot against him. From the shipwreck of his nocturnal reasoning, from a kind of determination that he had sworn he would adhere to, there still remained some anxiety about what his return might be like. The daylight, the discreet tinkling of silverware in the Hotel Mandarin coffee shop threw the mustache affair and its consequences into the realm of doubt, almost oblivion. But even though he was reassured, his presence in this coffee shop forced him to remember that irreversible events had occurred, that he'd crossed over and gone beyond the line, maybe to the point of no return. Since he'd remained without answers, the question for him had been displaced from the *why* to the *how*. But this *how* as soon as it no longer entailed putting one foot in front of the other, or coins in a slot or food in his mouth, also began to fluctuate. It was stripped of its verbal impact that was supposed to lead to some type of behavior. *How* should no longer be a question mark, like a *so what?*, a *now what?* whose paralyzing effects could only be countered one step at a time. He'd focused on immediate goals, and had been delighted to overcome these benign obstacles. Yet while they distracted his attention, they also stood in the way of the enormous obstacle of choice—whether to stay or to leave. At that moment, everything was wide open. But if he wrote to Agnes, he'd have to make a decision. Or else be satisfied with reassuring her, telling her not to worry, I'm just going through a phase, I'll fill you in on all the details soon. Put it off a little longer. The best thing would be to call, at least she'd know he was alive and wouldn't try to find him.

He decided against the letter for the time being, nevertheless making use of the hotel stationery to write down the phone numbers of his apartment, his parents, and his office, to make sure he wouldn't forget them. He folded the sheet of paper and slipped it into his jacket pocket. After paying for his breakfast, he made his way toward the phone booths he'd spotted in the corner of the lobby. An employee provided him with the country code for France, and he wrote it down. Then he dialed the three phone numbers, one after the other, but there was no answer. According to his calculations, it was eleven o'clock at night in Paris, which explained the silence at the office. But he still couldn't understand why Agnes hadn't turned on the answering machine. If she had, he could have listened to recent messages with his beeper, gotten an idea of the prevailing mood during his absence. That is, providing the beeper worked from such a long distance. He'd wondered about that when he'd first bought the machine. Was there a zone beyond which the beep tone would no longer function? Actually, there was no reason why not. And he could easily find out. There was scarcely a lack of electronic-equipment stores in Hong Kong. Even so, the answer would not yet solve the problem, as long as Agnes hadn't turned the answering machine back on. She'd eventually get around to it, unless it was broken, or—he smiled gloomily— unless Agnes assured him when they spoke to each other, if they ever spoke to each other again, that they'd never had an answering machine. Naturally, he remembered perfectly the way the machine looked, precisely when they'd bought it, the thousands of recorded and erased messages, among them the one from his father reminding them about Sunday lunch; naturally, he could put his hand in his pocket and run his finger along the metallic edges of the beeper—but what did that prove? He redialed his number and let it ring. Without letting go of the phone, which was still ringing monotonously, he took the small metal device out of his pocket. He carefully read the instructions:

1. Dial your phone number.
2. As soon as your message begins to play, place the beeper on the receiver and press for two to three seconds.
3. The tape will stop, the message cassette will rewind, and you will hear your recorded messages.

He mechanically glided his finger over the button on the side of the beeper, then pushed down, holding his finger there until the soft but steady shrillness of the tone became so unbearably ear-piercing to the corpulent Chinese man in the booth next to him that he began to pound on the glass with vehemence. Suddenly coming to his senses, he let go, put the beeper back into his pocket, hung up, and left. He was crushed, not so much by the silence on the other end as by the utter uselessness of a device with which he'd hoped to be able to test the waters and intercept the reactions to his escape. He felt defenseless, betrayed: assuming the very existence of the answering machine hadn't been thrown into the same pot with the mustache, his father, his friends—was it possible that Agnes had deliberately unplugged it when she realized that the beeper was missing? That she'd sacrificed the chance to hear from him simply to prevent him from being sneaky? Where was she? What was she thinking about? Was she still talking, eating, drinking, sleeping? Going about her daily routine, despite this unbearable uncertainty? Did she at least remember that he'd disappeared? That he'd ever existed?

While listening to the continual ringing, he'd been able to take a good look at himself in the engraved mirror on the wall behind the row of phone booths. He saw a worn jacket that was too heavy, a filthy and sweaty gray shirt, tousled hair, and a three-day beard. To calm himself down, he resolved to buy a change of clothes. He crossed the lobby to get to a patio surrounded by fancy shops. Taking his time, he selected a light-weight shirt with large breast pockets, which would save him the trouble of having to wear a jacket; a pair of linen trousers; two pairs of underwear; leather sandals; and finally, an elegant shaving kit. It all cost a fortune, but he didn't care, and after thinking about it, he even decided to change over to the Hotel Mandarin. The very fact of going on a shopping spree made him feel that he was making a decision. Besides, since he had nothing special to do in Kowloon, this move diverted him slightly from the temptation of the ferry. He had nothing better to do on the Hong Kong side, but so what? . . .

His new room was light, spacious and comfortable, with two twin beds. The windows, which were double and sealed shut, filtered out the commotion and looked out onto a side street instead of the wide avenue parallel to the docks. As soon as the bellboy had gone, he got undressed, took a shower, and shaved his beard, handling the old-fashioned razor with caution, since he was not accustomed to using one. His mustache was beginning to fill out, and the fact of its growing back sparked a bizarre hope within him—that the return to his former appearance would cause all the mysteries that he'd brought upon himself to vanish, cancel them out. All at once he would recover his integrity—physical, mental, and biographical. No trace of the disorder would remain. He would come back from Hong Kong, rightly convinced that he'd been on a business trip for an account from the office; in his briefcase, for he intended to buy one, he'd have the documents that substantiated his work and the contacts he'd established. Agnes would give him a tender welcome at the airport, she'd know the exact time of his return. She wouldn't remember a thing; neither would he. Everything would be back in its rightful place. Nothing incoherent would arise, the mystery would have been erased all by itself, it would never have actually happened. That was the best thing that could happen, and come to think of it, it wasn't any more or less impossible than what had already happened. He could even, he thought, thank the powers who, after playing with him, had now consented to put everything back into place. Heaven helps those who help themselves. . . . Yes, but in his case, helping himself meant gathering together the documents that proved the reality and usefulness of his business trip, telephoning Jerome to clarify the story that justified his impromptu departure, and asking him to mentally prepare Agnes so that she'd think she'd merely dreamed it. In short, it would mean beginning the farce all over again, providing new proof of his madness. He might as well call his own ambulance to come and meet him at the plane. . . . No, only heaven, if you could call it

heaven, would be able to help him: it was not a question of falsifying what was real, absolutely not, but of performing a mir-.
acle, making what had happened disappear. It would mean
erasing this part of their lives and the consequences, and also
erasing any trace of the eraser itself, and trace of that trace.
Not falsifying, not forgetting, but simply having nothing more
to falsify, to forget; otherwise, the memory would inevitably return, it would destroy them. . . . No, really, the only help within
his grasp, if he wanted to call upon the mercy of heaven, was to
let his mustache grow back, to take care of it, to trust this rem-
edy. As he lay there on the bed, he brushed his finger over his
upper lip, stroking the newly grown hair, his only chance.

Later on in the afternoon, he tried again to telephone Agnes
and his parents, with no more luck. Then he slipped on his new
clothes, rolled up the cuffs of his trousers since there was no
hem, and put his possessions in his front and back pockets:
passport, credit cards, some cash, and the piece of paper with
the phone numbers on it. He hesitated whether or not to carry
the beeper with him. Since it weighed him down, he ended up
wedging it between the bowl and the shaving brush in the
leather case of his razor kit, which he left in the bathroom. He
went out, used the overpasses above the avenues, and steered
himself toward the docks. The sky was gray; it was hot and
humid. Recognizing him, the ferry attendant waved his arms in
a sign of welcome. He got off in Kowloon and didn't take the
boat back until a half hour later, once he'd paid his bill at the
King Hotel and retrieved what was left of his carton of ciga-

rettes. Strangely enough, he hadn't smoked, hadn't even thought about it, since his arrival in Hong Kong.

Back on the island, he wandered aimlessly, trying to follow the docks, which proved impossible because of the numerous detours, construction sites, and overpasses, where he searched in vain for an opening to get a glimpse of the bay. The positions of the billboards on top of the skyscrapers towering over him enabled him to recognize neighborhoods that, from the ferry loading dock the night before, had seemed very far from the center of town. In another luxury hotel, the Causeway Bay Plaza, he tried phoning again, but there was still no answer. As night was falling, he took a taxi back to the Mandarin, drank a Singapore sling in the bar, then went up to his room to look at himself in the bathroom mirror, and shaved again, like a convalescent who is testing his strength. The smoother his cheeks were, the more the already-black patch stood out on his upper lip. He knew that, as usual, he'd have a difficult time getting through the night; that these particular, stubborn, contradictory ideas would begin to besiege his brain; that he'd alternate, without varying, between wanting to take the ferry again, dash back to the airport, and throw himself out the window; and that the trick was to do none of the above, so that he'd find himself alive and well the next morning with a healthy mustache, having contented himself simply with dreaming about irrevocable acts. What frightened him most was that, under the influence of some new whim, he might shave off his mustache again and then have to start all over. He envisaged a series of days and nights marked by alternately shaving and hoping it would grow back, a succession of contrary decisions, hopelessly perpetuated by the waiting and the indecision. Those bleak thoughts were coming back, of course, just as he'd predicted; the hardest part was to hold out. Hold out, nothing more.

He thought about getting drunk, but it was too dangerous. After trying to call Paris again, worried about what he'd say if, for some extraordinary reason, Agnes picked up, he went downstairs to look for a pharmacy where he could get some sleeping pills. But once he'd found one that was open and had explained what he wanted with the help of ridiculous gestures—folding his hands under an imaginary pillow and snoring loudly—the saleswoman looked at him reprovingly and made him understand that he needed a prescription.

With no appetite he ate some noodles and fish in an open-air restaurant. He walked for a long time, to make himself tired, then took a streetcar. Leaning out of the window on the upper level, smoking despite the prohibition that nobody respected, he watched the endless procession of building facades, lights, signs, neighborhoods, one after the other, some animated, some deserted; streetcars arriving from the opposite direction, passing so close that he'd have to jerk back his elbows each time. An unpleasant odor of fried food and fish streamed in through the windows. The line ran parallel to the port, across the length of the island, and when he'd reached the end, he was tempted to set out again in the opposite direction. He forced himself to descend. If he really wanted to exhaust all the possibilities of trips back and forth offered by city transportation, he'd still have the subway for the following day, and then the funicular, which would bring him to the top of the Peak. After that he could just start all over again, or else simply pace back and forth in his room. He could alternate between the two twin beds, and ask himself whether it was better to sleep with his mustache exposed or under the covers. He would always be able to find a physical substitute for the indecision that he was suffering from, but which he'd adopted nonetheless as part of his strategy. Only temporarily, he snickered, only until another idea, not necessarily a new one, forced him elsewhere. Nevertheless, on the whole, in spite of these sudden urges, which no longer surprised him, he was on his way to a kind of tranquil indifference, a definite improvement from the night before. Just temporary, he repeated as he walked along, just temporary.

Around two o'clock in the morning, almost by chance, he found himself back in front of his hotel, and shaved for the third time that day. Next, for the fifth time, he dialed the phone numbers that he'd written down on a piece of paper. When there was still no answer, he began to dial other numbers at random, prepared to wake up any anonymous Parisian, just to reassure himself that at least the city still existed. Several of the numbers that he was dialing indiscriminately must not have been assigned—but then he would have heard, "The number you have reached is not in service at the present time" or, "Your call cannot be completed as dialed. Please check directory assistance." He also called information, 411, time, a taxicab company, and the front desk of the hotel to check on the country code. This took up a good hour, during which time he smoked one cigarette after another. He retrieved his beeper from the shaving kit, clutching it like a useless fetish. The wave of panic he'd sensed was approaching had finally overcome him. It wasn't only his past, his memories, but the entire city of Paris that was sinking into the yawning chasm behind his every step. And what if tomorrow he were to go to the consulate? They'd undoubtedly tell him that the telephone lines worked perfectly well; should the occasion arise, they'd even go so far as to try to prove it, but the numbers he'd be trying to reach would still not answer. "It's because no one's home. Why don't you try again later," the obliging consul would logically conclude, perhaps the same one who would inform Agnes of his tragic death— and under the circumstances she'd pick up right away. He switched on the television that was in his room, turned down the sound, and kept dozing off, still fully dressed. When he opened his eyes, disgusted by the smell of stale tobacco, some well-dressed Chinese were moving their lips on the silent screen. Later on, cowboys on horseback rode into a sierra— probably reconstructed in Spain, if indeed Spain hadn't disappeared, as had been implied by the planisphere in Bahrain. The channels in Hong Kong probably stayed on all night, as in the United States, but maybe tomorrow he'd find out that no, the programs all went off the air at midnight. His obsession with the unverifiable had come back to torture him. He rolled over and groped for the telephone on the night table. At one point, just to hear a voice, he dialed a number without using a country code, holding the beeper tightly between his fingers. He woke someone up, probably in Hong Kong, who bawled him out, but he didn't understand a word. He hung up, got out of bed, shaved again, went back to bed.

At dawn he awoke, went out, and wandered through streets filled with morning gymnasts. He took the ferry once again, and to the visible satisfaction of the attendant, still the same one, he remained there all day. The jumble of masts in the bay, the shrill cry of birds circling the cloudy skies, the faces, the odor of tar, the glinting reflection of the buildings, the flow of what were now familiar sensations absorbed him completely. Whenever he felt the sudden inclination to go to the consulate or the airport, he waited for it to pass, and it soon did. He smoked a lot now, carrying his carton of cigarettes under his arm. As he sunbathed it occurred to him that he should buy some sunglasses, and he wondered in passing exactly when he had removed the ones that had been in his jacket pocket, the same ones he'd used several days ago on the Boulevard Voltaire to stage his fake blindness. He remembered the jacket he'd been wearing, which was now lying, rolled in a ball, at the bottom of the closet in his room. He'd taken them off in the café at République and put them into his pocket, but he could not remember taking them out again in the Jardin de la Paresse, in the apartment, or in Roissy Airport. He forced himself to re-situate this harmless gesture, to reconstitute the details of the twenty-four hours before his departure. But a kind of sluggishness kept him from taking stock of his actions, which were slipping into the domain of the unreal. They were now part of a hazy legend in which he was no longer the hero. With the same indolence, he quashed all future plans or long-term projects: a prolonged sojourn on the ferry; an adventure drifting from port to port in the China Sea; a verification visit to Java; a return home to conjugal life. He had become indifferent to all of it. Questions that had once been as trenchant as a razor had lost their edge. The urgency of choosing or not choosing had subsided.

Around midday an employee tapped him on the shoulder and told him, in something roughly resembling English, that if he so desired, he didn't have to get off at the landing dock; he could just pay him directly, give him a lump sum for all the trips back and forth. Whether this had been simply inspired by kindness or by the lure of a fraudulent profit, he declined the proposition. He explained that for him, getting on and off was all part of the fun, and it was true, he hardly gave a second thought to counting his change.

The continuous rhythm of his trips back and forth was broken just once, the time he gulped down a sizzling brochette of chicken, standing in front of a street stall where they also had cassettes of pop music on sale. Afterward he stopped by the Hotel Mandarin to retrieve his shaving kit, which he later used in the dirty bathroom of the ferry. When he wasn't on duty, the attendant would sometimes come over for a chat; he'd point out some detail in the landscape, would say, "Nice, nice," and he'd nod his approval. In the early evening a storm broke out, and the ferry began to rock violently. Once they'd landed, the passengers took shelter under red-and-black newspapers.

And then it was night, the last crossing, and just like two days ago, he found himself pacing the boardwalk. Embedded in the cement were lamps of frosted glass, blinking under a starless sky. As he continued along the quay, he soon arrived at another loading dock; this one was still open. He slid onto a bench across from a man who must have been about sixty. He had a florid complexion and was wearing a yellow linen suit with tennis shoes. The man immediately struck up a conversation. "Oh, Paris," he remarked, following the answer to the inevitable "Where are you from?" Given his pronunciation, he was from somewhere that could have been either Australia or Nazareth. "Nice place," he added dreamily. He was waiting for the one-thirty boat that was leaving for Macao, where he'd been living for the last two—or ten?—years. Was Macao nice? "Not bad, relaxing. Quieter than Hong Kong," the man said. And was it difficult to book a seat on the boat? No problem.

They fell silent and both climbed aboard when the boat arrived. He was obliged to take a berth, and given the choice between a dormitory for fifty people, a first-class cabin for four, and a VIP suite for two, his companion recommended the VIP suite, which they could share. Which was ultimately what he chose, but he did not share it. Instead he remained on deck, holding his shaving kit, watching the dark sea, the city lights as they faded in the distance, and then just the sea.

At times the wind would carry peals of strident laughter, probably from the dormitory, shrill voices, and above it all, the clacking of dominoes being thrown onto metal tables. It briefly occurred to him that he would have enjoyed this nocturnal crossing if Agnes had been along; he would have liked to put his arms around her shoulders. Mixed with the din of a new round of dominoes, he thought he heard the mournful sound of a telephone ringing endlessly in an empty apartment. He took the beeper out of his shaving kit and held it up to his ear. The tone rang out as he pushed down on the button. When he'd finally had enough, he stretched his hand over the railing and slowly uncurled his fingers, still squeezing the button. Because of the vibrations from the motor and the sound of the waves breaking against the hull, he could no longer hear the beep at arm's length, and of course he heard it even less when the device disappeared from his open hand. He only knew that he wouldn't be making any more phone calls, and ripped up the piece of paper with the numbers on it. A while later, when he thought about Agnes again, it had all become too distant; the absence of her body pressed against his, her laughing voice, excited by the diabolical advancement of the game, were nothing more than an inconsistent and suspended mirage. A mirage that had been swept in and quickly dissipated by the warm wind and by a weariness that could no longer strike out against empty air.

7

EARLY THAT MORNING THE BOAT DOCKED IN A KIND OF INDUSTRIAL
suburb that was sprawling with buildings under construction,
covered by bamboo scaffolds. At the end of the landing wharf,
taxi drivers were jostling one another, trying to attract the attention of travelers, who were, for the most part, Chinese. He
was just about to accept their services when his companion
from the night before, who'd gotten off after he had, offered to
drive him into the city. They took an overpass above one of
those multilane highways separated by barriers, which, unlike
the ones in Hong Kong, could only be crossed every ten kilo-
meters. They entered a parking lot, where a dusty four-wheel-
drive Toyota awaited them. During the ride, the Australian—if
that's what he really was—apologized that he wouldn't be able
to put him up, implying that certain amorous concerns had
upset his household. He suggested that instead of staying at the

Lisboa Hotel—where practically every taxi would have driven him in order to collect a commission—he ought to take a room at the Bela Vista Hotel, which was quieter, more typical, and he especially recommended the terrace. They could even meet there one night to have a drink.

A half hour after he'd been dropped off in front of the hotel, he was sitting on that very same terrace, his feet propped up on a whitewashed railing of the colonial balcony. There was a soothing row of ceiling fans; hanging beneath the four blades were four little decorative lamps edged with spunglass collarettes. Despite the brilliant sun, they remained lit. The China Sea spread before him, golden in contrast to the mint green and white pillars that supported the blackened paneled ceiling.

At the front desk they gave him a key to his room, which was hardly luxurious, but immense and cool, and a multilingual brochure on Macao that claimed, "The water in the hotel rooms is usually boiled, not for safety measures, but in order to reduce the taste of chlorine. Nevertheless, everyone, visitors and residents alike, prefers to respect the local custom and drink wine instead of water." Taking them at their word, he ordered a bottle of *vinho verde*. The neck of the bottle was sticking out of an enormous ice bucket. He drank it all. Aside from a vague feeling of contentment from the coolness, his mind was blank. Then he staggered to his room, where one window gave onto the terrace and the other, above the door, onto a spacious corridor that smelled of damp sheets, like a laundry. He turned off the air conditioner, one of those jobs that looked like a TV set and whose opulent and rusted bottom protruded from the hotel's shabby facade. He considered shaving but decided against it. Feeling drunk, he opened the window, lay down on the bed, and fell asleep. Occasionally he would stir, half awake, toying with the idea of getting up, shaving, and returning to the terrace, or going to one of those casinos the Australian had told him about in the car—the main local attraction along with the Crazy Horse cabaret imported from Paris—but his plans got entangled with confused dreams, as well as the absolute conviction that a typhoon was on its way. The tree branches were blowing, beating against the open window, and he could hear the rain and gusting winds. But in fact, it was only the blowing and dripping of the air conditioner, which he broke trying to turn off.

Later on he shaved in front of a mirror that was poised on the shelf above the sink—for one reason or another, they'd never fixed it to the wall, and that was generally the way things were at the hotel; everything was going to seed. Then he went out, feeling a little weak in the knees, and walked around the streets lined with little two-story cottages, pink or green, like hard candy. The streets, inhabited by the Chinese, were called *Rua del bom Jesu, Estrada do Repuso,* or something like that. There were baroque-style churches and large stone stairways, as well as modern buildings as one headed north, which was where he'd first landed. There were odors of incense and fried fish, an atmosphere of childish and gentle decrepitude, of a surging sea now at peace. He had a moment of sudden anxiety; how absurd to get lost in such a small town, and he repeated the name of his hotel several times to a Chinese policeman, whose face finally lit up. He nodded his head and declared, "Very fast." But it was impossible to know whether that meant that one could get there in no time at all, or whether one had to run there in order to get back, or else it might have meant that the hotel was "very far." The policeman wrote down the address in Chinese calligraphy on the cover of a matchbook that he'd just bought with a pack of local cigarettes. That way he could even ask those who didn't speak English for directions. The letters looked something like this:

However, he never got the opportunity to make use of this last recourse. Walking aimlessly, he ended up at the waterfront, within view of his hotel, which was on the outskirts of the city and looked like a dilapidated ferry in a dry dock.

He spent the late afternoon and evening on the terrace. There was a bronze bas-relief depicting Bonaparte on the Pont d'Arcole, headed with the inscription, "There is nothing impossible in my dictionary"—an approximation, he supposed, of the saying that was literally "impossible is not French." But the fact that it had been expressed in English, particularly to illustrate the effigy of a historical enemy, was fairly disconcerting, to say the least. He ate lightly, ordering dishes that reminded him of Brazilian cuisine, and also drank a lot, figuring it would help him get to sleep, and he was right.

8

TWO DAYS WENT BY IN THIS MANNER. HE SLEPT, SMOKED, ATE, drank *vinho verde*, strolled around the peninsula, and without wanting to, was frequenting what were probably the standard tourist attractions. He hung around the casinos: the elegant one in the Lisboa Hotel, and the floating casino, where the racket from the dominoes threw him into a kind of stupor, which would slowly dissipate once he was back outside. He dozed in the sun of the public gardens, walked along the border of Red China, visited the museum devoted to the seventeenth-century poet Camoëns, and later sat under a tree with a smug smile, recalling with astonishing clarity the Jules Verne novel in which the geographer Paganel takes it upon himself to learn Spanish in order to bone up on the epic poem of this same Portuguese poet.

Aside from ordering his meals, he didn't speak to a soul. The

Australian, undoubtedly overwhelmed with domestic problems, never showed up for the rendezvous on the terrace that he'd suggested. At times, in the far reaches of his numbed mind, menacing thoughts began to stir, concerning Agnes, his father, the relative proximity of Java, the search for his whereabouts, and the future that awaited him. But he'd only have to shake his head, close his eyes for a while, or take a few sips of wine to dispel those images, which had become more and more lifeless; they'd been emptied of their substance, they'd soon become ghosts, as innocuous as a drowned beeper in the China Sea, only a disturbing but fleeting impression of déjà vu. He made no more attempts to telephone, and contented himself with walks in the sun, bathing in the odor of dried fish and his sweat-drenched clothes. His aimless wandering was broken up by long naps. He would shave twice a day all the same, adapting humorous sayings for his own situation: happiness is listening to your beard grow. And he did listen to his mustache, but not very attentively; sometimes, while lying on a bench, he would relish the abstract but now uninspiring idea that he'd gotten through it. But he quickly forgot about these ideas as well.

9

THE THIRD DAY HE WENT TO THE BEACH. THERE WASN'T ONE IN Macao, but a recently constructed bridge linked the peninsula to two little islands, where, according to the affable reception-ist from the Bela Vista Hotel, one could go swimming. There was a minibus service that departed from the Lisboa Hotel three times a day, but he preferred to walk, and set out around eleven o'clock in the morning. He looked down at the pave-ment as he walked, and occasionally at the surrounding water, all alone on the bridge except for a few cars. One of them stopped; the driver opened the door, but he politely refused; he wasn't in any hurry. He had fish for lunch in a restaurant on the first island, called Taipa, facing the sea, then started out again around two o'clock. He followed the dusty yellow road until he noticed a black sand beach below him, which could be reached by taking a steep path. Several parked cars and Japanese motorcycles indicated that he wouldn't be alone, but he didn't mind. It was truly crowded, mostly young Chinese boys who were playing handball and shrieking with delight. The birds were shrieking as well. It was hot. Before going for a swim, he ordered a soda and smoked a cigarette at the little refreshment bar. Its straw roof was surrounded by speakers playing American pop songs; among others, he recognized Barbra Streisand's "Woman in Love." Next he took off his clothes, rolled them in a ball, placed his sandals on the little pile, and leisurely made his way into the warm water, which was almost opaque. He swam for a few minutes—you could touch bottom even very far from shore—and then headed back toward the beach. Remaining on his back, he stretched out at the shifting edge of the water, between the damp sand and the little waves lapping up against his sides. The tide was coming in, and he followed its movement by inching backward on his elbows, facing the sea. The glare was burning his eyes, but every now and then he'd squint at his clothes to make sure that they hadn't disappeared. About twenty yards away another European approximately his age was splashing around in the same position. At one point when he'd dozed off, he suddenly heard a very loud voice articulating words in English. He opened his eyes and looked around, a bit anxious since they'd apparently been addressed to him. And it was indeed the other white bather who was turned in his direction and kept shouting over the noise of the waves, "Did you see that?" He could scarcely distinguish his features, yet somehow he didn't think he was either English or American, and checked to see if anything special was happening on the beach. Nothing, just adolescents who were still playing ball, and a young man in shorts, also Chinese, taking a little stroll with a Walkman attached to the waistband of his swimsuit. "What?" he said, as a matter of form, and the European, still lying in the water, turned to him laughing, screaming at the top of his lungs, "Nothing. Forget it!" He closed his eyes again, relieved that the conversation had ended there.

Later on he got out of the water, dressed without bothering to dry himself, and set out on the road in the opposite direction. The minibus on its way back to Macao stopped for him in the middle of the road. This time, since he was tired, he decided to get in and took a seat in the back. From the prickly sensation of his skin, he could tell that he'd gotten a sunburn, and was looking forward to the cool sheets, which would feel a bit rough on his skin. Whenever the bus moved into the shade, he tried to see his reflection in the windows, which were covered with dust and dead insects. His hair was stuck together from the salt, his face was cut in two by the black line of his mustache, but this no longer held much meaning for him. He had no pressing plans, except the one to take a bath when he got back to the hotel, and then to settle in on the terrace, facing the China Sea.

On the board where he usually left it, his key was missing. The receptionist, an old Chinese man whose wispy frame was draped in a large white nylon shirt, said to him, smiling, "The lady is upstairs," and he felt a chill go down his sunburned back.

"The lady?"

"Yes, sir. Your wife. Didn't she like the beach?"

He didn't answer. Taken aback, he lingered in front of the brightly polished front desk. Then slowly he climbed the stairs. The carpet had been removed, probably in order to have it cleaned. The copper stair rods, lying in a bundle against the wall, reflected the glow of the setting sun. Dust particles danced in the slanting rays coming in through the large open window on the second floor. The door of his room, at the end of the hall, was slightly ajar. He pushed it open.

Stretched out on the bed, in that same golden light, Agnes was reading a magazine, *Time*, or perhaps *Asian Week*, which were available at the front desk. She was wearing a very short cotton dress that looked like an oversize T-shirt. Her tanned bare legs stood out against the white sheets.

"So," she said, when she heard him come in, "did you end up buying it?"

"What?"

"You know, the etching. . . ."

"No," he finally said, in tone that he thought sounded normal.

"The guy wouldn't come down on his price?"

She lit a cigarette and dragged the hotel's promotional ashtray over onto the bed.

"No, he wouldn't," he said, staring out the window at the sea. A cargo ship went by on the horizon. From his shirt pocket he pulled out his own pack of cigarettes and lit one, but it was damp; he'd probably gotten them wet when he'd dressed on the beach. He puffed vainly on the soggy filter, then stubbed it out in the ashtray, his hand brushing lightly against Agnes's bent knee. He said, "I'm going to take a bath."

"I'll take one after you," she answered as he walked into the bathroom, leaving the door open. Then she added, "Too bad the tub is so small."

He turned on the water, leaning against the rim of the bathtub, which was indeed too small. There was just enough room to sit, and obviously not enough for two. Moving toward the sink, he noticed on the shelf two toothbrushes, a half-empty tube of toothpaste made in Hong Kong, and several jars of moisturizing and cleansing creams. He almost knocked one over while removing them from the slightly crooked shelf on which they'd been sitting, and placed the rectangular mirror in the same slanted position, against the wall, right next to the bathtub. Having made sure that it was securely balanced, he got undressed, picked up his shaving kit, put it next to the mirror, and eased into the warm water. The only light in the bathroom came from a tiny window, the type you'd find in an attic. This aquatic atmosphere was dark and peaceful, harmonious with the sound of dripping water from the broken air conditioner. It was cool, a good place for a nap. Sitting in the tub waist-deep, he oriented the mirror toward him so that he could see his face. His mustache was nice and thick, like before. He smoothed it down.

"Are we going back to the casino tonight?" Agnes asked languidly.

"If you like."

Slowly and deliberately, he stirred the shaving brush in the bowl, covered his chin and cheeks with foam, and carefully shaved. Then, without pausing, he started in on his mustache. Lacking scissors, it took a while to clear the ground, but the old-fashioned razor worked quite well, and the hair fell into the bathtub. He took the mirror between his legs so that he could see what he was doing and lean into it. The edge of the mirror was digging into his stomach, which was propping it up. He applied a second coat of shaving cream, gave himself a closer shave. Five minutes later, he was clean-shaven once more, and this thought provoked no other, it was simply a fact: he had done the only thing possible. More shaving cream and little flecks of foam were dropping off, falling onto the water's surface or onto the mirror, which he wiped off with the edge of his hand. Again, he shaved the place where his mustache had been, so closely that he thought he'd discovered tiny irregularities on this narrow strip of skin that he'd never noticed before. By the same token, he noticed no difference in skin tone, even though his face had been tanned by these last few days in the sun, but perhaps it was due to the shadowy light of the bathroom. He set aside the razor for a moment but did not put it away, took hold of the mirror with his two hands, brought it very near to his face, so close that his breath made a little blur, then put it back on his knees. From his angled position, he could see leafy branches and even a patch of sky out the bathroom window. The dripping water from the air conditioner and the pages being turned by Agnes were the only sounds coming from the room. Had he twisted around and craned his neck, he could have stolen a glance through the half-open door, but he didn't.

Instead, he picked up the razor once again and continued to polish his upper lip. One time, he brought it up to his cheek, which reminded him of the way he used to caress Agnes, his tongue thrust inside her, he'd move away to kiss her inner thigh, then return to the spot where he'd buried his mustache. Now he'd adequately located the position that would permit him to press the blade exactly perpendicular to his skin. He forced himself not to close his eyes when, under this weight, the skin finally gave way and opened. He increased the pressure, watched the blood flow; it looked more black than red, but that was also because of the light. There was no pain, he was surprised he didn't feel it yet, but as he gripped the tortoiseshell handle his fingers were trembling so much that he was obliged to continue his incision laterally. As he'd expected, the blade slid in much more easily. He curled up his lip to stop the blackish trickle; however, several drops fell onto his tongue, and this grimace threw off his path. He was now feeling the pain, and realized that it would be risky to try and carry subtlety to its extreme, so he began to slice, not caring whether the gashes were neat. He clenched his teeth so he wouldn't cry out, especially when the blade reached his gums. The blood splashed into the dark water, onto his chest, onto his arms, onto the porcelain of the bathtub, and onto the mirror, which he wiped off with his free hand. His other hand, contrary to what he'd feared, did not lose its strength, as though it had been welded to the razor. And the only precaution he took was to keep the blade flush against his torn skin. Dark shreds, like small strips of spoiled meat, fell with a dull thud onto the mirror, then slowly slid down into the water, between his braced legs, rigid with pain, his feet pushing against the walls of the tub while he continued to maneuver in every direction, from top to bottom, from left to right, somehow managing not to scrape his nose and mouth, despite the blinding flow of blood. But he kept his eyes open, concentrated on the area of skin as the blade continued to dig. The hardest part was not to scream, to keep it up without screaming, without ever disturbing the stillness of the bathroom and bedroom, where he could hear Agnes turning the pages of the magazine. He was also afraid she might ask him a question, to which he could give no answer, his jaws clenched tightly together like a vise. But she remained silent, merely turned the pages, perhaps at a slightly faster pace, as though she were growing tired off it, and meanwhile the razor had started in on the bone. He could no longer see, he could only imagine the vibrant color of his burning jaw, and something clear and bright in the blackish pulp of the severed nerves, surrounded by brilliant flashes, whirling in front of his eyes, which he thought he hadn't closed when he'd actually squeezed his lids shut, clenched his teeth, arched his feet, contracted every single muscle in order to bear the scorching pain and not black out until the work was done, without further delay. His brain continued to function on its own, asking itself just how long it would continue to work, if it would carry on even further, before he lowered his arm to cut beyond the bone, to the bottom of his throat filled with blood. And when he realized that he'd inevitably choke, that he could never end it in this way, he pulled out the razor, fearing that he'd have no more strength to bring it to his neck, but he succeeded, he was still conscious, even if his gesture was weak, if the tetanic contraction of his entire body had receded from his arm, and he sliced blindly, without feeling a thing, under his chin, from one ear to the other, his spirit alive until the last second, rising above the gurgle, the sudden jolt of his legs and stomach, alive and appeased by the certitude that now it was over, everything was back in place.

Biarritz—Paris
April 22–May 27, 1985

LaVergne, TN USA
30 September 2010
199084LV00001B/2/P